DER DeRouen, J. A, author.
Waiting for Autumn

4/2019 FRA

WAITING FOR AUTUMN

J.A. DEROUEN

D1523093

ST. MARY PARISH LIBRARY
FRANKLIN, LOUISIANA

Waiting for Autumn
Copyright © 2018 by J.A. DeRouen
Cover Design by Oh So Novel Cover Design
Editing by Madison Seidler (http://www.madisonseidler.com/)
Proofreading by Mitzi Carroll (http://www.mitzicarrollediting.com/)

All rights reserved.

Without limiting the rights under copyright reserved above, no part of this
publication may be reproduced, stored in or introduced into a retrieval
system, or transmitted, in any form, or by any means (electronic, mechanical,
photocopying, recording, or otherwise) without the prior written permission
of both the copyright owner and the above publisher of this book.
This is a work of fiction. Names, characters, places, brands, media, and
incidents are either the product of the author's imagination or are used
fictitiously. The author acknowledges the trademarked status and trademark
owners of various products, bands, and/or restaurants referenced in this
work of fiction, which have been used without permission. The
publication/use of these trademarks is not authorized, associated with, or
sponsored by the trademark owners.

Library of Congress Cataloging-in-Publication Data

DeRouen, J.A.
Waiting for Autumn- 1st Edition
ISBN-13: 978-1728733982

🏵 Created with Vellum

PROLOGUE

Dear Seb,
Do you love me? Circle yes or no.
Love, Autumn
P.S. - If you show this to my brother, I'll tell everyone you cried at
the end of Where the Red Fern Grows.

Autumn
The Past
Prosper, LA

The afternoon sun hangs heavy in the Louisiana sky, like a fiery basketball drooping from a sleepy hammock. The blistering heat burned off any remnants of clouds hours ago and singed my exposed thighs right along with it.

Who wears cutoffs for a day of mudding with Sebastian Kelly? After all these years, I should know better than that. When he showed up on our doorstep bright and early with an ice chest, four-wheeler, and his jam-box, circa 1980, all signs pointed to this being an all-day affair. I threw on the first clothes I could find, wrapped my hair into a high bun,

1

and hit the fields with my boyfriend and my brother. Now, at the end of the day, my bun has taken a precarious plunge south, and sweaty, blonde curls stick to my flushed cheeks and neck.

"Ty Landry's having a bonfire behind his dad's old barn tonight. Who's in?" I ask, knowing exactly on which side of the fence both Brady and Sebastian will land. Brady, the altar boy, and Sebastian, the devil on Brady's shoulder. A hot, harmless devil ... well, mostly harmless.

Me? I'm the cheerleader for all hair-brained schemes. You only live once, and I plan to skid into those pearly gates with a boatload of epic tales. That's part of the reason why Seb and I are meant to be together. Well, that, and a thousand other reasons adding up to forever.

"I'll pass," Brady says after turning off his four-wheeler and running a hand over his neatly cropped hair. He swears the haircut helps to keep him cool. I say he looks like he battled with the clippers, and the clippers won. We agree to disagree.

"Like hell, you'll pass." Sebastian purposefully hits the brakes late so his tires bump into Brady's with a jolt and a muttered curse.

"Not this time."

My brother's clenched jaw and puffed chest only serve to amuse Sebastian. Brady's drank one beer too many if he thinks that'll be the end of it. Sebastian and I never take *no* for an answer. We're all too familiar with lassoing a reluctant Brady.

Cow-tipping in Old Man Johnson's field? What's the harm? Everyone conveniently forgot about Mr. Johnson's penchant for firing his shotgun first and asking questions later. I don't even need to mention his notoriously bad eyesight.

Driving lessons, better known as donuts, in the field

behind the neighborhood? At the age of twelve? Yeah, only Sebastian could make that one sound like a good idea. Good thing Seb's older brother came to the rescue with a four-wheel drive truck and an alibi.

Skinny-dipping in the country club's pool at midnight? Who'll ever know? Thanks to security cameras, the entire country club staff. The phone rang off the hook that summer when the girls in town got a peek of the goods. A gnarly case of the flu saved me from that fiasco, and I often thank Bernadette Jenkins for not covering her sneeze and saving my tits from going viral.

"What kind of friend would I be if I let you miss the biggest blowout of senior year?" Sebastian chides with a theatrical groan. Hands thrown up in frustration, his beer sloshes and splashes onto my bare thigh. He wipes the spill with his thumb, then sucks it into his mouth, shrugging his apology.

"And what kind of sister would that make me? I'm Team Seb on this one. You're comin', and that's the end of it."

"Come on, give it a rest. I'm tired as hell, and I've got to work at the feed store bright and early tomorrow. You know what's worse than schlepping fifty-pound bags of feed? Doing it hungover. I need to sleep off this beer." Brady peers at his watch and then throws back the rest of his Budweiser.

"All work and no play makes Brady *the worst best friend ever*. Am I right, Autumn? Brady the Buzzkill strikes again." Sebastian casts a glance over his shoulder, and I nod in agreement. I shrug and blow a kiss when Brady glares at me. "Our time for screwing off is coming to an end. Soon enough, you'll be neck-deep in two-a-days at LSU, wishing all you had to do was schlep bags of feed. Let's blow off some steam before you become the first freshman to win the Heisman Trophy for being the best fucking quarterback the SEC has ever seen!"

"Hell yeah!" I cheer, with a fist pump to the sky. My brother tips his head and sighs, while Sebastian pulls me closer and leans his weight against me.

My arms curl around his waist, and I lay a flushed cheek against his damp back. He tugs my hands to his lips and kisses my inner wrist. God, I'll miss this when he leaves for college in the fall. A day is too long to be away from him, let alone an entire year. It's a done deal; I'm all set to meet him next fall, but next fall feels so far away. As soon as that diploma hits my hand, I'll have lightning shooting out of my heels to get to him.

Truth is, I've been following Sebastian since the day I learned to crawl.

Trailing behind, griping for them to let me play, too.

Holding his hand as we ran down the block, narrowly beating the streetlights home.

Arms circling his waist as we splashed through mud and muck on his four-wheeler.

And finally, *finally*, my lips pressed to his, when he opened his eyes and saw the little girl with pigtails was more than just a tag-along.

"Hurry, Autumn. Catch up, I've been waiting for you."

He squeezes my clasped hands, and I slip my fingers under the seam of his shirt. His skin is warm and sticky, and his hair is drenched with sweat. I press my mouth to the curve of his neck and lick his salty taste from my lips. He lets out a low, tortured groan, only loud enough for me to hear.

"No play? We've been riding all damn day!" Brady raises up the empty twelve-pack carton and waves it in the air. "Beer gone. Sunburnt. Tired as hell. I'm tapping out, man. Y'all are gonna have to party without me. I'm sure you two can figure something out."

Honestly, a night alone with Sebastian sounds perfect to

me. I'm usually first in line for a party, but I feel our time together slipping through our fingers. I want every second with him to count in some indelible way. The future pulls and frays the ties that connect us, and I'm not the only one feeling it. It's all in his eyes—Seb wants us all together, all the time, the way we've been since we were kids. Like keeping those he loves close will dull the hurt when it's time to go. Brady leaves for LSU next month, and Sebastian moves the month after for Southern Louisiana University ... and I'll be all alone in Prosper without my partners-in-crime. My best friends.

The boy I love.

"How about this—" Seb starts.

"Nope," Brady interrupts, leaning back and crossing his arms.

"Race me for it."

"Screw you, man."

"I win, you come. You win, your momma can tuck you in before dark."

"*No*," Brady repeats.

And the silent stare down begins.

Softly, almost unintelligibly, Sebastian mutters under his breath, "Pussy."

The whispered taunt lingers in the air like the kicked-up dust dancing all around us. Brady fires up the four-wheeler with a kick of his heel, the sound piercing the silence around us. "You're on. First to the fence, and when I beat your ass, you're gonna clean my bike, too."

Sebastian barks out a laugh and cranks his bike while I hop off, kiss him fast and hard, then grab one of the empty cans out of his front crate. Standing between the two of them, I raise the crumpled beer can high in the air as their bikes growl on either side of me. Seb presses play on his damn near antique jam-box, and "Welcome to the Jungle" howls through the speakers. Guitar riffs amp up, and the air crackles with anticipation.

My hands stay high in the air as I look at Brady ... then Seb. I mouth "I love you" to him, and his eyes close as if he's caught the words mid-air. I grin, the excitement bubbling up inside me, as they both sit poised and ready for my cue.

"Ready ... set..." I bite my lip as two weighted seconds pass, then hurl the can high up into the air. *"GO!"*

Kicked-up dust swirls and grits between my teeth as I spin around to watch them shoot across the field. Axl Rose's primal cry pierces through the air, intertwining with the screaming engines as they're pushed past their limits. Chasing their trails of rolling dust, I race up the hill behind them.

"Faster Autumn, I'm right over here."

Tires devour dirt, and engines grind like a deafening thunder. Brady shoots to standing as he nears the hill, arm fisted in the air, and lets out a bellowing battle cry before he races over the top. Sebastian follows closely behind, and they both disappear from my view, as I race to catch up. My lungs burn from the effort, sucking in filthy air in short bursts as I squint to see what's ahead of me.

My legs pump harder once they vanish from sight, thighs burning with each pounding step. I race to the finish line without even a care about who wins, just caught up in the moment with my two best friends—my brother and the boy I love. The Fearsome Threesome.

The grinding hum of motors morphs into something high-pitched and sickly, turning my insides to acid. My gut twists as an engine whines in the distance, out of my range of sight. Something's not right ... something's very wrong ... something's—

An agonizing howl shoots from the other side of the hill and steals the breath from my lungs. I trip over my frantic feet, dirt and grass filling my mouth as I fly forward and hit the hard ground.

"I need you, Autumn. I need you, hurry!"

I stumble to my hands and knees, bits of stray rock piercing skin as I fight my way to standing ... running ... flying across the field.

"Brady, oh fuck, Brady! Christ!" Sebastian's voice sinks its teeth into the stagnant air and rips it wide open, all sounds bursting into high velocity and waves of technicolor horror.

I'm trudging through tar to get to them, stumbling the entire way as the world whips around me in a haze of terror. I round the top of the hill, and my knees buckle. I can't see ... I can't see ... I don't want to see ...

"Hurry, Autumn, help me. Fuck, help me get the bike off him. Please, Brady, do you hear me?" Sebastian howls like a wounded animal as he frantically wrenches the crumpled four-wheeler off my brother's limp body. "Please, please, please," he whispers as tears spill and splash onto my dusty cheeks, streaking them with rivulets of salty mud.

The sickening groan of the motor dies away, amplifying Sebastian's cries and a piercing scream I only then recognize as my own. I fall to my knees at Brady's side, drowning in paralyzing fear.

I will never forget Seb's frantic pleas as he heaves the four-wheeler off my brother ... or the absolute stillness of Brady's body twisted and contorted in a way that tells me, with utter certainty, our lives will never be the same again.

CHAPTER 1

Sebastian
Present Day - Five Years Later
Haven, LA

"Cappuccino, one sugar, light foam!" Lexi calls out, sliding the coffee mug to the edge of the pick-up counter. The customer doesn't notice her forced smile as she picks up her drink.

"Simmer down, woman. Your inner snob is showing," I whisper as I wrap a friendly arm around her shoulders and smile at the retreating customer.

"Light foam," she mutters, lowering and shaking her head. "A cappuccino is all about the foam, Seb. Who are these heathens we're serving?"

"Customers, Lex. Paying customers."

I slide the double shot espresso ticket in her direction, and she nods her approval.

"A man after my caffeinated heart," she sighs, her lips quirking up into a quasi-smile. She pushes up her sleeves, revealing a tiny sliver of the *Alice in Wonderland* mural tattooed on her forearms, and gets to work.

We're all mad here. Truer words ...

Lexi's been with me from the very beginning when Fuel was a run-down coffee shop named Marge's Cup of Joe, run by ... Joe and Marge Reynolds, of course. Joe is an ornery old man with glass packs in his lungs and a weathered saddlebag for skin due to centuries of smoking. Marge has never met anyone she didn't want to mother to death and is as tall as she is wide. I take that back—there's one person Marge doesn't want to mother—Joe. Her favorite pastime is nagging the old man to death. Luckily, she mothered the hell out of me the day I showed up in Haven five years ago, broke and broken.

Marge took one look at me holding her *help wanted* sign and realized I needed a shitload more than just a job. She started with an unfinished apartment upstairs and an offer for free rent in exchange for fixing up the place. Once my apartment was transformed from open walls and concrete to exposed beams and graffiti murals, I got to work on down-stairs. Diner chairs with cracked and frayed vinyl were swapped out for galvanized metal barstools. Stained Formica tables were replaced with distressed wooden plank tables and benches. And when Marge and Joe were ready to retire, a lease-to-own agreement between a generous couple and their wayward employee transformed me into a business owner. The exiled black sheep of Prosper, LA turning into a contributing member of society. Who would have thought it was possible? Definitely not me.

And that was when the big changes came.

Espresso machine instead of old drip coffee pots.

Eminem instead of Chuck Berry.

Fuel instead of Cup of Joe.

And with every addition, every step in the direction of

making this place my own, I became less of a dejected boy and more of a confident man. A confident man with a chip on his shoulder, but miles away from the screwup I used to be. Hell, on a good day, that ever-present chip looked more like a tiny speck of lint.

Brush that shit off, man. You can't rewrite the past.

On a bad day ... well, we won't talk about the bad days.

"Hey, welcome to Fuel. What can I get started for you?" I ask the striking brunette opposite me. Her blue eyes saunter over my lips, chest, colorful arm art, then land squarely on my dick. I smirk at her appreciation and resist the urge to return the perusal. When her eyes return to mine, I raise my eyebrows in the universal "like what you see?" gesture.

She chuckles and leans closer, like she's got a secret she's dying to tell. I meet her halfway, all too eager to hear where she plans to meet me later. Her lips curve up, and she whispers, "Your barn door is open. Thought you'd want to know."

I can't help it—I grin and let out a laugh. I place my hand on my zipper and watch her eyes make their descent ... again.

"Thanks for the tip. We wouldn't want the rooster to get loose," I quip, slowly pulling up my zipper as I smirk. "Cock-a-doodle-dooooooooo," I singsong.

Lexi's groan drowns out my rooster crow, and we both turn in her direction. "Seriously, have you no shame? And that goes for the both of you, since I have no doubt she'll be handing over her number shortly. It's hard to watch sometimes."

After taking her order and getting her to sign her receipt, which she wrote both her signature and phone number on, I might add, I narrow my eyes at my insolent employee.

"Cock-block much?"

"Cock-a-doodle-doooo," she sings, and then bursts out laughing.

I open my mouth to ban her from speaking for the rest of the morning when the ringing phone interrupts me. I grab the portable off the back counter and check the caller ID. If the 318 area code doesn't grab my attention at first, the Prosper, LA across the screen punches me square in the gut. No name, just Prosper, LA.

I don't give a fuck who it is—there's no one in Prosper who's got anything good to say to me. And there's nothing I can do or say to change that.

"Telemarketer. Let it ring," I say in a clipped tone as I toss the stick of dynamite on the counter and stalk to the back.

I pace the storage room as the incessant ringing rattles my brain. I clench my eyes shut and push out every thought of that godforsaken town. Over the last few years, I've become adept at locking those memories away in the deepest part of my heart, never letting them see the light of day. It's funny how a two-inch-by-four-inch illuminated screen can dismantle five years' worth of work ... suppression ... denial ... whatever.

When the ringing finally stops, I fold in half, hands gripping my neck and head hanging between my knees.

If I could just breathe.

The answering machine flips on, and my recorded voice ricochets off the walls, punctuated at the end with an ear-piercing beep. My lungs seize in my chest as a voice I'd know from anywhere fills the room, deliberate and somber.

"Seb? It's Lance ... your brother." He sighs into the phone, sounding like a harsh, piercing whistle. "I'm here ... in Prosper. Look man, you're gonna need to come home."

Home. Home. *Home.*

The unrelenting guilt I battle every time I think of Prosper rushes over me. There's a reason I've shoved those memories to the furthermost corner of my mind. Tentacles of regret pull me under like a thousand-pound cinder block at the bottom of the Black Sea. Memories, emotions, and sorrow for the mistakes I've made barrel through me. Brady ... my parents ... Autumn ... *my Autumn.*

One phone call unravels me as I'm pummeled with the only truth I know with any amount of certainty.

I lost my home on a summer day five years ago, and I'll never get it back.

CHAPTER 2

Sebastian
The Past
Prosper, LA

I shut the front door and slam my fist into the wood, feeling every frustration and fear barreling through me without mercy or filter. The images of Brady's crumpled body, Autumn's bloodcurdling screams, and that fucking music blaring while my world fell apart assault me in graphic detail.

What I wouldn't give to be winning the race? Then my bike would have hit the stray scrap of log on the other side of the hill. I would have gone airborne, only to be thrown to the ground, my bike following with a sickening thud. Then I would have laid there, contorted and broken. *Me*, instead of Brady.

Images flash through my mind like a macabre picture show, a constant loop of gruesome regret, never giving me a moment's peace. Peace is the last thing I deserve, anyway.

Bloodied knuckles and exhaustion slow me down, and I

slide to the floor, head in hands and heart utterly crushed. The foyer is filled with nothing but my labored breaths.

It's been a week since the accident. Seven days since my stupid idea left my best friend mangled and bleeding. Seven days since I've seen Autumn or Brady.

Seven days ... more like an eternity.

Brady was airlifted to Shreveport after the local hospital assessed his injuries. His father, stone-faced and haggard, made an appearance in the crowded waiting room, bursting at the seams with the entirety of Prosper High's student population. He let us know Brady was being transferred to a higher-level facility, our prayers were appreciated, but we all needed to go on home. Every day since then, I've driven the two hours to Shreveport and camped out in the hospital waiting room, asked for updates at the nurses' station, called Autumn's phone—and nothing. I've tried everything I can think of and get nothing but silence in return.

Until today, that is, when I was escorted out by hospital security and told to leave and not come back.

How did things spiral so out of control? Brady and I had raced hundreds of times—on foot, bicycle, skateboard, four-wheeler. You name it, and we've turned it into a competition. The worst thing that had ever happened was a scraped knee or a bruised ego.

Until last week. God, what I wouldn't give to hit rewind and make a different choice. Say something other than the all-too-familiar challenge between best friends.

Race you for it.

I clench my eyes shut and dig my fists into my sockets, either trying to hold the flaying pieces of myself together or push the racing thoughts away. I'm not sure which, but it doesn't work on either count.

Too focused inward on my hurricane of thoughts, I don't

notice my dad's approach until he's right in front of me, clearing his throat.

"Son, we need to talk."

~

"I-I-I don't understand," I stammer, holding back the burgeoning tears as my father sits across from me with powerless eyes and a ticking jaw. "Am I being arrested? I-I-I know I shouldn't have taken that beer from the house, but—"

"It's not that kind of lawsuit, Sebastian," he interrupts, letting out a frustrated sigh and shaking his head. "They aren't threatening criminal charges. They're talking about a civil lawsuit. The punishment wouldn't be jail time. If you're found guilty, the punishment would be restitution to the family. Money." He leans forward, elbows to his knees, his expression more somber than I've ever seen. "A lot of money. More money than I've seen in my life, if I had to guess."

"What are you saying? Dad, I don't have any money. Other than a hundred bucks of Christmas money and my savings bonds you've got in the safe, I-I'm broke."

God knows, if I had any money … if it would fix the hurt I've caused Brady and his family, I'd gladly hand over every last cent.

"But *we* do." My dad narrows his eyes and waits for his words to sink in. "Yeah, Seb, they'll take it all. The house, the little savings we have, the business … I've already lost five long-standing clients because of this. They said they couldn't do business with 'people like us.'"

A single tear, hot and shameful, escapes and tracks down my cheek as I look away. Disgrace washes over me as I think of all the years my dad has spent building his lawn services company. For my entire life, he's been up before dawn, chasing sunlight as he sweats and slaves to keep his family afloat. And I've unraveled all those years in one afternoon.

"I'm sorry, Dad. Tell me what I can do to make it right. I'll talk to Brady's parents. Apologize," I plead, already knowing an apology is as useful as placing a Band-Aid on a bullet hole.

"Their son may never walk again." He raises his hands in exasperation and glares. "Do you get that? Can you fathom how your little stunt caused something that has forever changed that boy? That family? You're the last person they want to see right now."

A stack of envelopes hits the coffee table with a stinging slap, and I look up in question.

"Death threats. Six in the last two days, not to mention the gashes in your mother's car. It's been keyed multiple times this week." He shakes his head and sighs. "Son, you can't destroy the golden boy, the football prodigy of Prosper, and come away unscathed. They want retribution. Revenge."

My dam of control collapses, and the tears flow freely down my cheeks. Crushing sobs rack my body as my fingers twist and pull at my hair. I think of all the people I've hurt. Brady. His parents. My father. Autumn.

Autumn … she'll never be able to look at me again without remembering what I've done.

My dad reaches over and grips my shoulder as my whole body quakes. "Son, I'm sorry, but I need you to understand the magnitude of this. As much as you want it to, this thing isn't going away. What happened out in that field … it's not going away."

"What do I do? What do I do? What do I do?" I chant softly to no one.

As if on cue, I hear the suitcases hit the floor beside me. My eyes travel up the trembling hands of my mother to see her tearstained face etched with exhaustion and despair.

"There's only one way out of this, Sebastian, so I need you to listen to me carefully," my dad says with steely resolve.

I listen with rapt attention as the cell door slides firmly shut on every hope I had for my future. I hear the sliding of steel and the clicking of the lock, loud and clear. No, I may not be going to prison, but my life will become a prison all the same.

CHAPTER 3

Sebastian
Present Day
Prosper, LA

I stand on the edge of the sidewalk, not daring to step a toe into my father's yard, body poised to bolt at the slightest provocation. I stare at my charred childhood home with a mixture of sorrow and dread. I dreaded coming, never planned on showing my face in my so-called hometown ever again. But there are things to be done, papers to be signed, and a helluva lot more cleanup than I could leave to just my brother.

I look to the left. To the right. I wait for the angry mob to descend, telling my worthless ass to go back to where I ran off. The street remains silent, but memories, some cherished, others dreaded, race unfiltered through my thoughts.

Mr. Jansen's yard, where I kissed Autumn for the first time.

Mr. Alfred's greenhouse, our favorite hide-and-seek spot.

This exact spot, five years ago, where I drove off with nothing but a duffel bag and a beater car, never to return.

Until now.

Nausea stirs in my gut as Lance emerges from the nonexistent wall that used to be my parents' bedroom, smudged with grime and soot.

Did they wake up right in the thick of it, unable to escape? I clench my eyes shut and suck in a sharp breath at the very thought.

Lance dusts his hands off on his jeans and makes his way toward me. Good thing, because my feet are still cemented to the spot. His tightly tucked-in shirt, buzzed hair, and stern eat-shit-and-die expression serve to remind me some things never change. The fight-or-flight response I feel being back in Prosper makes me think *nothing* ever changes. Time means nada, and sins are marked in tattoos, not chalk. At least that's how it is in this unforgiving town.

Lance squeezes my shoulder, and the gesture releases a small bit of tension stretched tight throughout my body. It takes long seconds before I can tear my gaze away from the nightmare of soot and ash and meet his eyes. The pitiful expression he gives me says everything. I look lost and floundering through his eyes. Not surprising, since that's exactly how I feel.

My emotions are a house of precariously teetering cards, threatening to topple under the pressure of being in Prosper after five long years, suddenly losing my parents, never mending our relationship while they were alive, and a hundred other emotions that refuse to stay bottled up where they belong.

"I know what you're thinking, man, because I thought the same thing. They didn't bu—" He chokes and presses his lips together to stave off the wave of emotion. He takes a sobering breath and continues. "They didn't burn. It was smoke inhalation that got them. Old electrical wiring is what did it. He'd mentioned rewiring the house before but hadn't gotten to it yet."

I nod my head, unable to speak, grateful for the small bit of peace his words bring me. My parents are still gone, our relationship still left in unamendable shambles, but the thought of them burning rips at my insides. When all is said and done, setting aside my mistakes and their dismissal, I loved my parents, and I know they loved me the best they knew how. Yes, they sent me away with whatever quick money they could muster, and that will probably always sting. It's taken a long time, more years than I care to admit, to swallow that bitter pill. I'm not sure I actually have.

We haven't spoken since the day I left, and I'll admit I'm partly responsible for that. I've always kept in touch with my brother, but he's deployed most months of the year and lives in Texas when he's not. That is the extent of my contact with my old life. My parents never looked for me, never sought me out after that day, and I staunchly refused to make the first move. What felt like pride and self-respect back then now holds the bitter taste of arrogance and stupidity. Death has an uncanny way of flushing out the bullshit and leaving you reeling.

"So what," I choke out. "What are we—"

A crash from inside the house interrupts my stammering, and Isaac, Lance's son and my nephew, peers his head out of the makeshift hole.

"My bad, sorry!" he calls out with a wave and disappears back into the blackened cave.

Lance brings his attention back to me and frowns. "It's a total demo, Seb. We're just looking through the rubble for mementos, things that we may want to keep that didn't burn. Your room is probably in the best shape ..."

I jerk back, shaking my head, and Lance grips my

shoulder more tightly. "I don't want anything out of there. Nothing."

The last thing I need to do is sift through my old life, ruminating over all the things I've missed. That would serve no purpose other than rubbing salt in a reopened wound.

Lance shakes his head, jaw clenched, looking as stubborn, if not more so, than I do. "Not letting you do it anymore, man. They may have sent you away, but you've been running ever since. Enough."

The petulant teenager who lives and breathes inside of me wants to say, "screw you," and "you don't know me," but the half-evolved adult I've become knows that's a lie. The facade and bravado I wear like a suit of armor melted away the second I hit the Prosper city limit sign. Part of me is still that kid, guilt-ridden and so fucking sorry. Sitting pretty in Haven, the ghosts of my past look much smaller, like I'm in an airline jet, watching ant people at thirty thousand feet. Here in Prosper, it's me who's the ant, and my demons are poised to stamp me out like the little pest I am.

"When you're chased out of town, what choice do you have but to run? Don't really see how that's on me, brother."

"I'm not talking about running from this town ... running from these people. I'm talking about running from yourself," he says, with a firm shove to my chest. "Pretending that shit from the past isn't there while it slowly rots you from the inside out."

I look to the setting sun and sniff, pushing down the emotions boiling over inside of me. Shove it down deep, just like every time before. That's the only way I've made it through these past few years. Choke it down deep and move forward. Maybe there's some truth to what Lance is saying. Maybe each step wouldn't be so hard if I let go of some of the baggage weighing me down.

Maybe chucking old luggage out the window is much

easier said than done. Maybe looking ahead instead of fixating on the rearview mirror is an impossibility.

Fuck, I need to get out of this town.

As if reading my mind, Lance starts back toward the rubble, knowing I'll follow. "Let's put the demons to rest. Throw out that old shit that doesn't serve you anymore. You never know, man, you may just find some things worth coming back for."

And maybe that's what I'm most afraid of ...

My navy-blue plaid comforter still lays neatly on top of my old bed, beaded up and faded, but soft and comfortable as ever. I run a hand over it and smile, trying to remember when this used to be home, and push back the overpowering smell of soot and smoke burning my nostrils.

I lean down and grab the yearbook off my bookshelf, open it to a random page, and chuckle. Me, armed with a paintball gun, and Brady, running for his life, while he looks back at me with a shit-eating grin.

Running. He was running. Damn ...

Emotion burns the back of my nose, and for once, I don't swallow it down. Moisture builds behind my eyes as the familiar feeling of regret takes over. I know he never wanted to hear from me, that was made crystal clear back then, but I've looked him up a few times over the years. Sometimes, when I felt especially self-deprecating, I'd venture onto Brady's social media accounts. Even though they were set to private, a few profile pics were available for public viewing. In the photos, he always had that same steady grin, ready to take on the world, except now he was doing it with the aid of a wheelchair. Part of me felt triumphant for him, watching my best friend soar despite the hurdles placed before him.

But the part of me that lived in the real world knew these pictures only showed half the story—the pretty part. If you pull back the perfectly painted curtain, I'm sure there are cries of frustration and grunts of despair ... all created by yours truly.

And if that wasn't enough to warn me away, then the sight of Autumn was the final nail in the coffin of my heart. The first photo I came across was of brother and sister on a basketball court, both sporting wheelchairs and expressions brimming with laughter. The basketball rested in Brady's lap as he looked over his shoulder at his obviously gaining-on-him sister. Tendrils of Autumn's hair had stuck to her neck, shiny and slick with sweat. Her full lips were curved up into the widest grin, one degree shy of busting out laughing. Flushed cheeks and mischief—that's my girl. That *was* my girl, at least. Every single thing screams life went on without me, and I'm nothing but a terrible nightmare for both of them to overcome. From the looks of things, they're both well on their way.

I only wish I could say the same.

The similarity between the two photos is not lost on me. I may be absent from the more recent pic, but I left one helluva souvenir in my place. Extricate the suck-ass best friend, and in return, Brady, you get a hunk of metal signifying Sebastian's failures and a lifetime of hardship to boot. Irony sure is a motherfucker these days.

My fingers twitch to turn the page, turn to *the* page, half of me knowing it's a terrible idea and the other half of me knowing I have no choice in the matter. I've only seen the words once in my life, when I snuck a peek just days before the accident. Autumn told me I wasn't allowed to look at her inscription until I got to college in the fall—I lasted a day. She had known my dodgy relationship with rule following and all things authority. I can't imagine she'd be surprised I gave in.

In one swift move, I flip to the back of the yearbook and run my fingers over the fluid loops and swirls of the ink. The first time my eyes drank in her words, they were stolen kisses, stomach drops, and whispered "I-love-yous." Now, all these years later, I feel that strong and hopeful heart cracking under the pressure.

Sebastian Parker Kelly,

I fight back tears every time I think of us being apart. How can I go even a day without seeing the boy who's held my heart for as long as I can remember? Where in the world else would I be, if not with you?

Then I close my eyes and think of the feel of your fingers interlacing with mine. I hear the steady beat of your heart as I rest my head on your chest. And more than anything, I feel what we are to each other.

And I know the truth ...

No amount of distance can separate a love that started with pigtails and skinned knees. No amount of time can erase a feeling that's as ingrained as breathing.

A year is nothing when we have a lifetime ahead of us. And I can't wait to live my life with you.

Remember, wherever you go, I'll follow, Seb. I'll always be by your side.

Wait for me.

I love you,
   Autumn

A sharp rap on the door rips me from my thoughts. I blink away the memories and look up at a curious Isaac.

"No need to knock, dude. It's not like there's a door anymore," I say with a humorless laugh.

He shrugs and takes a quick look around the room. Isaac's unruly hair, relaxed smile, and laid-back attitude are so opposite from my straight-laced and rigid brother, it's actually jarring. But today, he's a bit punchy, overly tense and seemingly at a loss for words. Given the circumstances, it's completely understandable. Losing your grandparents in such a tragic accident, regardless of how well you knew them, is enough to rattle any kid.

I assume Isaac spends most of his time living with his mom and stepdad since Lance is career military, always off to the next deployment. The thought makes me feel a sort of camaraderie with him, knowing how stifling it can be to follow in the shadow of the great and disciplined Lance Kelly. With a fourteen-year difference between us, there were many times when Lance felt more like a father to me than a brother.

"Dad asked me to check on you," he says, rubbing a nervous hand over his neck and not quite meeting my eyes. "Do you need any help loading up or packing?"

His eyes dart to the stack of empty boxes against the wall and quickly move back to the floor. Part of Isaac's unease is undoubtedly from losing his grandparents, but it may also be due to me acting like an unlit stick of dynamite. He hasn't had enough happen to him to waltz into the shit-storm of emotions swirling around this room without flinching.

Lucky kid.

I close the yearbook and clench it shut, trying to stop the flood of memories as I shake my head and chuckle. "Nah, Isaac. Thanks, but there's nothing you can do to help me."

CHAPTER 4

Dear Autumn,
Meet me behind the pool house after the public swim. Travis says
we aren't real boyfriend and girlfriend unless we kiss.
P.S. - I don't really care what Travis has to say. I just want to
kiss you.
Seb

Autumn - Thirteen Years Old
The Past
Prosper, LA

"Do you think he'll stick his tongue in your mouth?"

Sandy squeals at the thought, but I freeze in terror. What if he *does* stick his tongue in my mouth? I've never French-kissed a boy before … I've never regular kissed a boy before. The only experience my lips have comes in the form of Gramps and Grams, and there was definitely no tongue involved.

Oh God, I'm going to be sick.

If I could titty-twist that stupid Travis Mottley, I swear I would, the meddling jerk. This isn't how my first kiss was supposed to go, and it's all his fault for being the bully that he is. If it weren't for him, Seb's and my first kiss would be under twinkle lights, in my best purple dress. My hair would be braided and twisted, and my lips would shine with strawberry Lip Smackers gloss.

I had it all planned out. We would be just like Edward and Bella at the prom.

"I'm going to be sick," I say, clutching my stomach through my damp bathing suit and dropping my head between my knees.

The humid air of the pool house dressing room feels too thick to breathe. Goose bumps erupt on my tight, sunburnt skin and my stringy, half-dried hair sticks to my neck. I run a hand over my head and feel the baby curls cork-screwing around my forehead like a frizzy crown of straw.

Just great. Sebastian Kelly, *the* Sebastian Kelly, wants to kiss me, and I look like a sunburnt, one-piece wearing, poodle-headed chump. He's going to take one look at me and realize I'm still too young to be his girlfriend. I sure as heck have no idea what to do if he sticks his tongue in my mouth. I should have practiced with my pillow, but my stupid baby brain didn't even think about French kisses.

"Here," Sandy says as she hands me half of a chocolate bar. "I don't have any mints, but chocolate breath is the next best thing."

I shove the candy into my mouth and shimmy my flip flops onto my damp feet. The chocolate dissolves into a sweet, goopy mess, but I'm afraid the galloping horses in my belly will toss it back up if I swallow.

"What if he does, Sandy? I don't know how to kiss like that." I pull my cover-up over my body and throw my swimming bag over my slumped shoulders. I swallow the candy with a forced gulp before standing to leave.

Sandy grabs my hand before I make it very far and huffs out a laugh. "Autumn, calm down. This is Seb we're talking about. You've lived down the street from him your whole life. He's taught you how to pop a wheelie on your bike, how to fish, how to sneak out for Friday night hide-and-seek. So, he's going to teach you how to kiss today … so what? Seems kind of perfect to me." She shrugs and rolls her eyes.

My racing heart calms and a warmth washes over me because, of course, she's right. I've got nothing to be afraid of because Sebastian Kelly has been teaching me things all my life. I wouldn't want it any other way.

"And, I mean, he's fourteen. I'm sure he's practically an expert kisser by now."

My jumbled nerves are replaced with grating jealousy, and I give Sandy's shoulder a shove.

"I doubt he's an expert," I mutter. "I mean, I'm thirteen, and I'm completely clueless."

There may have been a couple of meaningless girls before me, but I know the truth. Seb has always been biding his time, waiting for me.

I run my hands over the paint-chipped cinder block of the pool house and peer around the corner. Travis's pinched face comes into view just as he lets out a pig-like snort. My lips curl in disgust, and I think of a hundred ways to knock that jerk down a couple of pegs. John and Pierre laugh right along with him like they always do, and their groupies, Reagan and Ruthie let out a spray of giggles.

I spot Seb at the exact moment he spots me, and my lips curve into an excited smile, the doofuses beside him completely forgotten. He's got a foot propped against the wall and his hands shoved into the pockets of his bathing suit. He didn't bother to put on a shirt, and his worn-out running shoes cover his sockless feet. He tips his head in my direction and smirks.

Why does he always look like he's got a master plan brewing behind those eyes? Probably because he does. Why am I always game for whatever he has planned? Because whether we're having fun, getting in trouble, or doing nothing at all, by his side is the very best place to be. Always.

Sandy grabs my shoulders as she peers over me, and I nearly topple to the ground. I catch myself before falling to my knees, but I'm no longer hidden behind the side of the pool house. All the laughing and tittering stops, and I shoot a nasty look over my shoulder at Sandy.

She shrugs and scrunches up her nose. "Oops."

"Right," I grit out.

"Well, look who decided to show up," Travis says, slow-clapping like the little jerk he is. He separates himself from his group of friends and puts a hand on Sebastian's shoulder. "I told Seb you probably wouldn't show. I told him you were just a scared little sixth grader—"

"I'm going to the seventh grade," I interrupt, putting a shaky hand on my hip. I keep my grip tight so he won't see the tremble. I smile, eyes slits and my voice steady. "And I'm not scared of anything."

"That's my girl." Seb's voice is barely louder than a whisper, but my confidence soars at his words.

He pushes off the wall and saunters toward me, smirk firmly in place and his hands still shoved in his pockets. He stops about a foot away, and I tip my head up to meet his eyes. The insignificant voices and fake laughter fade into the background, right where they belong.

"Hi." He waggles his eyebrows, and I giggle.

"Hey." I bite my lip and my gaze darts to the ground, the awkwardness of this situation making me cringe.

Sebastian Kelly has seen every bum knee, snotty nose, and temper tantrum I've ever thrown. Our lives are too interlaced, too singular for this kind of awkward. I shoot another scathing look behind Seb at that fat-faced dill hole.

He tosses an annoyed look over his shoulder in Travis's direction, then turns back to me. He leans closer and whispers in my ear, "I don't like people telling us what to do."

His arms slide out of his pockets, and he sets them in between us. Two writhing lizards jump and skitter in his palms as he holds them in place between his thumbs and forefingers. He hunches his shoulders to hide his prize and grins at me.

"You ready to run?"

"I'm always ready," I whisper, a giggle of anticipation bubbling up in my chest. Matching smiles ... mischievous grins ... flipping, flopping reptiles ... it all swirls between us and the air feels charged with anticipation.

"Are you two gonna suck face or what?" Travis taunts, shooting a conspiratorial glance at his band of idiots.

Seb holds my gaze and gives me a nod before shouting over his shoulder. "Hey Trav, think fast!"

Seb whips around, his hands shooting out in front of him, and Travis looks momentarily stunned, totally confused until ... He reaches for his neck, feeling a tickle or touch of some kind. When his fingers close around the culprit, and his mind, ever so slowly, does the math, all hell breaks loose.

The most pansy-assed, girlish screech I've ever heard rips from Travis's lips as he slaps himself silly, flopping to the ground. He'd make a two-day old kitten with a pink bow look downright manly right about now.

Momentarily stunned by the spectacle that is Travis, Seb tugs my arm to get my attention. I peel my eyes away from the carnage and catch a quick glance at Sandy, eyes wide, mouth in an astonished O. My feet tumble forward with another tug from Sebastian.

"Time to bounce," he says over his shoulder as he darts across the park toward our neighborhood. I trail behind him, laughing the entire way as I keep peeking back at Travis sputtering in a dusty pile.

"I'm going to kill you, Sebastian!" Travis whines as he finally gets up off the ground. He takes off in our direction, but lucky for us, we've got a good lead. "Brady's not here to save you this time!"

"Do your worst, girly-man!" Seb shouts over his shoulder, then howls with laughter.

Our feet pound the pavement, and I struggle to keep up and hold onto my flip-flops. We zig and zag through fences and backyards until the sounds of Travis and his gang become as distant as cars passing on the highway out of town. We round the corner of my street, and the fuchsia crepe myrtle in my front yard shines like a beacon.

Olly olly oxen free!

We're almost to the cul-de-sac when Seb gives my arm a hard tug, pulling me between Mr. Jansen's fence and the holly bushes. The weather-beaten wood pricks my back as he presses against me, fingers tangling in my damp hair. His panting breath brushes across my lips like the whisper of a touch, and I wish that it was. I want to feel the pressure of his lips on mine more than anything. And yeah, he better put his tongue in my mouth. My eyes drop to his parted lips, and all I can think about is bridging the distance between us. With a belly full of Pop Rocks and a heart set on fairy tales, my lashes flutter shut, and I surrender to him.

His thumbs dust over my cheeks, and he leans in closer. "No way was I going to let our first kiss happen that way," he whispers, then lowers his mouth to mine.

The gentle pressure of his lips, the curl of his fingers in

my hair, the thud of his heart beating in tandem against mine; I've dreamed of kissing Sebastian Kelly hundreds of times—thousands even—but nothing can compare with the real thing. On contact, his breath hitches, his fingers clench my hair, and we settle into the sweetness.

And when his tongue enters my mouth and slides against mine, a yip of surprise crawls up my throat, and I sag against him in a heap of gelatinous goo.

And when he pulls away, I'm out of breath and left with nothing but air between my ears. Hot air. And I whisper the only word I can pull from my jumbled brain.

"Wow."

The drunken expression on Seb's face tells me he agrees.

CHAPTER 5

Sebastian
Present Day
Prosper, LA

I hear the rustle of fabric and hushed condolences behind me as people exchange hugs and handshakes, but I keep my eyes trained ahead. My mere presence makes people in this town twitchy, so it's better this way. I ignore them, and they silently admonish me. I won't give them the courtesy of my thoughts. Not today.

With one hand resting on my parents' coffins, I do what I should have done years ago. I open my heart to them in a way that they couldn't do for me.

I should have called. I should have come back. I'm sorry I was too proud to right the wrongs between us.

I've always thought that one day my parents would show up in Haven to see their cast-out son. Maybe hoped is a better word. They would walk through the door of Fuel, take one look around at what I've accomplished, and they would finally be proud of me. They would look around and see how I'd turned failure into fortune. God, I'm such a fool.

Yes, Sebastian, you've ruined people's lives, but this cappuccino is delicious. Great job, son.

Lance interrupts my thoughts with a firm hand on my shoulder. "Seb, time to wrap it up, man. Everybody's clearing out, and these guys have a job to do. Mom and Dad know what's in your head—you don't have to stand here all day. *They know.*"

I didn't notice the cemetery workers just a few yards away until now. They appear restless and more than a little put out. I meet Lance's gaze, and he gives me a nod of understanding. Except I don't buy it, because no way does he understand what's going on in my head.

"Not all of us have a spit-shined halo hanging on our bedposts, big brother. My halo, for example, is rusty, dusty, and bent into the shape of a question mark. A goodbye from me is going to take a little longer than yours."

"Bullshit. It's time you stop doing this to yourself, man. You're not that kid anymore. You may not have bridged the gap with Mom and Dad before they died, but I talked about you all the time. They asked about you. All. The. Time. And they were proud of what you're doing in Haven. They were proud of you, man." Lance moves to stand in front of me, and his expression softens a bit. "You haven't been that kid for years, and it's time you see that for yourself. I know you've changed, whether you believe it or not, and screw anybody who can't accept it and move on."

"I thought I had, then I drive back into this shit-stain of a town, and the years between me and that kid melt away." I release a humorless chuckle. "Move on. It sounds so easy when *you* say it."

"Because it is. Let go of the demons. *They* already have," he says with a look in the direction of the coffins. "It's time you do the same. You're already here in the belly of the beast. Do what you need to do ... then you need to let it go."

A large part of me wants to get the hell out of this town before it strips away all the walls and masks I've built, and there's nothing left but the ugly truth of it all. There's another part of me, one that I've only recently become acquainted with, that knows I can't just walk away. They may have run me out of town when I was a stupid, gullible kid, but I'm a man now. It won't be so easy this time around. And the threats of the past no longer hold the same weight they once did.

In hindsight, I've given too much energy and thought to the people of this town. Back then, they felt like giants hovering over a helpless kid, but not anymore. Their anger and hatred hold little significance in my life. I now know what's important. What ... and who?

Brady. Autumn. Mr. and Mrs. Norris.

My parents.

The son in me wants my parents' forgiveness, even after all this time. The man in me needs to pardon them as well. Things were said and done that can never be taken back, but if there is ever a time to move on and let go, this has got to be it. Maybe they were just as sorry as I am ... or maybe not. I guess I'll never know. But my heart can't hold onto this anger anymore. It's needless and toxic, and it'll rot me from the inside out if I let it.

Sometimes forgiveness is about letting go—taking that five-ton boulder off your chest and heaving it into the abyss. I've carried this weight for far too long.

Lance walks away from me without another word. I clench my hands into fists and give the varnished wood a gentle tap of my knuckles, a silent goodbye ... I'm sorry ... I love you.

It's a start.

I turn toward the gravel road that snakes through the center of the cemetery and follow my brother. My gaze falls on the only other vehicle left from the service, and my heart seizes in my chest.

She folds up the wheelchair and loads it into the back of the SUV, unaware of my eyes drinking in every single part of her like she's finely-aged whiskey. I savor this moment, letting the warmth run a path from my throat, down to the empty pit in my stomach. Her hair is shorter, lighter than it used to be—almost a white-blonde. She looks different, but also exactly the same. I'd know her anywhere. Five years, ten ... blonde hair or black. It makes no difference. Autumn Norris will always have a direct line straight to my heart.

The edges of her black dress dance around her thighs as she walks to the passenger door and climbs into the seat. Only then does she turn her head. Only then do our eyes find each other, years of love, laughter, tears, and heartbreak reeling between us with one heavy blink.

"Hurry up, Autumn. I've been waiting ... I've been waiting for so long ..."

I don't know what I want her to do next, but I'm craving ... *something*. After all these years, after all this time, I wholly reject the notion that we could lock eyes and just walk away. Who we are, what we've always been to each other deserves more than that. Demands it, even.

I don't know what I'd say if she gave me the chance, but my heart wells with intense longing. The need to say something choking me, words left unsaid for far too long grappling to break free. Anything to make her stay where she is right now and just let me savor the sight of her. To make the time drift away like wisps of smoke, along with guilt, regret, and every bad decision I've ever made in my life.

Screw it. I can't come this close to the future I squandered and not at least try to right some wrongs, close the gap even a little bit. I have to *try*.

I raise my eyebrows in a show of hope, or maybe vulnerability, and step toward her. Before I can take the second step, I watch her face crumple. Her expression is painted in grief at the mere sight of me. I shouldn't be surprised. It shouldn't hurt like a punch to the gut, but it does all the same. She turns her head toward the driver, breaking our connection. The ignition cranks, and the tires inch forward.

I focus on the driver and only then do I remember the wheelchair Autumn hauled into the back of the SUV. Only then do I remember the reason why nothing I do will ever make up for the things I've already done. You can't throw a dozen roses on top of a nuclear explosion and call it good. And that's what I did to their family—I rocked them to their foundation.

Autumn refuses to meet my eyes again, keeping her gaze firmly trained on her lap. But Brady doesn't shy away as the gravel crunches underneath the rolling tires. He throws up a hand in a cheerful wave that is all Brady. Then the five finger wave morphs into a one finger salute.

And for the first time today, I laugh.

CHAPTER 6

Autumn
Past
Prosper, LA

"Where is that damn nurse? He should have already gone to CT and been back by now. This is ridiculous." Spittles of saliva collect in the corners of my dad's lips as he rages. And rages.

He vacillates between furiously pacing the room and providing a running commentary of the inept medical staff at Prosper Medical Center. The one thing he's yet to do is take a good look at his son.

My brother, who's laying strapped to a board, collared, and freaking the hell out. I see it in the frantic way his eyes dart from one part of the tiled ceiling to the other, nostrils flaring as he drags in one ragged breath after another.

Another stray tear burns a trail as it tracks down my sunburnt cheek.

This is all my fault. This is all my fault. This is all my fault.

My mother trembles uncontrollably in the corner,

stunned and silent. She checked out before she ever stepped foot into the hospital.

I brush a lock of Brady's sweat-drenched hair back and wipe the dirt smeared across his forehead. He clenches his eyes shut and presses his lips together, holding back ... something.

Everything.

"It's going ..." I suck in a breath and squeeze my eyes shut. I hold back the words, the lies sitting on the tip of my tongue.

I don't know if everything is going to be all right. I don't know anything at all. And I certainly don't know what to say to Brady to help him get through this. One glimpse at my spiraling dad and helpless mom tells me they don't either.

I settle on, "I'm here." It's the only solace I can give him as we wait. "I'm here for you, Brady."

"I-I-I ..."

I lace my fingers with his, fisting them together, careful not to move or jostle him in any way. I've done enough damage today. I wait patiently for him to finish his sentence, but he's stuck on that single syllable, over and over and over again.

"I-I-I ..."

"Shhh," I coax as I squeeze our gritty, sweat-soaked fingers together. "I've got you, Brady."

"Are you building the goddamn machine?" My dad hollers down the hallway to whoever will listen.

The monitor above the stretcher beeps, beeps, beeps as I watch the numbers, meaning God knows what, rise with each furious outburst from my father.

I've got to get this situation under control before we cause any more damage. It doesn't take a doctor to know this isn't helping Brady at all.

I know who can help. Who we need. And I'm positive he needs us, too.

"Where's Seb?" I ask, patting my pockets, searching for my phone that's probably crushed into a million pieces in the field at this point. "We need to call him. He needs to be here."

After calling 911, we were flooded with blinking lights, blaring sirens, and a barrage of organized chaos. Policemen barked orders and EMTs worked on Brady and whisked him into the ambulance at breakneck speed. I ran along with the stretcher, never leaving his side as the door clicked shut and peeled off to the hospital.

We were halfway there before I realized Seb wasn't with us.

Before I can reach my mom's purse sitting on the bedside table, it's swiped out of my reach. My father glares daggers at me as he clutches it to his chest. He shakes his head slowly as his knuckles whiten from his grip.

"Don't. You. Dare."

"Give me the purse, Dad. He's got to be worried sick—"

He leans into me, eyes bulging, face crimson and twitching with fury.

"I don't give a shit what he is!" His voice booms with such force, I step back for cover. "That boy has ruined our lives for the last time. Beer drinking, cow tipping, sneaking out … how stupid your mother and I have been. I should have *known* where it all would lead."

"You can't blame—"

"I can and I will!" The purse hits the cabinet across the room with a bang, flinging it open. Medical supplies tumble to the floor as my dad rips at his hair with one hand and points accusingly at me with the other. "It should be him lying in this bed. *Him!*"

"Dad!" I cry, shaking my head, trying to erase the venomous words from my mind.

He doesn't mean it. He doesn't mean it.

He continues to point at me as I hover close to Brady, not sure if I'm trying to protect him or seek protection for myself.

"He will never touch my family again. You hear me?" he whispers, the furious rage cooling into quiet vengeance. "If I see his face, I *promise* you, he'll need a stretcher of his own."

For once, I don't answer back, my body thrumming with an emotion I never thought I'd feel toward my dad.

Fear.

His expression flips back to frenzy, all signs of menace wiped clean. So quick and complete, I wonder if I'd imagined the entire thing. He drops his eyes to the floor and walks across the room and into the hallway.

"Nurse? Nurse!"

"I-I-I-"

"I'm right here, Brady. Don't worry about Dad, okay?"

I lace our fingers once again and shoot a frantic look in my mother's direction for her to *do something*. She never even meets my gaze.

"Autumn!" Brady's voice wraps around my name like a thorny branch, and I jump to attention.

I raise up on my toes to hover over him, looking directly into his eyes. He blinks frantically, then inhales a deep breath.

Then his face crumples. My brother, the hero ... the all-star ... the town legend falls to pieces in front of my eyes.

"I-I-I-," he whispers, loud enough for me to hear, but low enough to make me lean in closer. A single tear slips free, sliding down his temple into the stiff collar around his neck. "I can't feel my legs."

CHAPTER 7

Seb,

This shit has gone on long enough. A few miles won't change what you and Autumn have.

She's not budging, man. You have to go.

Fix this shit,

Brady

P.S. - If Autumn makes me watch one more second of Lifetime television, I'm going to go find your balls in her purse and pulverize them.

Sebastian - Seventeen Years Old
The Past
Prosper, LA

"Come on, Autumn, open up," I whisper, my light tapping on her window becoming more insistent. "I'm not leaving until you talk to me."

Her only response is to flick off her bedroom light and leave me in total darkness. Autumn made her wishes known the second I peeked through her bedroom window. With a

43

furious scowl and red-rimmed eyes, she pulled the blinds closed right in my pleading face.

Any other girl would have called me romantic for deferring my college enrollment. Any other girl would be happy to have a boyfriend who couldn't bear to be away from her. She might even reward her boyfriend for such acts of selflessness, possibly with gratuitous sexual favors.

Autumn is obviously not most girls.

When she found my acceptance letter to Southern Louisiana University jammed in the back of my sock drawer, she was livid. Why hadn't I told her I was accepted? Why would I keep something so important a secret? What other secrets was I keeping from her?

The answer was simple. I never told her about my acceptance because I didn't plan on going. At least not this year. From the moment I unfolded the letter and read "Congratulations" on the first line, I knew what I wanted to do. I also knew what I didn't want to do.

I didn't want to be where Autumn wasn't. It's as simple as that.

I would defer for a year, take a few classes at the local community college, and save up some extra cash while helping my dad with his lawn business. Then once Autumn graduated high school, we'd both take off for Haven in the fall.

So, who's the most romantic and caring boyfriend in the world? This dipshit right here—the one with his shoes suctioned to a pile of mud, sweating his ass off, tapping on a vacant, dark window while his girlfriend pouts about … what in the hell is she pouting about again?

Let's just ignore the fact that she was digging in my things when she found the letter. I'm perfectly willing to forgive that complete invasion of my privacy if she'd only start acting like a rational human being again. If her head would stop spinning like Regan's in *The Exorcist* long enough to listen to me, I'm sure she'd give in to reason.

"Open the damn window, Autumn, or I'm going to ring the doorbell and wake up the whole house, I swear to God—"

"I wouldn't do that if I were you."

I turn as best I can with my feet cemented into the muddy ground and see Mr. Norris in his robe, leaning over the porch railing, amused eyes trained on me. Busted.

"I'm not trying to cause any trouble, I promise. But she won't listen to reason, Mr. Norris," I explain with a frustrated sigh.

"Son, I've been married for longer than you've been alive, so trust me when I tell you this. Females were absent the day God handed out reason. They've got their own way of thinking of things and listen closely to what I'm telling you. Their way is the right way."

Wait … what?

"Now hold on a minute—"

Mr. Norris shakes his head and frowns. "The sooner it seeps into that stubborn skull of yours, the happier you'll be. Now come up here on the porch with me before we wake up the neighbors. Mrs. Coletti keeps a loaded shotgun by the front door, but never remembers to wear those Coke-bottle glasses of hers when she's waving the damn thing around."

I meet him on the front porch steps, and he takes a seat beside me. We both remain quiet for a bit, me thinking about his unreasonable daughter, and him hopefully thinking up the perfect answer to my problem. Obviously, my approach of *"I'm staying here for a year, so deal with it"* had gone over like a gift-wrapped box of rocks, so I'm counting on him to bring this one home for me.

The long-suffering sigh he releases while frowning and shaking his head leaves me doubtful.

"Women are a mystery, Sebastian, and I assure you, my

daughter is no exception. With Mrs. Norris, when I'm wrong, I'm wrong. And when I'm right ..." He looks over to me and shrugs. "You guessed it. I'm still wrong."

"Excuse me for saying so, sir, but that's just crazy."

"That's life with a woman. But in this case, you deferring for a year and staying here in Prosper?" He smiles grimly and meets my gaze. "Any which way you slice it, you're wrong on this one, son."

I slump my shoulders and lower my head in defeat. "How can wanting to be with her be wrong?"

"You think you're giving something up and that's proving your love to Autumn, but you're wrong. You think that's what love is—wanting to be with her all the time and making it happen, no matter the cost." He lets out a labored sigh. "And I guess in some ways it is, but it's an immature kind of love."

My spine goes ramrod straight, and I gnaw my cheek to keep from mouthing off to Autumn's dad. I'm trying to keep us together, and he's calling me immature? Screw that.

"I feel your hackles going up, but just hear me out. Real love is about hard work and sacrifice. It's about doing the things you need to do to make a future. Staying here, waiting around? It's effortless, Sebastian. It's the easy way out. Going to college, showing her you love her enough to make long distance work, that's what real love looks like. Doing what feels good at the time is the easy part. Doing what's right for the future? That's what a real man does."

"If I stay here, I'll save some money, take a few college classes ..."

"But that's not moving forward, son. It's a holding pattern." He slaps a firm palm to my knee and nods. "You know what you gotta do. You gotta do the work."

Do the work. I've heard him say those words a thousand times, but always to Brady. Tossing balls, lifting weights, on the field, no matter where, *do the work*. Mr. Norris is a great motivator for his son, but I never thought he'd take on the role of my relationship coach. I feel honored and kind of creeped out all at the same time.

Or maybe his evil genius plan is to send me far away from his daughter, hoping our relationship will implode and he'll finally be rid of me. With all the hell the three of us have raised over the years, I can't rule out the possibility completely. Except ... deep down I think the old man really likes me. And he can't scare me off so easily—I'm sure he realizes that by now.

"Do the work, huh?"

"You know what you need to do. My daughter is one helluva person, and she could never live with herself if you put your life on hold for her. That girl doesn't have a selfish bone in her body, so it's no matter that she's gonna miss the hell out of you, she still knows in her heart of hearts she's got to let you go." Mr. Norris lifts to standing and places a hand on my shoulder. "And when the two of you make it through that year apart, you'll both be stronger for it. And that's how you build a relationship that lasts."

"Yeah," I say, as a thousand random thoughts circle my brain and my plans make a complete one-eighty.

Mr. Norris chuckles. "Scary shit, huh? I can hear it in your voice. That's how you know you're doing the right thing. Now go find my daughter and make things right, okay? She's making the rest of us miserable. And I wouldn't object to you telling Mrs. Norris that I was the one who fixed everything; ya hear me? Let me be the one that's right for a change."

CHAPTER 8

Sebastian
Present Day
Prosper, LA

The boards groan beneath my feet when I hit the third step, and I smile. Some things never change. Mrs. Norris has her fall chrysanthemums proudly displayed on the porch, *The Prosper Daily* is still on the doormat waiting to be picked up and read, and Mr. Norris will never get around to fixing that third step on the porch. The creak sounds more like a welcome than a nuisance at this point. I should savor it since it's definitely the only welcome I'll receive. Regardless, I'm here to say my piece.

Like Lance said, do what I need to do, and then finally, *finally* let it go.

I wish it were as easy as that. I wish I could say what I came here to say, then leave my baggage on the Norris's creaky third step. Just walk away, for better or worse and get on with my life. Moving to Haven, starting fresh and growing the fuck up, has healed pieces of my heart, but there's always that part, shoved way back in the corner, festering with the knowledge that things are still unresolved. Words have been left unsaid. That knowledge feels like a tether, holding me hostage in so many ways.

Marge's all too familiar words of wisdom come to mind— words she's told me dozens of times since the day I washed up on her and Joe's doorstep.

Do what you've always done, and you'll get what you've always got.

So here I stand, doing something I never thought I'd have the guts to do, expecting ... well, I'm not entirely sure what I'm expecting, really. But it seems like the first step in the direction of healing.

As I knock on the front door, I try to stifle the hope simmering up to the surface. I can't help but notice the SUV in the driveway—the same SUV from the cemetery earlier. I'd give anything for either Autumn or Brady to answer the door, but there's little chance of that. Mr. and Mrs. Norris warned me away all those years ago, and there's no way they'll let me waltz back into town, and back into their lives, without a fight. History proves they don't fight fair, and today won't be any different.

Mr. Norris steps onto the porch, arms crossed and face impassive. The door clicks shut behind him, and he doesn't say a single word.

Hello, stone wall...

"I'm not here to cause trouble," I say, raising my hands as a gesture of truce.

"Aren't you?" He releases a dragon breath and shakes his head. "Son, I'm sorry for your loss, but ... I can't imagine why you'd think showing up here would be a good idea." His tone is clipped, and I barely recognize the man in front of me.

I'm fully aware that my foolish actions caused this change in him. I've had years to ruminate on how my actions would affect his opinion of me, but I've never experienced it first-hand. I was sent away without ever seeing the full force of his anger, and today, it feels like a close-range gunshot. Time has done nothing to heal the gaping wound I've left behind.

I'd always thought of Mr. Norris as a fair man, almost a second father to me. I've sat at their dinner table, had sleep-overs and campouts with their son, tagged along to Sunday Mass ... loved their daughter. I'd cared for Brady and Autumn's parents all those years ago, and I know they'd cared about me, too. I know he cared for me, but that was a long time ago. A lifetime ago, it seems.

"I know I'm the last person you want to see ..." He lets out a sarcastic huff and shakes his head. "But I only came here to apologize. I never got the chance back then, and I want you and your family to know how deeply sorry I am for the pain I've caused."

"Sorry? You're sorry?" He throws up his hands in exasper-ation and barks out a humorless laugh. "Well, since you're sorry, we'll forget all about it—"

"That's not what I mean," I interrupt, feeling my temper bristle at the insinuation that my words are careless and flippant.

"Since you're sorry, we can erase all Brady's years of frus-tration and physical therapy. I'll grab the phone and call LSU right now. Let them know Sebastian Kelly is sorry, so my son will be on the field and ready to practice next week."

His words wheeze out in a long, labored exhale. The diatribe expels like a deflating balloon, and at the end, Mr. Norris looks spent. The silence between us feels insur-mountable. He inspects me, like a hateful child making the most of a magnifying glass and the burning sun, for no other reason than he can.

It's clear that nothing I say will penetrate the blame and anger that's been carefully crafted and nurtured over the years. I did as they said—I left and never contacted them. Today, it seems as if that may have been the worst mistake I could have made. The passage of time and my silence only allowed the hurt to fester and grow. My hope for a different future withers away with each of his menacing glares.

"Since you're sorry," he whispers.

"You don't get to act like I don't care. You don't get to send me away, then stand here and berate me for not being here for Brady. It's unfair and you know it."

"What's unfair is that you get to waltz into town and apologize and have this weight lifted from you. You get to be free from all of this, but what about my boy?" Mr. Norris's voice cracks, and I resist the urge to touch his shoulder. Grab his hand. Share this pain with him, because yes, I hurt for Brady, too. I think of what he's lost, and I'm overcome with the desire to turn back the clock.

But I'm the last person he wants comfort from.

"You think I came here today to be what? Absolved? To be set free?" I can't leech the incredulous tone from my voice because what the fuck? This man has no clue who I am. "That's not what I want. It's *never* what I've wanted. It's what *you* demanded of me."

Another weighty silence falls between us, and I release a frustrated breath.

"I don't want to be free. That's not what I wanted then, and it's definitely not what I want now. I needed to be in the thick of it, right alongside Brady, doing whatever I could to help my best friend. And it wouldn't have been a penance—it would have been a privilege. Still would. Helping Brady, being there for him, is all I've ever wanted. He was my *best friend*, Mr. Norris. Autumn was my—"

"Don't say it. Don't you even dare say her name." He stabs a finger into my chest, then recoils like my chest is made of hot coals. He drops his chin to his chest and shakes his head.

Just when I think he's going to walk away from me, he sucks in a tortured breath and meets my gaze.

"If I could just see them," I whisper, unashamed of the pleading in my voice.

"We had a deal. You stay the hell out of town and away from my family. In return, I don't sue you for every penny you've got. If you want me to keep up my end of the bargain, I suggest you get the hell off my property, get into your car, and *drive*." His eyes burn with anger and saliva collects in the corners of his mouth as he points to the road behind me. "Just drive and don't stop until you see the Prosper city limit sign fading in your rearview mirror."

I pull my keys out of my pocket and squeeze the jagged edges into the flesh of my palm. Mr. Norris and I will never understand each other, and this conversation could go in wicked circles for eternity. I need to back off ... for now.

"I'll leave, and I'll never bother Autumn or Brady again, if that's their wish. But if it's not ..." I say, pausing until I have his full attention. "If that's not what they want, though, then all bets are off. Circumstances have changed. You can't hurt my family anymore, Mr. Norris. So, I won't promise to stay away from yours."

My parents' death wounded me in many ways. Never feeling their acceptance, knowing they'll never see the man I've become ... so many regrets. I'll live with that in some way for the rest of my life, whether it be open wounds or mended scars. But there's no denying it freed me in others. I didn't leave Prosper out of fear for my own well-being. I left to spare my parents. My father didn't deserve to have everything he'd worked his entire life for ripped away because of me.

But now, here I stand, a man with nothing to lose—a loose cannon. And if the expression on Mr. Norris's face is any indication, he knows it. And he doesn't like it one bit.

Without another word, he turns on his foot and reenters the house, leaving me staring at my second childhood home with jumbled feelings of regret laced with the tiniest amount of hope. What did he say to spark hope in me? Not a damn thing, if I'm honest, but the dreamer in me is a resilient little bastard, able to survive on faith and fumes.

I back away, watching the third window on the right, willing a certain pair of blue eyes to peek through and meet mine. Wishing she would crack open her window like she'd done a thousand times before, and race into my arms.

A sharp whistle jerks me back into reality, staring at the vacant window and steeling away my aching heart. My head jerks, and I do a double take at the scene before me.

Brady motions me closer with a wave of his hand as he sits perched in the driver's side of the SUV. The door is swung open, and his wheelchair occupies the space on the ground.

He throws a thumb behind him and jerks his head. "Throw the wheels in the back and get in. I've had to use this piece of shit all week since my van's in the shop. Pain in my ass."

"Wh-what?" I stammer, shaking my head in confusion.

"Hurry the fuck up, dude," Brady chides sarcastically while shooting me a what-are-you-waiting-for grin.

I continue shaking my head, hoping the motion will unclog my brain. "If I get in the car with you, your dad will call the police and have my ass thrown in jail for kidnapping. Not sure how you've missed it, but the guy hates my guts."

"I'm a cripple, you fool, not a child. You can't kidnap a willing, *grown ass* man."

"Brady, I'm trying to show your parents that I'm not the same stupid kid. I seriously doubt taking off with you right now is a step in the right direction ..." My voice tapers off, hoping Brady will hear the voice of reason and agree to a friendly driveway chat.

When he stays silent for five seconds, then ten seconds, I think I've gotten through.

Brady's lips curve into a mischievous smile, and he mutters under his breath, "Pussy."

Shit ...

I begrudgingly grab the wheelchair, toss it in the back, and climb into the passenger's seat. I'm impressed with the modified handles and controls made to accommodate Brady. He cranks the engine as I slide my seat belt into place.

"Let's hope your 'crippled' ass can drive," I mutter, throwing his choice of words right back at him as the SUV jerks into reverse.

CHAPTER 9

Dear Autumn,
Halloween—I'll be Westley, and you'll be my Buttercup. My
princess bride. I'll protect you at the haunted house tonight.
Unless you tell anyone the costumes were my idea. Then I'll leave
you for dead in the Hillbilly Hell Room.
As you wish,
Seb

Autumn - Sixteen Years Old
The Past
Prosper, LA

Sandy's high-pitched shriek blows out my eardrums, and I stumble as she shoves me forward. With my ringing ears and the struggle to stay upright, I barely register the snarling zombies clawing at us from behind the steel cage. Another piece of my dress rips under my heel, and I groan.

"Sandy, you've got to get it together, or I'm gonna walk out of this haunted house buck naked."

"Is it over? Is it over? We've got to be close to the end,

right?" I reach around and pull her close behind me as I inch toward the buzzing of a chainsaw. She cries, "Oh no, that can't be good!"

"Just stay behind me, tuck your head into my neck, and close your dang eyes." She does as I ask and whimpers. I blow out a frustrated breath. "I don't know why you ever thought this was a good idea. You get twitchy watching *Criminal Minds*."

"Because it's creepy! If *Criminal Minds* doesn't scare the shit out of you, then there's something wrong."

"Stop screeching, or I'm going to throw you in the cage with the zombies." I laugh as she trembles behind me.

The Prosperians for Change, the local civic organization, sponsor the annual fright house and cornfield maze every year. Sandy always begs me to go with her, and every year she all but pees her pants as we make our way through. Usually Seb likes a front row seat to the freak show—Sandy, not the haunted house—but he was nowhere to be found when we got here. This Buttercup is without her Westley, and I've been itching to find him. The best part of Halloween is getting "lost" in the corn maze with Seb.

The "transplant-gone-wrong" scene is the last stop, and the ice chest is overflowing with entrails as the vampire nurse reaches inside and takes a whopping bite of large intestine.

Sandy clutches her chest and dry heaves. "I'm go-go-gonna—"

"If you paint my back with the Baconator you scarfed down earlier, I swear on all that is holy, I will *cut* you, you hear me?" I reach back, grab ahold of her arm, and jerk her forward. "Keep it moving."

The cool October air crashes into us as we step onto the creaky front porch, and Sandy holds herself up with one hand pressed against the house and the other clutching my shoulder. Watching her catch her breath with her Vote for Pedro T-shirt, oversized eyeglasses, and her slightly askew afro feels like my reward for enduring the haunted house with her. My doofus of a best friend is in rare form, but I love her.

"You gonna make it, Napoleon?" I ask as I hand her a few tissues to wipe her sweaty forehead.

She narrows her eyes at me, but before she can deliver a snarky response, I hear Seb calling my name. I raise a finger in her direction as I turn around, and she huffs.

Sebastian, my own, personal Westley, stands below the porch, gripping the railing as he drinks me in. His hair is darker than the original Westley, but he's feathered it perfectly. The ties of his flowy man-shirt hang loose, exposing a bit of his chest. He even grew a teeny mustache to look the part. It's perfect. He's perfect.

"Wow," he breathes as the corner of his mouth quirks up into a lopsided grin. "You take my breath away, Buttercup."

I lower my head and flutter my lashes bashfully. "Thank you, kind sir," I whisper as I lift the sides of my dress and lower into a deep curtsy.

"I should throw you over my shoulder right now and steal you away."

"To the cornfield? Yes, please." A little shiver runs down my spine at the thought, but it stops short when I catch Seb's frown. "What's wrong?"

He reaches out a hand to me. "We've got a little problem." He flinches and lifts his shoulders in a resigned shrug. "Actually, we've got a two-hundred-pound problem ... and it's time sensitive."

"Oh no." I round the railing and walk down the front porch steps, wondering what Brady has gotten up to. "What did he do?"

This football season has been the most stressful of Brady's

life. The whole town is counting on him to bring home the championship. My dad has constant video, along with unhelpful commentary, going at home—last week's game tape, the other team's game tape, highlights and low points of Brady's game play. The scouts are in the stands most Friday nights. And Brady looks like a pressure cooker, ready to blow at any second. I had a feeling it was just a matter of time before he would implode.

Everyone thinks being the football star is the greatest thing there is, but that's not what I see when I look at my older brother these days. Being the town hero looks like misery if you ask me.

Seb salutes Sandy. "So long, Napoleon. I'll take a rain check on your dance routine."

"Huh?"

"Are you serious?" he scoffs. "You can't dress up as Napoleon Dynamite if you can't rock the ending dance number."

Sandy rights her afro and pushes her glasses up her nose. "You don't think I can rock it?"

Her eyebrows lift in challenge just as her hips start to gyrate in her skintight Wranglers. When she throws in the jazz hands, there's no doubt she's in touch with her inner geek. She stops abruptly and points at Seb. "To be continued."

"You gotta stand for somefin …"

I hear Brady's drunken, off-key singing before I actually see him and shoot Seb a weary glance. We round the corner, and a muddied pair of work boots are all that's sticking out from underneath the house.

"You gotta be your own man …"

The boots shuffle in the dirt, and a loud clanging comes

from underneath the house. I assume his routine includes gestures, too, and Seb jumps into action to grab a bottle from the booted doofus.

Wild Turkey ... yeah, not the greatest idea my brother's ever had.

"You don' haveta call me darlin' ... *hey* ... where's ma whiskey?" Brady slurs. He starts to shuffle out from underneath the house, but a big thud causes him to stop short. A pained groan fills the night air. "Yup, thas gonna leave a mark."

A giggle escapes my lips before I can muffle it with my hand. "Dude is toast."

"That's an understatement. His eyeballs are floating in a pool of whiskey."

As ridiculous as Brady sounds holding a one-man, off-tune country concert, nobody's going to be laughing if he gets caught. Grounded at home, possibly suspended from the team ... things will go downhill quickly if we don't do something.

"We've got to get him out of here before someone sees him. Coach ... Principal Higgins ... God, my dad. He'll kill him, Seb," I whisper while trying to figure out the least conspicuous route from where we are to the parking lot.

Seb bends down, takes hold of Brady's ankles, and pulls with all of his might. My brother appears from under the house, a whole lot of dusty with a lopsided gorilla mask on his head. His groan gets louder as Seb grabs his arms and heaves him up to a sitting position. He lets out a wet and nasty burp as the gorilla mask falls to the ground.

"If you're gonna hurl, do it now, brother. Before we get in the truck," Seb warns as he hauls him up to standing.

Brady throws an arm around Seb's shoulder and teeters on unsteady feet. "S'all good, man. I'm feeling good. So fine."

I shove the gorilla mask back on Brady's bobbing head, then wrap his other arm around my shoulders for support.

"The mask makes it easier to hide you while we're getting out of here."

"Also muzzles that ninety-proof breath," Seb mutters under his breath, and I giggle.

∼

I toss the muddy boots, gorilla mask, and sweaty T-shirt into the corner of Brady's room as he lays sprawled on the bed.

"Safe and sound, and nobody's the wiser," I say as I draw a quilt over him. "Sorry, but the jeans stay. Drunk or not, you're still my brother."

Brady catches my wrist as I try to stand and levels me with a defeated look in his eyes. At this moment, he looks way more sober than I thought he could.

"What if they would have found me? Would that be so bad?"

"Oh, I don't know. Suspended from the team, grounded for life, more yelling from Dad than either of our eardrums can withstand. Don't even get me started on the scouts. Doesn't get much worse than that, does it?" I pull the quilt up to his chin and tuck it tightly around his body all the way to his waist. I gently tap his chest and let out a relieved laugh. "But no worries, right? Crisis averted."

He should be thankful we saved his drunk ass. He should be freaking overcome with gratitude.

Whew, Autumn, that was a close one! Thank you so much for looking out for me. I don't know what I'd do without y'all.

Brady says none of that. He places an arm over his forehead, shielding his face, and releases a heavy sigh.

"I hear you say suspended from the team, and I know I should be relieved I wasn't caught." He mashes his palms into his eyes and groans. "I should be fucking relieved, Autumn. But the truth is I feel like my chest is being squeezed by an iron fist."

I drop down to sit on the bed beside him, dumbfounded. "What are you saying, Brady?"

I take a long look at the person in front of me, because no way is this my brother talking. He can't mean what he's saying. He'd never toss away his lifelong dream like that. No amount of pressure or stress can erase what's he's worked so hard for. He's got a knack for taking all the crap that's thrown at him and spinning it into one helluva Friday night highlight reel. The guy sitting in front of me doesn't look anything like the brother I know.

He scrubs his face in frustration and waves me off. "Shit. Don't listen to me. It's just the whiskey talking. Don't believe a word I say," he says as he shakes his head. "I'm just tired and feeling sorry for myself."

There's more truth to his words than either of us would like to admit, but I wouldn't know where to start with *that* land mine. I wrack my brain for the right words, but everything comes up short.

So I settle for, "Okay."

God, I'm such an idiot.

"Okay," Brady returns with a slightly more cheerful smile. It's obvious it's only for my benefit, but I'll take it.

"I'm gonna …" I say, throwing a thumb behind me. "Seb's waiting for me at the corner. So …"

He wrenches the covers out from underneath me, and I stumble to standing with the force. The wall breaks my fall, and I grace my big brother with a one finger salute. "Get outta here. And don't you dare get caught sneaking out. We've dodged one bullet tonight; I doubt we'd be so lucky a second time."

"Don't worry about me, big brother. As long as the golden

boy is tucked safely in bed, no one notices what the baby sister does," I say with a lightness I try my best to feel. "Pay no attention to the sister on the sidelines."

Isn't it funny how the boy who carries the world on his shoulders dreams of letting it all go, and the girl with all the freedom at her fingertips just wants someone to care if she comes home? Or maybe it isn't funny at all.

I'm out the door and down the street without so much as a peep from my parents. When I round the block and see Seb waiting for me on the tailgate of his truck, I break out into a run. His solid body absorbs the shock when I launch myself at him. My arms latch around his neck, my feet lock behind his back, and my lips meet his for a kiss that's long overdue.

I open my eyes to find him gazing back at me, and we both laugh.

"Hi," I whisper as my lips brush his.

"Hey," he returns, tucking a lock of hair behind my ear.

And suddenly, I'm not the invisible little sister anymore. There is someone in this world—the one who matters most —who sees me just fine.

CHAPTER 10

Dear Autumn,
What do you say to the girl who stole your heart before you even
knew what to do with it? How do you apologize for breaking hers
when she trusted you to protect it? The answer is I don't have a
clue, but I'll spend every day of the rest of my life figuring it out if
you'd only let me. I've done a lot of things that I'm not proud of, but
you were always the one good thing in my life. I hope one day you
can forgive me for the hurt I've caused. I'm a different man than
the scared boy who left, and I'll always be here, hoping you give me
the chance to prove it to you.
Always waiting,
Sebastian

Autumn
Present Day
Providence, LA

"What did the letter say?" Brady asks for the millionth time.

"Oh, I didn't tell you about it?" I throw my toothbrush

and hairdryer into the duffel bag and start shuffling through drawers. "Probably because it's none of your business."

Before I can throw my ratty jeans into the bag, Brady swipes it away and puts it behind his back. He shakes his head and glares.

"Who gave you that little love note? Me! Now it *is* a love note, right?" I cross my arms and pinch my lips shut. "Autumn, I am literally the messenger. People kill the messenger. They, at the very least, tell them what is in the note before sending them to the guillotine. So?"

I reach behind him and retrieve my bag, all the while continuing to pack and ignore him completely. He releases a long sigh, letting me know he's in it for the long haul.

Relentless. My brother will peck something to death until there is nothing left but dust and gravel. As my hand runs over Seb's note, tucked safely in the side zipper of the duffel, I'm certain that's all that's left of the two of us. Dust, gravel, and a deep-seated resentment.

His letter? Just pretty words. The ugly swirling in my gut after Seb skipped town without a word is still alive and well inside me. No amount of ink and paper can make up for actions that sliced, scarred down deep into my heart, not to mention my family.

Not to mention my own actions after the accident. I did what I had to do to make a life for myself, and I can't apologize for that now. When the love of your life hightails it without a word, you move on. You make do. And you never let those words of betrayal see the tip of a pen or top of a page. Some things are better left unsaid, and some wrongs are best left unforgiven.

Until fate tap dances in and shuffle-ball-steps all over your best laid plans.

After years of no contact and no clue where Sebastian Kelly ran off to, there he was, back in our hometown. When

Brady asked me to attend the Kellys' funeral with him, I was hesitant at first but figured there was no way he'd actually show.

Heel toe ... well done, karma.

Then Brady tells me he lives in Haven. Haven—home to Southern Louisiana University. The only college in the state of Louisiana with a graduate program in physical therapy. And it just so happens he's got a great apartment for rent at nearly half the rate of any other apartments in the area.

Heel toe step heel ... Seriously, karma, can't I get a break?

"I see that drawn-up, crotchety face you're putting on, and I don't like it, sis. Things aren't—" He pulls the bag away from me again and waits for me to meet his eye. "Things didn't happen the way we thought they did back then."

"Really, Brady? It was all a bad dream? You weren't hurt. He didn't run. I-I-"

"You and me? Yeah, that shit happened. But he didn't run, at least not like you think he did."

I shake my head, rejecting his words. No matter how much I protest, he keeps talking, breaking down the carefully crafted world I live in.

All the tears ... all the lies ... how? How in the hell did we end up in this mess?

With every word Brady utters, karma keeps on tap dancing. Shuffle-ball-step ... heel toe ... heel toe step heel.

I'm just not sure if it's fracturing my heart or breaking down my resolve.

Only time will tell.

CHAPTER 11

Sebastian
Two Months Later
Haven, LA

"If you ever let one slip in class, just pawn it off on whoever's sitting behind you. I mean, don't fart if you can help it, but things happen sometimes."

"Temple is an all-boys school, Uncle Seb. If I were to guess, they probably hold farting contests at lunch every day," Isaac says, chuckling to himself.

"You're right, I bet they do. Still good advice, though," I say, and Isaac keeps doodling in his notebook. "If you go skinny dipping, be sure you stash your clothes in a secret hiding spot. Nothing like walking out of a cold pond to find your shit's been snatched. You know, because it's *cold*."

"Oh God," Isaac whispers, and I see the splotchy red crawling up his neck.

"I'm not trying to embarrass you, man, but I feel like I have all this knowledge to impart on you. God knows your dad probably never did. He's strung so tight, I seriously doubt he's able to fart. And I'm pretty sure that GI Joe getup is stitched directly onto his skin, so no skinny dipping either. For the next couple of years, it's me and you, kid. That's not a lot of time to give you the keys to the kingdom, but I sure want to try."

"I swear, Uncle Seb, I'm *good*." Isaac chuckles and closes his notebook. "I won't fart when I shouldn't, and I'll keep the shrinkage under wraps. Okay?"

"Okay. Oh! And remember, a buzz only lasts so long, but the photographic evidence is forever." I cringe at the thought of what was probably floating around Prosper when I was a kid. Since his neck is already flaming red, I'll keep those stories to myself for now.

Isaac's only been living with me for a week, but he's settling in nicely. I was hesitant at first, when Lance called, saying his son needed a place to live for his last two years of high school. I've only met the kid a handful of times. But Isaac's only options were moving in with me or moving to Germany with his mom and stepdad. I remember being out of options all too well, so in the end, I was happy to give Isaac another alternative. He still had to move away from home, but Louisiana's a shitload closer to Texas than Germany.

My house is nearly twice the size of my old apartment above the coffee shop. Because of that, I expedited the move so we could have a bit more leg room. Most nights, I come home to find the laundry and dishes all taken care of. The most rebellious thing he's done this week is go through my record collection. The kid's got great taste in music, so I even showed him where I keep my record player. He's the most well-behaved roommate a man could ask for.

Above all else, he's funny and kind, and very aware of the people around him. I don't think that can be said for most teenagers. I was happy to open my home to Isaac, but I hadn't counted on really liking the kid. But I do. And I want to give him sixteen years' worth of uncle wisdom as quickly as possible, no matter how embarrassed he gets.

Isaac looks around the deserted coffee house and shrugs. The last of the customers filtered out about twenty minutes ago.

"Mind if I head to the house, Uncle Seb? Mom's supposed to call me in thirty minutes, and I want to shower before then."

He shoves the notebook into his book sack and tosses it over his shoulder. School doesn't start for another month, and the kid's already toting his book sack around. See what I mean? Perfect.

The coffee shop is only a few blocks from the house, so he pops in when he's bored, or the fridge is lacking. I'm working on my domestic tendencies, but I'm still a bachelor at heart. A jar of pickles and a bag of beef jerky usually sum up the contents of my fridge and pantry. Isaac and I have mastered the art of take-out.

"Yeah, that's fine. Just flip the sign to closed on your way out. I think I'll shut down a little early tonight," I say, as I walk to the back to turn out the lights. I hear the jingle of the door as Issac walks out, and I wait to hear it click shut behind him.

"Sorry, we're closed for the night," I hear him say, but I keep walking, hoping the straggling customer will take his cue and leave so I can get everything cleaned up for the night.

"Oh ... I-I thought you were open until nine."

The hair on the back of my neck stands on end because I know that voice. *I'll never forget that voice.*

I'm halfway across the shop before I even realize I'm moving. "Wait," I call out, petrified she'll leave or vanish into thin air before I can rejoice in the fact that she came to me. She came to me—that has to mean *something*.

I pull the door from Isaac's grasp and open it wide.

"One more lesson for the night, Isaac. When a girl shows up … when *the* girl shows up, you're always open," I say, never tearing my eyes away from Autumn.

I watch her teeth tug at her bottom lip. I memorize the curve of her neck, the wisps of hair brushing against it. I breathe in every piece of her I've loved since I was a boy and hold it close to my heart.

Delicate, fidgeting fingers. Nails painted, but always chipped.

Freckles dancing across the bridge of her nose, no matter how hard she tries to hide them.

Azure eyes, fierce even in sorrow, because nothing and no one can steal her fire.

Home. Autumn will always be home to me.

"O … kay…" Isaac says as he stands between me and everything I've ever wanted.

"See you at home, Isaac." I give him a gentle nudge in the right direction—the right direction being out of my damn way.

"Oh, right!" His body jolts into action, and he waves awkwardly at Autumn before taking off.

We stare at each other for long seconds, and I revel at the mere sight of her. After starving for all those years, no matter how long I stare, it'll never be enough. It's always been that way with her—never enough time, never enough kisses … never enough. A smile tugs at my lips, and my heart stutters in my chest as if the cocoon protecting me for years cracks open and withers away, leaving me vibrant, alive, and ready to take on the world.

Autumn's mood obviously doesn't match mine, her expression more a mixture of fear and hesitation. She looks on the verge of throwing herself into my arms and running in the other direction, all at the same time. She wrings her hands in front of her stomach, and my eyes zero in on the piece of paper fisted in them.

Seeing her feels amazing, but strained and uneasy at the same time. The energy between us feels forced and unnatural —when being with Autumn, loving her, has been the most natural thing in my life.

Being here with her today feels like coming home again, only to find the photos taken off the wall and the design a cold, impersonal art deco.

"Part of me is confused. And sorry. But the biggest part, after all this time, is still so angry," she whispers.

"Come inside, Autumn, please."

"And I don't know how to stop," she says, ignoring my request. She holds up the paper in her fist and frowns. "I've read this letter, more times than I care to admit, and I want a chance to see what's next, but I know I'm not ready to take it. So many regrets that can't be forgiven. There are things, Seb … things you don't know …"

"I know," I whisper. I reach out to take her hand, but she shies away from me. "Just … come inside and let's—"

"How could you just leave me?" Her voice cracks on the last word, and she sucks in a sharp breath.

I suck in my lips, attempting to hide the flinch. Hearing the question I've asked myself a hundred, no, a thousand times over hurts as much as it always has. It hurts that much more coming from her.

Why did you leave? You should've gone back. You never ever should have left.

Cue the self-deprecating ramblings of my regretful mind.

"It wasn't that simple. I was wrong, and I'm so sorry, but it just wasn't that simple."

I want to say a thousand things, explain to her every

single thought bottled up inside of me since the day my parents kicked me out. But the look on her face tells me I don't have that kind of time. One wrong move and she'll run. One wrong move and I'll lose her forever.

"I know it wasn't. It wasn't simple for you to leave and it wasn't easy for me to stay. My brain knows you're sorry, but my heart just can't catch up," she says with a humorless smile. "You know, things weren't simple at home either. You didn't take all the complications with you when you left." She sighs and shakes her head. "And here we are."

"Yes. Here we are." I smile and shrug. "But that's something. Right?"

She huffs, and her lips turn down into a resigned frown. "Brady told me you have an apartment for rent. I've been searching for a place, but they're all way out of my price range. I didn't realize the rent prices were this high in Haven. I start school in a month, and I've got nowhere to live." She sounds exasperated and more than a little put-out. She shrugs and lets out a frustrated sigh. "It seems I'm out of options."

"It's yours," I say quickly.

"Wait. I don't even know where it—"

"We'll work all that out later, but the location is great. It's in a safe area, and it's newly remodeled. It'll be perfect for you, I promise."

"How many bedrooms?"

"One. Well, one bedroom and a smaller room I always used as an office," I explain. "But the walls are partial. They're tall, but don't go all the way up to the ceiling, so I wouldn't suggest a roommate."

She nods, and I exhale a relieved breath. "Okay. Thank you," she says, sounding relieved. She chews her lip nervously, and her steely eyes settle on mine. "It's just an apartment. Right? I need it to be just an apartment."

71

"Yeah, of course," I answer too quickly and with a nod resembling a bobble head with a loose spring.

I choose to ignore the edge of reluctance in her posture and the firm set of her jaw. Autumn may not be able to forgive me today, but if she takes the apartment, I have every day for the foreseeable future to convince her I'm the only one for her. I always have been, and I always will be. The fact that she doesn't realize the apartment is above the coffee shop I own? Just a minor detail.

She tosses a thumb over her shoulder and crinkles her nose. "Isaac? Lance's son, right?"

"Right. His mom moved overseas with her husband, and Lance is always on tour. He's going to live with me for the next couple of years. Uncle Sebastian to the rescue." I shoot her a sheepish smile and shrug. "Let's hope I don't corrupt him. How much damage can I do in two years, right?"

Autumn raises her eyebrows and presses her lips together, then we both laugh. Together. And it feels like home. It feels like after years of being on the outside, afraid to look in, I may finally get to come home.

Her mood sobers, and she gives me a soft smile. "I didn't have a chance to tell you before, but your parents, Seb... Well, you know how I felt about your mom ... about both of them, really. I'm so sorry."

"Thanks," I say, resisting the urge to reach out and squeeze her hand. "That means a lot."

We talk about rent and move-in dates, and somehow, I'm able to skirt the tiny issue of location. We talk logistics, and my mind reels with all the unspoken words hanging between us.

I've missed you like crazy.

I don't want to spend another day without you.

A love this strong was never meant to end.

But she gives me a terse wave over her shoulder, and I

return it with a hopeful smile and wait. There will be a time for everything I want to say to her, and it's fast approaching. I've opened the door today. Now I only need to get her to walk through it. And I'll wait for that day. I'll always wait for Autumn.

CHAPTER 12

Dear Seb,
When your fingers slide between mine, I break into a full body
shiver.
When our chests press together, I feel our hearts beat as one.
When your lips brush against mine, I hear the whisper of every
promise you've ever made to me.
You are mine, and I am yours. No amount of distance will ever
change that.
Forever,
Autumn

Autumn - Sixteen Years Old
The Past
Prosper, LA

"I think we should run away tonight." Nuzzled into Seb's neck, I feel the chuckle bubbling in his chest. "With the championship game next week, no one would even notice we were gone until it was too late."

His thumb circles over my bare hip, and the sensation is

like a hundred first kisses rolled into one touch. His hands running up my bare legs; the brush of his chest against mine as he hovers over me; the feel of our bodies coming together on a gasp, then a contented sigh. We've lived a lifetime of memories in the making, and tonight feels like the culmination of every kiss, touch, and secret we've shared.

"Who needs high school diplomas? We'll just live on love." He pauses, his words and his thumb. "Love and squeeze cheese. Our skin will have an orange tint from all the dye and plastic we've eaten, but orange people need love too, right?"

"Yes, yes they do."

When I found Sebastian's first note earlier this afternoon, I never imagined we would end up here.

You are my first and last thought, and that's no lie,
You'll find the next clue where lizards fly.

The folded-up note peeked out from between the bricks of the pool house. With each clue, he walked me through our memories. Our favorite hide-and-seek spot; the stop sign that marked how far we could venture on our bikes, even though we never listened; Mr. Janson's fence where we kissed for the first time. And the last clue led me here.

I'll always be with you, this I've solemnly vowed.
Come and find me where girls aren't allowed.

Like some stupid sign written by stinky boys could ever keep me away. The cabin hadn't started out as much—just a few pieces of plywood lodged between tree roots with a corrugated metal roof resting on top. Over time, our death trap of a hideaway got makeover after makeover. Today, it's got an honest-to-goodness floor, windows, and roof that doesn't blow away at the whisper of a rain storm. I'd even made curtains, although I was nearly outvoted on that one. It helps when you stick your tongue down the swing-vote's throat.

I saw the candles glowing in the window as I made my way through the trees. When I peeked my head inside, I couldn't believe my eyes. Rose petals littered the floor and photos spanning a decade covered the unfinished walls. Gone was the cracked ice chest where we used to hide the beer. In its place was a picnic basket and my favorite person sitting cross-legged next to it wearing the sweetest, most vulnerable expression I've ever seen.

Fisting the stack of notes in my hand and hurling the crumpled mess at his head, I hollered, "It's about time!"

He busted out laughing and reached for me.

I'd been throwing myself at my boyfriend for months. *Months.* Honestly, I was beginning to feel like that little girl with lopsided braids and dirty knees again.

He wanted everything to be perfect. He wanted it to be the right time. Honestly, there had been moments when I'd been a hair's breadth away from yelling, "The right time is right the hell now!" I couldn't make him see that it would be perfect because it was us, not because of the time or place.

"And we'll have little orange babies. Two of them, I think."

His words snap me back to the present, and my eyes widen. The burn of emotion pricks behind my eyes as I beat back happy tears. I know it's just a silly daydream, two teenagers thinking of a faraway future, but it's been *my* dream for so long. To know Sebastian thinks about those things, looks at his life and sees me there by his side, is surreal.

"Yeah, two kids," I whisper, failing to hide the smile in my voice as I tip my forehead into his chest. "We'll name them Aria and Wyatt."

"Aria and Wyatt? Hmm, I think I like that." He brushes my hair behind my ear and tips my chin to meet his eyes.

"Doesn't the name Aria sound delicate and angelic? You can't even say it without sounding reverent. Aria ... Aria ... Aria." I giggle when he pinches my side. "Isn't it so pretty?"

His face breaks into a wide grin. "I think I love it. And you."

Our lips crash together, hungry and hot, as if we haven't spent the night devouring each other. As if no one else in the world has ever wanted another person so badly, loved someone this much. And it's hard to believe that anyone has. What I feel for Seb is too big to fit inside the confines of my body. My chest could explode with it. My fingers vibrate with the need to touch him, feel his warmth. My body is a feeble cage, and my heart is ripping at its seams.

My breaths come out in short bursts as I rest my forehead against his. "Do you think anyone else has ever felt this way?"

"Never." He wraps an arm around my waist and squeezes. "Are you sore? Did I hurt you?"

"I'm a little sore, yeah, but nothing worth fussing over. I feel wonderful."

"I'll be better next time, I promise. I'll get better." Seb nods his head, his lips pressed into a thin, determined line.

"How could it be any better? It was perfect," I say, then press my lips to his. "*You* were perfect."

Sebastian has been my first in all things, and today I was a first for him, too. I feel like the luckiest girl in the world.

"Yeah?"

"Yeah," I say with a reassuring smile, then slide into the

crook of his arm. "Maybe we don't have to go anywhere. We can hole up here and sneak into our houses for food while everyone's gone. It would be perfection."

Seb chuckles. "Until summer comes around and that hot-as-fuck, after-sex sheen you've got going on your skin right now turns into swamp ass."

"You love my ass."

A grabby hand squeezes my right cheek, then gives it a playful slap.

"That I do." He hesitates for a moment before pushing up to sitting, then cradling me in his lap. "I know I'm not the best at telling you how I feel. My heart doesn't come through in my words, but I hope you can see it in my eyes, feel it when I touch you … hold you … kiss you. Because you are my future, Autumn."

He levels me with his tender gaze—so vulnerable and loving. He shows me how he feels in so many ways every day. How could I ever doubt that?

"And you're my future, Sebastian. Don't ever doubt it—I know how you feel. And don't ever doubt me, because every plan I have includes you. Tomorrow, next month, next year … forever."

"It's you and me huh?"

"And Wyatt," I say with a raise of an eyebrow.

"And angelic Aria." He runs a hand through my hair, watching the strands slip through his fingers.

"And Gatsby."

His hand stops midair, eyes darting to mine. "No way in hell I'm naming my kid Gatsby. Kids will take a number for the chance to give him a swirly."

"What the heck is a swirly?"

"A nosedive into the toilet, which a kid named Gatsby will have on his regular schedule of activities."

"Gatsby's our dog, doofus, not a kid."

"Oh." Seb breathes a sigh of relief. "Well, in that case, I approve."

"Well, that's good. I'd hate to have to swirly you into submission."

I laugh as Seb hauls me off his lap and onto my back, hands above my head as he hovers over me. "I can think of a great many other ways you can make me submit to you."

"Tell me more..."

CHAPTER 13

Sebastian
Move-In Week
Haven, LA

"Is there something you'd like to tell me, Seb?"

I cringe at the tone of Autumn's voice, bordering on screechy, but full-on pissed.

Hmm ... I'm guessing she got my package.

"Tell you? What do you mean?" I infuse innocence into every word. I dart to the back of the shop when I realize my eyes are wide and my hand is splayed across my chest in mock disbelief. The last thing this conversation needs is one of Lexi's perfectly placed insults about my Academy award-winning performance.

I pull the phone a few inches away from my ear before she gets started again. My eardrums will undoubtedly thank me later.

"Something you failed to mention? Like the fact that the address of my new apartment is one-and-the-same with the address I punched into my GPS to get to your *coffee shop?*"

Each word punches like a shove to my shoulder, which is exactly what she'd be doing if she was standing here with me.

If there were any way to send Autumn the key to her new apartment sans address, I would have made that shit happen. God knows I tried.

Just meet me at the coffee shop, and you can follow me. I'll help you unpack. No need to get lost in a new town.

She stonewalled every one of my attempts. My solution? Wait until the very last minute to send her the key. Wait until every apartment in a thirty-mile radius that isn't infested with bedbugs or sporting an outhouse was taken.

I never said I'd play fair.

"Well, in my defense, the address is slightly different," I hedge, daring to put the phone back to my ear. "You see that letter 'B' after the address number? My coffee shop has a letter 'A.'"

Muffled huffs and puffs filter through the phone, and I picture her wearing a hole in the floor as she paces back and forth. Autumn's always been a tomboy at heart, but there's a little bit of drama sprinkled in there, too. The drama is amped up to one hundred today, because *seriously*? She's a grad student with a coffee shop right downstairs. That's the equivalent of heaven on Earth.

So, she'll run into me every once in a while. It's not the end of the world, is it? Some women would be ecstatic at the prospect. Some would be downright delighted.

But not this woman. And she's the only one who counts.

"I need to call Aunt Dorothy and tell her plans have changed," she mutters, talking more to herself than me.

"Whoa, hold the fuck up. Plans haven't changed. It's a great apartment, Autumn, you don't have to back out," I say, my words coming in a rush. I feel as if I have thirty seconds to change the trajectory of the Titanic. "I'll have Lexi bring you coffee every morning before classes. The fancy shit."

"Lexi? Who's Lexi?"

"Huh? My barista. That's not important." And now *I'm* wearing a hole in the floor. I run a frustrated hand over my face. "What's important is you've got a great apartment, cheap-as-shit rent, and unlimited amount of coffee at your fingertips. What more could a grad student need?"

Complete silence. I hold my breath, hoping my hard sell was good enough to dodge the iceberg. To come this close and watch my chance crumble and sink—I can't think about it.

"You don't know me anymore, Sebastian," she whispers. "You have no idea what I need."

"Wait, Autumn, please don't hang up. You're making a bigger deal about this—"

"It's fine," she clips, finding her voice again, screechy, pissed-off tone and all. "I still need a place to stay. I'll just have to … I'll have to juggle a few things."

Her words grate. They're a jab in a wound that hasn't completely healed—probably never *will* completely heal. Is my mere presence that much of a chore to her? Here I sit, fucking elated at the thought of getting glimpses of her, and she's acting like I'm the tagalong little brother, cramping her style.

After leaving Prosper for the second time, I left that miserable guy behind me—watched him fade away in the rearview mirror. I've made peace with the relationship with my parents, I've reunited with the best friend I'd never really lost, and made the conscious decision to look to the future instead of drowning in the past. Autumn's aggravation is dredging up old feelings I'm not willing to let surface.

No matter what she thinks, I'm not that guy anymore. And if her words keep digging up that grave, then she's another thing that may be better left in the past.

God, it kills me to even think it.

"Sebastian, you there?"

"Yeah, I'm here," I say, more resigned than I was just five minutes ago. "Look, don't feel like you have to *juggle* anything on my account, okay? I'll stay out of your way, Autumn. No need to worry."

And with those final words, I say goodbye. That conversation ended a helluva lot worse than it began—that's saying something since it began with Autumn wanting to throttle me.

CHAPTER 14

Sebastian
Present Day
Haven, LA

"I'd like an extra-large macchiato, with almond-flavored whipped cream, and sprinkles in the shape of unicorn horns." I'd know that voice from anywhere, even before Brady lets out his telltale snicker. "Unicorn horns ..."

"I'll take that unicorn horn and stick—"

"I knew I should have blocked off the ramp this morning to keep out the undesirables," I interrupt with my back still turned, trying to put a quick end to Lexi's verbal bloodbath.

"I don't think I'm what you could call undesirable, Mr. Kelly. Wouldn't you agree, honey?"

"Look, if you think those wheels will stop me—"

"Lexi, would you please get an Americano for my *oldest friend*. Cut him a break, he didn't realize you have fangs in the daylight, too," I joke, then turn to Brady. "You don't want that fancy shit—keep it manly, my friend. And don't fuck with the wildlife. This is a counter, not a cage. And I don't think you've had your rabies shot."

Brady smirks but doesn't spare me a glance. He only has eyes for my prickly barista, who is ignoring him with impressive focus. He slaps some bills on the counter and follows Lexi to the espresso machine. He raises himself a few inches out of his chair, perusing every inch of her. Her spiky black hair, blood red lips, and that pale white skin dancing with colorful rabbits, hatters, and teacups.

"Oh, I don't know, Seb. I think I may fair pretty well taking a trip down the rabbit hole."

Lexi's eyes widen in shock, and I believe I see blush creeping up her neck and pinking her cheeks. Brady deserves a high-five because in all the years I've known her, I've never seen Lexi embarrassed. Pissed off and fiery as hell, absolutely. But never embarrassed.

"Keep talking and my boot will find a much less agreeable hole to lodge itself into. And so help me, if you call me Alice, I'll—"

"Never!" Brady shakes his head, then his lips split into a wide grin as he swipes his coffee off the counter. "You're obviously the Queen of Hearts in this scenario."

I come around the counter and stuff Brady's bills into his front pocket with a laugh. "Your money's no good here. Plus, you'll need it for your hospital bills if you keep dancing with the she-devil."

A sharp slam on the counter grabs our attention, and Lexi's furious glare is focused solely on Brady. He shrugs and takes a sip of his coffee. He moans.

"But she sure makes a mean macchiato."

"Americano," she growls.

"Whatever."

The faintest hint of a smile dances on Lexi's lips when she thinks we're not looking.

I move to the table farthest away from the register, and thankfully Brady follows. I watch him sip his coffee and take in my shop with all kinds of nostalgia bubbling inside me as my two worlds collide.

It feels good. And weird. But mostly really, really good.

I knew he was coming in today, but I didn't expect him quite so early. "Did you get up before the sun, man? I didn't expect you for a couple more hours."

"Feels like it. We ate a quick breakfast and got on the road about six. Lord knows, my slave-driving sister can't deviate from her blessed schedule." He clutches his stomach and shoots a longing glance at the bakery counter. "Hey, maybe I should have gotten a muffin or something. Now that I think about it, I may need to refuel."

Some things never change.

I roll my eyes, and he huffs when I don't hop to attention to grab a snack for him. He knows me better than that. I drum a nervous beat on the table as I keep watch on the front door. Brady told me Autumn would be driving her car and he'd be in his van, but I can't imagine she's very far behind.

"Has she made it here yet?" I silently applaud myself for waiting a full five minutes to ask that question. God knows I don't want to sound overeager to see her when my mere presence is the equivalent of a root canal for her.

"She should be here any minute. She's probably ten minutes behind me. She's such a do-gooder, refusing to go one mile over the speed limit. She doesn't have a get out of jail free card, like me." Brady points to his legs and chuckles.

She never called or messaged about exactly when she would be moving in, but Brady and I have been in constant contact. Although she hired movers to do the heavy lifting, Brady offered to help her unpack and get things set up. There's only one problem with that —

"The apartment is upstairs?" And here we go with the

shrieking again. Autumn glares from the doorway, arms crossed and scowl firmly in place. "Brady, you can't help me unpack. You can't even visit! There's no way for you to get up there! Somebody failed to mention the apartment is on the second floor, with a narrow, outdoor stairway."

She's flustered. And breathless. And so fucking cute.

From her wispy, white blonde hair with her aviators perched on top, to her used-to-be-white Chucks that have seen better days … every piece of her, old and new, still holds me hostage. In a flash, I see it all again. Dirty feet and clasped hands … skinned knees and broken curfews … faint whispers and broken promises.

"Calm down, little sis, it's no biggie," Brady chides, not grasping that the least effective way to get a woman to calm down is to tell her to *calm down*. Autumn's irritated growl and foot stomp prove I'm one hundred percent right. He leans back in his chair and puts his hands behind his head. "I'm crashing at Seb's house. He and I are going to chill like old times. It's been decided. The boys need to catch up."

She narrows her gaze at Brady, reading between his not-so-subtle lines. "It's been decided, huh? And when exactly did you decide this?"

His eyes flit to mine for a split second before he hits her with his widest grin. "Just now, little sister, just now. Look, I'm sorry I can't help, but it's not a total loss, right? You've got a new apartment, I get to see my best friend …"

He waggles his eyebrows and shrugs sheepishly. It only takes seconds for Autumn to fold. She never could resist Brady when he turned on the charm. It used to be the same for me, but I doubt that still holds true. If recent run-ins are any indication, she'd incinerate my balls regardless of charm level.

"Well," she sighs and throws up her hands. "I guess there's nothing to be done about it, right? I mean, I wish you could help me with the boxes and get the furniture put back together, but I'll manage."

And there it is. The tiniest crack appears.

Sure, baby, the door to your heart may be shut tight, but I'm a resourceful man.

"I'd be happy to help," I offer, with the most unassuming smile I can muster. Her pursed lips say she's half-buying it. But her narrowed gaze tells me my balls may be in danger after all. "I can lug boxes with the best of them, and I'm a master at putting together bed frames. I even have a toolbox."

She bites her lip and runs the bottom of one shoe over the top of the other. That mindless motion, shoes twisting and tapping nervously on top of each other, has me mesmerized. If that's all it takes for her to grab my attention, I don't stand a chance.

And when her lips quirk up into the tiniest of smiles, I think maybe, just maybe, neither does she.

CHAPTER 15

Sebastian
Present Day
Haven, LA

The first time we kissed, Autumn's fingers trembled as she
ran her hands up my chest. When she snuck out her
bedroom window with her parents only two doors away, her
widened eyes looked as if she was waiting for the SWAT
team to light up the yard and cuff us both. The first time we
made love, her stuttering breath and racing heart were off
the charts.

But when I closed the apartment door behind us, leaving
nothing between us but a shit ton of boxes, four walls, and
utter silence, Autumn redefined the meaning of anxious. I'd
never seen her this keyed up. A bundle of exposed nerves and
unspoken words pulse around us as she flits from box to box.

"Wait, stop."

"No, don't touch that one!"

"I've got it."

I've relegated myself to the corner, patiently awaiting my

89

instructions. Or for Autumn's head to explode from the pressure—whichever comes first. It takes her a good ten minutes to notice the lack of movement on my part, and she shoots me a quizzical look. She throws her arms out and shrugs. I cross mine and do the same.

"What are you doing over there?" She huffs.

"Waiting for my marching orders."

She narrows her eyes. "You don't have to be a jerk, you know."

"What? I'm not … what are you talking about? Look, I'm here to help, Autumn. I'm not trying to upset you or unnerve you or do whatever *that* is to you," I wave a hand in her direction. "Tell me where you want me, and that's where I'll be."

If she gets my double meaning, she doesn't show it as she runs a frustrated hand over her face. She shakes out her hands and gives me a tight smile.

"You're right, I'm sorry. I'm just … gah!" She smiles her apology, and like the whipped idiot that I am, I melt. "It's just that … I mean, this is hard, right? Don't you think this is hard?"

Is it hard to hold back the urge to eat up the space between us and wrap my arms around her? Yeah. Is it hard to swallow the words held hostage in my gut for the last five years? Hell yeah. But "hard" is all relative, because nothing, and I mean nothing, could be harder than walking away, *staying* away from her all this time.

"It doesn't have to be, Autumn. Come on, it's me," I say with a gentle smile. "It's just me. So, put me to work."

She sucks in a nervous breath and blows it out with a shake of her head. "Okay, sorry. I guess you can start by bringing the dresser into the bedroom and putting together the bed frame. And thank you."

I walk over to the dresser and pluck the hot pink, fuzzy pillow off the top. It looks like the top of a troll's head, and the backside is silver sequins. I run my hand over the fuzz and laugh.

"Looks like a unicorn barfed up a hairball in your new apartment." I toss the pillow at her head, and she catches it with a grin. "Quick, get rid of it before it multiplies."

"Whatever." She rolls her eyes and places the pillow on the counter next to her.

"Never in a million years did I think I'd find a pink, fuzzy anything in your possession. That thing," I say, pointing at the glob in question, "is the anti-Autumn."

I expect her to throw the damn thing back in my face. Maybe shoot me the bird and tell me to piss off. What I don't expect is for her lips to turn down into a frown as she averts my gaze.

"Things change," she whispers, her nerves creeping back into her words. "A lot has changed in the last five years, Sebastian."

"Furniture assembled. Kitchen unpacked. Cable and Wi-Fi wired and ready to go." I lean against the doorframe of Autumn's new bedroom and cross my arms. "You sure you don't want me to help you in here? Or work in the spare bedroom? I assembled the twin bed you brought, but I could unpack the boxes ..."

She stands up and brushes off her shorts, shaking her head. "No, no I've got it. Really, you've done more than enough. Thank you for the help."

She brushes past me and into the living room, and her tone and demeanor feel so formal all of a sudden. She's already headed to the door like I'm the hired help she needs to see out. I half expect her to hand me a check.

She stops in front of the graffiti mural in the living room and glances back at me.

"This is amazing."

"It is."

She traces a finger along the tattered devil's wing, then turns her attention to the opposite side, a curved angel's wing in pristine condition. Good and evil. Light and dark. Yin and yang. The art nearly takes up an entire wall in the living room.

"I told the artist to choose whatever she wanted. She said there's light and dark in all of us. It's the ultimate balance. She thought I needed a reminder. Or maybe she thought I needed saving." I shrug as I take in the yin and the yang of it all. "I just think it looks cool."

"I suppose she's right," she whispers, then walks the length of the room.

Our time together has ended.

"I'm sure Brady and Isaac are starving, and so am I. What do you say I order takeout and we can all have dinner at my place?"

She shakes her head as she swings open the door, not even turning around to look me in the eye.

"I've got way too much to do. And you shouldn't feed that idiot—it's like rewarding bad behavior. He should starve for his deceit."

I raise my eyebrows and smirk, silently admitting, "Maybe he wasn't the only one involved in said deceit."

Her return smirk and playful glare say, "No shit, Sherlock."

God, I miss our silent conversations.

I'm halfway down the stairs when she calls my name. I turn around and smile, feeling way more hopeful than I have any right to be.

"We need to talk," she says. I wait while she fumbles. "I

mean, not right now. Of course, not right now, but soon. I just think we should, you know, have a conversation. That's all I'm saying."

She blows out a breath of frustration, shaking her head and laughing at herself. I can't help but join in.

"Sure thing," I say with a chuckle. "When you're ready, you know where to find me."

"What?"

I point to the coffee shop below us, and she gives me a goofy smile. There she is. Behind the bluster and nerves, there's the Autumn I remember.

"Duh ..."

If she were interested in a second chance, she'd have walked right into my arms and kissed me. The only reason she'd want to have a "talk" is to make sure we're on the same page, which is no fucking page at all. As I walk away, I know I should bury my burgeoning hope under a big steaming pile of realism.

I'm a lot of things—scrappy, sarcastic, too broody for my own good. And I'm one helluva sweet talker.

But one thing I've never been is a realist. And this isn't over.

~

"I hope five pounds is enough for you, my friend, because Isaac and I have done a number on these crawfish," Brady says as I meet them on my back porch.

I peer into the garbage bag they've been filling and scoff. "How many pounds have you two eaten already? This is easily fifteen pounds in this trash can."

"Who can remember?" Brady points a gloved finger at Isaac. "Do you remember?"

"Nope, I don't remember," Isaac says with a somber shake of his head.

"Plus, Isaac is a growing boy."

He meets my eyes and gives me an apologetic shrug. "I'll do all the cleanup, Uncle Seb."

"And what kind of pussy wears gloves to eat his crawfish?"

"The smart kind," Brady mutters, sucking and tossing another head into his pile of destruction. "I've got hangnails and the cayenne pepper burns like a mother! Leave me alone."

"You say hangnails, I hear pussy." I grab an empty tray and fill it with crawfish as Brady mutters unintelligible insults under his breath. When I grab his dipping sauce and put it between our two trays, I dare him with my eyes to touch it.

"Miserable fucker." Brady laughs and elbows Isaac. "How do you live with this guy?"

"Lesson of the day, my dear nephew," I cut in before Isaac can respond. "When there's someone out there who knows where all your skeletons are hidden—like in the deep end of Mrs. O'Malley's pool after her unfortunate divorce from her husband, for example, that's a bear you don't want to poke."

Isaac looks from me to Brady, then back to me again while we both sit in utter silence.

"Which one of you was it?" Isaac asks, kicking me under the table.

Brady and I answer at the same time.

"I don't know what he's talking about."

"No one ... I made the whole thing up."

Isaac resumes peeling crawfish ... while quietly humming the opening ditty to Mrs. Robinson.

And Brady and I burst out laughing.

CHAPTER 16

Sebastian
Present Day
Haven, LA

"Tomorrow's the big day. You've got your game face on?"

I keep my eyes trained on the boxing match highlights lighting up the television. Teenagers are like wild animals. Direct eye contact scares the shit out of them, and they dart out of sight at the first hint of a threat.

The kids in my high school class were the same kids eating glue beside me in kindergarten. I'm definitely not an expert on the subject, but I'd bet switching schools in your junior year of high school sucks balls. Big hairy ones, if I had to guess.

"Yeah."

That's it. *Yeah.* Chatty Cathy, this one.

Don't get me wrong, I've enjoyed getting to know the kid. He's low maintenance, no frills, and he helps around the house and coffee shop like it's his job—hell, Lexi could learn a thing or two from him—not that I'd ever make the mistake of suggesting it. I'd like my big, hairy balls to stay intact, thank you very much.

But it's not only that. Sure, I appreciate the help, but I've also enjoyed the company. Issac and I shoot the shit about all sorts of things, and we agree on what's important—Pearl Jam is the greatest rock band to ever live, Scarlett Johansson is what spank banks are made of, and Drew Brees is the best quarterback in the NFL. Everything else in life is negotiable.

But when the conversation turns to him, what he's doing, or God forbid, his *feelings*, I've got to treat my otherwise amiable nephew as a hostile witness.

"Did you meet anybody yesterday in orientation?"

"Yeah."

Eyes still trained forward, I grab the throw pillow next to me and smash it into the side of Isaac's face.

"Wha—Come on, stop it, Uncle Seb," he chuckles, wrenching the pillow out of my grip.

"Swear to God, man, if you say 'yeah' one more time, I'll line your path to the bathroom with rat traps tonight."

"Stop it."

"I'm serious. Not mouse traps—*rat traps*. Strong enough to snap a toe bone like a splintered toothpick," I say, serious as a motherfucker. "Now, how did orientation go yesterday? Think long and hard about your answer. Your toes are depending on you."

He lets out a long-suffering sigh, shrugs, and mirrors the posture of Eeyore. I've learned Eeyore is the actual mascot for the teenage condition. Lucky for me, Isaac usually keeps a tight leash on his inner donkey.

"It was good, I guess." Another shrug. "I mean, the other guys were cool, but I don't really know them, you know?" Sigh. "Some of them were kind of showing off and acting douchey, but I don't know. It might just be me." Shrug—seriously, if he keeps this up, he may need a chiropractor. "I'm sure they're fine, and I'm being a dick. I'll get on board, Uncle Seb, don't worry."

"I know you will," I say, then reach out and rub his shoulder.

Isaac looks down at my hand and scrunches his face. "Why are you rubbing me?"

"Shut up. I'm not flirting with you, man. I just figured your shoulder was sore, with all that shrugging and shit."

He flutters his lashes at me and cocks his head to the side. "Are we having a moment? Should I braid your hair?"

My grip on his shoulder tightens until he lets out a lady-like squeak. "Like a splintered toothpick."

"All right, all right," he chuckles and squirms out of my hold.

"But seriously, I get it. It sucks to switch schools with only two years left, have to meet a whole new group of people, start over from scratch. Hell, I'd have a bad attitude, too. But I bet you'll like them more once you get to know them."

"Yeah. I'm sure I will." Shrug. "I guess we're both out of our comfort zones, aren't we?"

My first reaction to his statement is *damn straight*, but the thought grates. Autumn is warmth, comfort, and every happy memory from the first two decades of my life. I'll always consider her and Brady my best friends, no matter time, distance, or circumstance. After years of separation, Brady and I picked up our friendship, dusted it off, and moved on as if we were never really apart.

Autumn and I, on the other hand, feel like a bloody hangnail. Something that desperately needs mending but hurts too badly to touch. I look at her and feel every-thing—the accident, the guilt, the bad decisions, the longing—separating us, making a few steps feel like miles. I look at her and the mountain range I've erected between us and think, *"Take a good look. This is all your doing."*

How can the accident and everything after be water under the bridge for Brady and me, but feel like a brewing thunderstorm with Autumn? *He* was the one who was injured. *He* was the one who lost his career ... his legs ... his independence. If he can forgive me, then everything else should just fall into place, right? If only that were true ...

They were both my best friends, but our relationships were obviously very different. In a twisted way, I've always felt I ruined Brady's life, and losing Autumn was part of my punishment. If I couldn't protect those I cared about most, then I didn't deserve them.

Whatever the reason, and as much as I hate to admit it, Isaac is right. What was once my greatest comfort is now so unclear. And I either have to live with what we've become or fix it. But how?

"Uncle Seb? Where'd you go?"

"Huh? Yeah, I'm here. Sorry. I guess you're right. I've got some things to figure out, too."

~

"What in the hell are you doing?" Lexi storms toward me, all the while shooting daggers. "And why are you fondling my muffins?"

"Okay, first of all, your death glare has lost effectiveness due to gross overuse." Eyeroll. "And eyerolls never worked to begin with. Second, you said I was fondling your muffins."

I chuckle. She doesn't. I've always wondered about that girl's sense of humor. She probably tortures clowns to get her rocks off.

She says nothing and continues to glare.

"If you must know, I'm attempting to lure Autumn into

the shop. And don't look at me like that because I know it works. I used to live up there, remember? I know she can smell all this baked goodness, and sooner or later, she'll take the bait."

It's been almost a week, and other than an occasional glimpse through the shop window, there's been no sign of my new tenant. No coffee runs, no muffin grabs, and no further mention of the talk she very specifically told me we needed to have. I'm beginning to think she intended to kill me slowly with curiosity.

It's working splendidly.

Undeterred, I keep holding the tray up to the fan, pointed directly at the air vent. My thumb slips a centimeter off the pot holder and onto the scorching muffin pan, and I yelp. Lexi rushes over to save her baked goods just as I drop them clumsily to the counter. One of the muffins jumps ship and rolls to the floor. Lexi rips the pot holders from me and pulls the pan out of my reach.

"Ugh, you can be such a doofus. At least there was only one casualty from your failed fiasco."

Pulling my blistered thumb from my mouth, I gape. "One casualty? What about me and my thumb?"

I lift my hand in her direction for closer inspection, and she pinches it.

"Why are you acting like a little pussy?"

"Why are you a grown woman wearing a tutu?" Death glare. "What? It's a legitimate question. And when did you become such a sadistic little thing?"

Her blood red lips quirk up into a smile. "Oh, come on now. I've always been a sadistic little thing. And I think my tutu is adorable." She fingers the glittered, black netting and pouts like I've hurt her feelings. Like she has any.

"I'm sorry I insulted your dance recital costume," I say and then motion for her to take her turn. "This is the part where *you* apologize to *me* for insulting my manhood. And also causing me bodily injury, because my scorched appendage is obviously your fault."

"Scorched appendage? Really, Sebastian, must you make it so easy for me?"

I run a frustrated hand over my face and cringe when my scruff stabs my newly forming blister. "Why are you back here, anyway? And who's watching the front counter while you harass me?"

She glares *again* and places a hand on her popped-out, tutu-ed hip.

"I came back here to tell you to stop your little wooing project."

"I think we need to redraw the lines of our employee..." I point to her. "And employer..." I point to me. "Relationship."

"Oh, shut up before you really piss me off. I'm telling you to stop because she's standing at the front counter that I'm supposed to be watching." She crosses her arms and smirks.

"W-w-wait, what?"

Lexi spins on her heels and saunters away from me, completely ignoring my stammering. As she reaches the doorway that opens into the front of the store, she looks back at me and winks.

"And she's asking for you."

CHAPTER 17

Autumn
Present Day
Haven, LA

"Mmm, it smells great in here," Seb says as he clicks my apartment door shut behind him. He inhales deeply and shoots me a cheesy smile.

"I never thought living on top of a coffee shop would be such an exercise in willpower. I keep dreaming of cupcakes and banana bread." We both chuckle as we avoid each other's eyes. I wring my hands and turn to the kitchen, searching for anything to release some of this nervous energy. "Can I make you some coffee? Wait ... sorry ... that's a dumb question."

"Nah, not dumb at all. I'd love to have a cup of coffee with you."

It's just the two of us. Nowhere to hide. And truthfully, I've been hiding from Seb since the day I moved to Haven. If I avoided seeing him, I'd have more time. More time for what, I don't know. If I've learned anything in the past five years, it's that nothing can change what's already been done. Of course, knowing this doesn't make things any easier.

My smile is tight, and my movements feel robotic, like someone or something is pushing me forward. And I guess that's true. After weeks of procrastinating, time has me cornered.

Seb returns my smile and gives the apartment an appraising look. "Looks great. You've really settled in."

I'm too keyed up to volley back the canned response he expects. Present day Autumn and Sebastian wear cloaks of polite conversation and propriety, and it's nauseating. *Lovely weather we're having ... how was your day ... would you mind terribly if I stuck this fork in my eye?* My thoughts are held prisoner inside my head, and I can't break through the barrier. When those cloaks fall away, every word holds too much emotion, frustration, uncertainty—just too much of everything.

When the niceties fall away, we'll only have the truth, no matter how it stings. The words we haven't spoken, the memories we've kept lying in wait—they'll all come rushing to the surface. To the here and now. And I don't know if I'm ready.

If I'll ever be ready.

I sip my coffee and watch him over the rim, lounging on the barstool, elbows leaning on the counter. He fiddles with the handle of his coffee cup, waiting for me to make the first move. I long to lean into him, bridge the gap between us, all the while knowing it would break me. I shove the thought aside and walk stiffly to the living room, grabbing the photo I know will crush his heart. It'll also crush this tentative truce he and I share.

I clutch the frame to my chest and squeeze my eyes shut while my insides churn.

"OK, you're starting to scare me. What's wrong? You look

like you've seen a ghost." He chuckles nervously and reaches out to me.

I shuffle forward, right into the space between his legs. He tugs my arm until it comes loose from my belly and the frame in my hand unfolds. He takes it from me and stares in confusion, his eyes darting from the picture, back to me, and to the picture again.

Bouncy, brown curls ... button nose ... a dimple in her right cheek deep enough to stick her pinky in (which she often does) ... brown eyes dancing with all-too-familiar mischief.

My eyes well with tears as all the explanations I'd practiced detonate into ash. There's no explanation for this—no words to make it okay. I step backward, creating space between us and push the words past the fist clenching my throat.

"She's four years old. H-h-her name is Aria."

It takes only a split second, but I see the exact moment he recognizes the name. Realization dawns in his eyes, and the air in the room shifts. The light, nervous energy evaporates, leaving behind something equivalent to a black hole. Confusion ... hurt ... anger ... betrayal ... I see it all playing across his face in rapid succession.

Yes, the cloaks of courtesy lay in tattered piles at our feet, and if Sebastian's glare is any indication, they've been replaced with swords.

"Sh-she's mine?"

A tear splashes onto my cheek, and I nod.

CHAPTER 18

Autumn
Present Day
Haven, LA

Lifetimes pass as Sebastian says nothing. One moment, he stares at the photograph in his hand with complete adoration, and the next, he shoots death glares in my direction. Regardless of the circumstances, I deserve his anger. I swallow back the urge to go to him, to fill the empty space with explanation and apology. He needs time to feel whatever he's feeling right now, without interruption from me.

His head whips around, and he drops the picture on the counter. Stalking across the living room, he swings open the bedroom door. HER bedroom door.

A strangled cry erupts from his chest as he braces himself against the doorframe. I stand behind him as he takes it all in, not saying a word.

The crystal chandelier, sparkling with pink hearts. The princess vanity set with a velvet covered stool. The pink, pleated quilt smoothed over the tiny twin bed, complete with the hot pink fuzzy pillow Seb saw the day he helped me move in.

Like he needed an extra kick in the balls today. Shit ...

He shuffles across the room and lowers himself onto Aria's bed. Closing his eyes, he brings the pillow to his nose and inhales.

And my heart breaks in two.

It's hell to watch, to see him lose four years with his daughter in a matter of minutes, but I won't look away. I played a part in paving our path, and I don't have the luxury of taking a time out.

"You started our life without me," he whispers, his head falling between his knees. He clutches the pillow into his stomach and wraps his arms protectively around it. "Like I didn't even exist."

"I didn't have a choice." My voice catches on the ball of emotion lodged in my throat. "You took off without a word."

"You know it wasn't like that." Angry, red-rimmed eyes glare at me. "You don't get to say that to me. Not anymore."

"It sure felt that way at the time. It's easy to look back on things now and judge what I did or didn't do, but I didn't have that luxury. I was pregnant and alone, and you had vanished into thin air. What was I supposed to do?"

"Not keeping my daughter away from me for four fucking years would have been a great start. I don't even know her, Autumn! Do you get that?"

"Yes, of course, I get it. I do, but—"

Seb stands to full height and paces the length of the room. He's too big for the tiny space—like a Great Dane in a Chihuahua's cage. Fists clench and unclench as he fights for calm. Unfortunately, it's a losing battle.

"Do you have any idea what the last five years have been like for me? Do you have the first fucking clue?"

"And what about me, Sebastian? Huh? Do you have any

idea how hard it's been? Being a single mother, going to school—"

"That was your choice! Don't you put that shit on me—" Seb stalks forward, his finger hitting the center of my chest. He looms over me, and I step back into the hallway, shaking my head.

He jerks back when he sees the fear etched across my face and curses under his breath. Turning his back to me, he runs his hands through his mussed hair and tips his head to the ceiling. Hands gripping the back of his neck, he lets out a frustrated groan.

"I didn't know," I start, but a sob breaks free, stealing the breath from my lungs. "I didn't know until I was twenty weeks p-pregnant. Long after the accident. A-after ... God, I was so lost, Seb. I was lost and alone and scared out of my mind."

Tears roll down my face unchecked as Sebastian studies the floor, hands on hips, shoulders slowing rising and falling as he searches for calm.

My emotions are a jumbled mess. Part of me will always be that frightened girl with nowhere to turn and no one to talk to. I will always hurt for her because I felt that pain down to my soul. That pit resting like a sizzling boulder in my gut, holding me hostage. Dread like that leaves a permanent scar.

The woman I am today knows I stole something from Seb that he'll never get back. Did I have a choice? At the time, I'd say no, absolutely not. I was trapped by my parents, and he was nowhere to be found. What was I supposed to do?

But when I look at him now, standing shattered in front of me, doubt creeps in and whispers "but maybe…"

I don't know ... I don't know ... I don't know.

Life seems so much simpler through the rearview mirror,

but when you're there, in the thick of it, nothing could be further from the truth.

"Look, I need some time to think, or I'm going to say things I can't take back." His voice is lower than before, but I can feel the tension in each syllable, the over-stretched reins of his emotions, threatening to snap at the slightest provocation.

"Th-that's totally understandable. Take all the time you need—"

"Where is she?"

"What?"

"My daughter, Autumn." My name sounds like cyanide on his tongue, and I flinch. "Where is my daughter?"

I cower at the accusation in his tone. I've gone from single mother to kidnapper in a matter of minutes, and I feel the sting. I'm the girl who's been keeping him away from his daughter for all these years.

I pray that he can see nothing in our lives is so black and white.

"She's with my Aunt Dorothy in Providence." I cross my arms protectively over my chest and frown. "I'm leaving in a few minutes to pick her up. We both start school Monday morning."

"Unbelievable. I've got to get out of here," he mutters as he stalks to the door. He grabs the doorknob but then turns to me. "Waited until the last possible minute, didn't you? Seriously, Autumn, the human decency train is blowing its horn, seconds away from leaving the station. I guess I should thank you for hopping on—you know, not letting me run into my daughter on the street without a word of explanation."

"Well, since it's gone so splendidly, I truly wish I'd done it sooner," I mutter, the words flying out of my mouth before I can catch them.

"Nice," he scoffs and pulls the door open.

"There's no rule book for telling your ex-boyfriend who you haven't seen in five years he's got a daughter. Dr. Spock left that part out of the child-rearing book, okay? I don't have all the answers; hell, I don't even know the questions, but I'm trying to do the right thing here."

"Then I'll see you tomorrow night, so I can finally meet my daughter. I'll be here at six."

"W-w-wait, hold on," I stammer as I push back my overwhelming anxiety. "I think we should take this slow, Seb. I don't want to rush things."

"Things have been at a standstill for four years. That's slow enough, don't you think?" He quirks a sarcastic eyebrow and steps over the threshold. "I'll be here tomorrow night. Thanks for the coffee."

It's only after he leaves that I realize the picture from the counter is gone.

CHAPTER 19

Sebastian
Present Day
Haven, LA

"What's up douchebag?" Brady quips, his booming voice in direct contrast with my stormy mood.

"I talked to your sister."

"Yeah?" He sounds expectant, as if he's waiting for me to spell it out for him. Like he has every intention of keeping her "secret" if she hasn't come clean.

"Yeah."

"Shit … give me a minute, man. Hold on."

Cheers and whistle blows fade away as he presumably finds a quieter place to receive his verbal beatdown. Silence replaces the background noise, and Brady lets out a labored sigh.

"Before you say anything, I want you to know I've been pushing her to find you for years. She was so lost and angry, Seb. In her eyes, you abandoned her." He lets out a labored sigh. "Now, since the funeral, since I found out my dad's hand in all of this, my push turned into an out-and-out ultimatum. I've been relentless, I swear. I told her enough was enough. Either she told you or I would." His tone is laced with contrition, but it does little to control my temper.

"This isn't high school, Brady. Autumn didn't flirt with another guy after the fucking football game. This is my life we're talking about here," I growl, wearing a hole in the carpet.

"Her life."

"What?"

"It's *her* life. Aria's, I mean. My niece is the entire reason I didn't tell you myself. I wanted you and Autumn to sit down like calm adults and figure this shit out together. That's what should have happened from the beginning—it's what *needs* to happen now. Because nothing is more important than that sweet, little girl, including you and your temper. So, dial it back, brother."

Leave it to Brady to level me in sixty seconds flat. Don't be fooled by the light heart and sarcastic comebacks. He's the most levelheaded guy I know, and he won't hesitate to call me out for being a self-centered asshole.

"I didn't mean it that way. Of course, Aria is the most important thing." I close my eyes and let the consequences and ramifications of my situation, past and present, race at high speed. "How do I even begin to process this? I'm just overwhelmed and shocked and pissed. God, I don't know. And then I think of the last four years of her life, four years I completely missed, and I'm so fucking sad. Brady, I have a *daughter.*"

I've spent the last five years basically alone, estranged from my family, separated from my friends. When I left Prosper, I gathered up all I had left, which wasn't much, and created something new. I'd had no other choice. I'd blocked out all I'd left behind and moved forward—otherwise, the depression would have crushed me.

To know while I was building a new life, my daughter's life was just beginning. To know I'd missed Autumn's growing belly, Aria's birth, her first steps … first words…

How do I get over that and look forward? And will I be too late? The past and the future are two treacherous mountain ranges, and I'm standing smack dab between the two. Looking back and looking forward both scare the shit out of me at this point. Every time I think of Aria and having the chance to be her father, the years I've been absent hit me square in the gut.

I trace Aria's cheek in her photo, and my heart grows three sizes in an instant. Through the swirl of emotions engulfing me, there's only one thing I know for sure. "Too late" isn't an option for me.

A bang in the kitchen catches my attention, and I turn to see Isaac watching me with wide eyes. He holds up a spoon as an excuse for why he's got front row seats to my meltdown but makes no attempt to make himself scarce.

"Wanna have a seat? Grab some popcorn for the show?"

Isaac jolts at my sarcasm and takes off like a shot. He forgot the bowl of whatever he was eating on the counter, but I'd bet my ass he won't be coming back.

"All of that shit is real. I'm not saying it isn't, Seb. You have every right to be angry, upset, and whatever the hell else you're feeling about all this. But you need to put that shit aside for now and just take it all in. You've got a *daughter*." Brady chuckles, and I can almost picture him shaking his head and smirking. "And just wait 'til you meet her, man. It's like God took the best parts of you and Autumn and smushed them into the cutest fucking person I've ever seen. When she laughs? Swear to God, my chest cracks open and I bleed on the floor. That little girl knows how to make it rain candy when her Uncle Brady's around."

I hear the sheer awe in his voice, and it lays me out.

"Stop," I whisper, doing everything I can to hold the "what-ifs" at bay. "And if you ever say my daughter's name and 'make it rain' in the same sentence again, I'll shave your eyebrows again. Both of them this time."

Brady's belly laugh on the other end of the line splinters the cord of tension in my spine, and I let out a long sigh.

"Look, Autumn's angry because you left. Understandable. You're pissed because you didn't know about Aria. Also understandable. Nobody is disputing you've both been wronged, whether intentional or by the bitch of circumstance. But in the midst of all this butt-hurt is a little girl who deserves to know her father. Let the past go for now—you've got all the time in the world to deal with your shit, and Autumn's shit, and whatever else is twisting your britches. But you not knowing Aria? It's gone on for far too long, and that's where every bit of your energy needs to be. With Aria. With my niece."

"When I woke up this morning, my biggest worry was getting to the shower before Isaac stunk the place up with his rotten, teenaged guts." Brady laughs, and I shake my head. "Seriously, it's like he's fermenting roadkill in there. Armadillo scraps, with a side of skunk juice."

"And we smelled like fucking daisies?"

"I did. You smelled like a mixture of pork rinds and corn chips."

"Some things never change." He chuckles and lets out a little sniff. "A couple of hours on the basketball court and I'm sporting an aroma even a mother couldn't love."

The easy back-and-forth between us shows me Brady's right—some things never change. I never could stay mad at Brady. And I'm one lucky son of a bitch because he can't ever stay mad at me either. Even when he's been a party to hiding my daughter from me.

"I can't even begin to wrap my head around the last five years. How did this never come out? My parents would have known. The gossips of the town would have known." I rack my brain for a logical explanation and come up empty. "There's no way my parents kept this from me. As disappointed as they may have been, they'd never—"

"Nah, they didn't know anything. My parents, Seb, you know how they are. They can be very resourceful if need be. They pulled a throwback move from the 1950s and sent Autumn to stay with Aunt Dorothy in Providence. Home school for her senior year, then she stayed in Providence for college." Brady laughs, but there's no humor in it. "Let's just say we spent a ton of holidays in Providence rather than having the girls come to Prosper."

Fists clenched and temper flaring, I rein in my fury. "So, they treated Autumn and Aria like their dirty little secret? Are you kidding me?"

"Look, I love my parents, faults and all, and I don't want to believe the worst of them. But, yeah, I guess it felt that way sometimes. Somehow, it was always more convenient for us to go to them. I don't know if Autumn ever felt the sting of it or if that's even what was going on, but I can't lie—it grated on me. But again, not my story to tell."

Would the Norrises ever stop pushing Autumn to the back burner? They've been doing it for so long, I hardly expect them to realize it. And to hide my daughter away like a dirty secret? I don't foresee a happy reunion between Autumn's parents and me. They've hated me for years, and right now, the feeling is mutual.

If only I'd known … Autumn and Aria would never have felt even the hint of a slight. I'd have been so proud to have them by my side.

Both of them ... though the thought seemed to pop out of thin air. Surely, I only mean Aria.

"Knowing these things isn't helping me to let shit go," I say with an irritated growl. "I'd say it's having the exact opposite effect."

"Then forget I said anything. Besides, that's only how I saw it. You'd have to ask Autumn to get the real story." A barrage of whistles comes through the earpiece, and Brady hollers a muffled reply. "Look, I've got to get back to the game. Just remember, nobody knows better than me how your life can change in an instant. It doesn't necessarily have to be all bad. Actually, for you, with Aria? I have a feeling it'll be the best thing that's ever happened to you, man."

"Lie to me again, trust me, they'll never find the body."

"Yours or mine?"

I shake my head and laugh. Honestly, if time has taught me anything, it's that you can never count Brady Norris out.

"Hey, Brady?"

"Yeah?"

"I meet my daughter tomorrow," I whisper, taking in every feeling those words elicit and holding them close.

"Yeah, you are. Prepare to fall in love, man. Tell my niece I miss her like crazy."

CHAPTER 20

Sebastian
Present Day
Haven, LA

Loving Autumn was never a conscious decision. No, our relationship was a living, breathing thing, constantly morphing and changing through the years. Maybe that was why losing her rocked me to my very core. Because loving her was like a golden thread of memories woven into the deepest part of me.

When five-year-old Autumn gave me half of her Fun Dip —all purple-stained teeth and lopsided pigtails.

At ten years old, her fingers laced with mine as we huddled together in our favorite hide-and-seek spot. I couldn't put my finger on it, but I knew I wanted to get closer to her.

Then the summer I broke my leg. That year was the final stitch—the summer I fell. While Autumn made it her mission to salvage my vacation, day by cooped-up day, I fell in love with my best friend's little sister.

The falling was slow and sweet and permanent. Every kiss, touch, and whispered word was a building block added to the mountain of *I love you*. There was no zing of electricity or love at first sight. I've never really believed in such things.

Until the moment I lay eyes on my daughter.

Watching my little girl tangled in her mother's legs, stealing peeks at me, a complete stranger, through her unruly curls, my heart can barely stand the pressure. I'm overrun ... floored ... completely overwhelmed by the gigantic feeling of *there you are.*

And I stand frozen in the doorway as she watches me with guarded eyes.

I'm a likable guy—a real charmer, if I'm being honest. I'm usually gifted with the ability to suck the awkward out of most situations. It's a useful skill most days. But today, when it really counts, I've got nothing. I should know what to do, what to say to make my daughter fall instantly in love with me the way I have with her, but I come up empty. I'm left here, holding a pizza box and a look of sheer terror. All I can do is stare dumbfounded at the most beautiful little girl I've ever seen. It takes every ounce of effort to hold back the competing emotions of unimaginable loss and sheer awe.

"Aria, this is the visitor I told you about earlier," Autumn says, trying to grab her attention as she burrows deeper into her skirt. "Can you tell Sebastian hello?"

"Hi." She releases the word as a labored huff and doesn't dare meet my gaze.

"H-hey Aria, it's nice to meet you," I stammer, then raise up the box in my hand. "I brought pizza."

I brought pizza? THOSE are my first words to my daughter?

Aria tugs on Autumn's skirt, and when her mom bends down to her level, she whispers into her ear. Her eyes stray to me once, for a split second, then she darts across the apartment, her glittered shoes streaking in a flash of sparkle.

Autumn smiles sympathetically, grabs the box from my hand, and squeezes my shoulder.

"Breathe, Sebastian, it's going to be fine."

I brush off the apprehension bubbling inside my gut and shake my head. "You wouldn't be saying that if you knew how close I am to puking on your shoes."

Her eyes widen like saucers as she places the pizza on the counter. We're alone in the kitchen, but the wonderful whisper of a little voice filters from Aria's bedroom. I crane my neck to try and catch a glimpse inside.

"She always does that. Talks to herself constantly. To her stuffed animals, imaginary friends, her hairbrush." Autumn chuckles. "Quiet isn't really her thing."

"She gave me one syllable. One." I scowl, feeling deflated.

"It'll take time. Some kids are like dogs. They aim to please and are always excited to see you." She tosses her head in the direction of Aria's bedroom. "That one in there? She's a cat. Makes you work for it."

"You'd think two Cocker Spaniels like us would—"

"Siamese cat all the way." Autumn laughs, crossing her arms.

Our effortless banter eases a bit of the tension knotted between my shoulder blades. Tonight is a mountain climb without safety gear, so I'm happy to see at least one thing will go smoothly. Quite frankly, I'm too keyed up to be angry at Autumn right now. Kindness on her part may be the product of sheer pity, but hey, I'll take what I can get at this point.

"So, what did you tell her?"

"I kept it vague. I told her a new family member would be stopping by to meet her tonight." Autumn wrings her hands and sighs. "Look, I know you probably wanted more, but I feel like this is the starting point she'd be okay with. I have to protect her, Seb."

"No, no I respect your decision," I say, waving off her

hesitations. "I've had some time to think—and talk to Brady—"

"Lord, do I even want to know what he said?"

"Oh, he had a lot to say. You know Brady. But he made a lot of sense. Talked me down off the ledge like only he can. I was harsh yesterday, and I apologize." I put my hand up to stop her from interrupting. She presses her lips together and frowns. "Wait, just let me say this. I'm still angry and frustrated and all those things we talked about yesterday. And you've got your own reasons for hating me, too. But I'm not going let those emotions lead me, and I hope you agree. I respect your decision because I know you have Aria's best interests at heart. And so do I. The rest of it? All of that can wait until later. Right now, I just want to get to know my daughter. Okay?"

Autumn offers me a thin smile and nods. "Okay."

"Do you think I can..." I motion toward Aria's door, and Autumn nods.

"Yeah, sure. I'll just get the pizza on plates." She runs her palms down the front of her dress and shuffles to the kitchen. "Sebastian?"

"Yeah?" I turn back to the kitchen to find Autumn wringing her hands and staring a hole in the floor.

"I don't hate you," she whispers, only meeting my eyes for a split second before looking away.

I nod because I understand. No, that's all wrong. I don't understand anything at all, and I know she doesn't either.

I wish I could hate Autumn. Hate would be easy. Simple. A singular emotion I could identify and understand as opposed to this tangled mess.

If I'm honest with myself, hate isn't the emotion I wish to single out when I see Autumn standing across the room.

"Me either."

And I turn and walk away.

I peek around the doorframe into Aria's room, and she's half hidden in her closet as she reaches up on her tippy toes to get … something. I see my "in" and take it.

"Can I help you get something?" I ask with a hopefully helpful-looking smile.

She eyes me warily but points to a pink book bag hanging from a tad too high hook. I remove it from the hook and hand it to her. She clutches it to her chest and backs away from me like I've kicked her puppy.

"First day of school tomorrow?" I gesture to the bag in her hand, and she nods as she crawls up onto her bed.

Unicorn. Fuzzy heart. Some kind of troll with the wildest mop of pink hair I've ever seen. One by one, Aria loads her book bag full of stuffed animals as she keeps her back turned to me. Yeah, I have a feeling Autumn will be unloading all of this later.

"Momma says you're part of our family. Like Uncle Brady," she says without stopping what she's doing.

"I sure am."

"So where ya been?"

Her question is more accusatory than I expected, coming from a four-year-old. She looks over her shoulder for a moment and gives me a once-over. I lower myself onto the farthest edge of her bed, and she watches me with guarded curiosity. Her hard gaze is in direct contrast with the soft brown curls framing her face, falling like loosely coiled springs down her back. Yes, Aria is a formidable opponent.

"I-I was lost." How do you explain something so complicated in a simple way? "Both me and your mom were lost, and we didn't know how to find each other. But now that we have, I hope you don't mind if I stick around."

She zips up the book bag and turns around, feet dangling off the side of the bed, giving me nothing but her profile.

"Momma told me when you lose somefing, you should try to 'member the last place you had it."

"Oh, believe me, I am. I'm starting to remember lots of things."

Aria releases the tiniest giggle as her feet sway off the side of the bed, and her fingers lay clasped gently in her lap. The sound hits me square in the chest, and I swear to God, time slows to a crawl as I take it all in.

Everything comes into focus, like one of those graphics with a hidden picture that was there all along. The love between Autumn and me was an ongoing fairy tale, carefully weaving its way into the fabric of my life. But falling in love with my daughter is a rush of emotion, washing over me like a tsunami.

Autumn is the story I've known my entire life.

Aria? She is a revelation.

CHAPTER 21

Sebastian
Present Day
Haven, LA

"Whatddaya say, old man? Theo's Ribs & Legs for lunch today? Just me, you, and Marge." Lexi places a steaming cup of black coffee in front of Joe while he coughs up a lung.

"Oh, I don't know, Lexi-Lou. Marge ain't feeling so hot these days. Doesn't like to get out much." He tries to lift his mouth into a smile, but it isn't quite up to the task. The lines etched in Joe's face used to tell the story of a life well-lived, but lately, he looks more weary than weathered.

It's been a few years since I bought the coffee shop from Joe and Marge, and we all hoped they would take to the road. Buy an RV and ride off on an epic US national park tour. But instead of reviving the old couple, selling the shop seems to have taken the wind out of their sails. Their bodies are shoddy makeshift tents, and retirement was a storm that blew in with a vengeance.

This realization hit us all hard, but no one harder than

Lexi. While I don't know the whole story, I wasn't the first wayward kid Joe and Marge swooped in and saved. When I first came to Haven, Lexi lived with the Reynolds and only moved out on her own in the last couple of years. I think Joe and Marge are the parents Lexi always wished she'd had. They're the only people who can get through her tough exterior, that's for sure.

"How about you and me then, old man? Let's grab a movie at the cinema. Popcorn, Sno-Caps ... I'll even sneak in a few of my kitchen sink cookies for you to munch on." She waggles her eyebrows at Joe, but he isn't taking the bait.

"All those picture shows are loaded with subliminal messages from the liberal agenda." He lets out a crackled sigh and pushes his barstool back. The veins in his forehead pop while his neck flushes a deep red. Yep, the old man's blood pressure is creeping higher by the second. "Nope, the only entertainment left for an old man like me is scratch-off lotto tickets at the Stop-N-Grab."

Lexi places her hands on her hips just as I touch her shoulder. She peers back at me with fiery eyes, and I shake my head and frown. Joe's been the man he is for more decades than Lexi and I have been on this earth combined. Some fights aren't worth having, and some ships will never change course.

"How about Lexi and I stop by and visit later. I bet Marge would like some company," I say, trying to meet in the middle.

"She'd like that lots. Maybe it'll raise her spirits some. You could bring those cookies you were talking about, Lexi Lou." He stands to leave, and his smile looks a tad more believable now. Just a tad.

As he walks out, Lexi elbows me in the ribs. Hard.

"The man thinks people are feeding him hidden messages

in the movies, and you want me to keep my mouth shut? Have you met me?"

"Ok, give it to me," I say, waving her on. "Tell me your argument. What were you about to say to Joe that would make him respond, 'You're absolutely right, Lexi. The liberals aren't out to get me. I've been completely wrong for the last seventy years of my life.'"

She narrows her eyes at me, then stomps her foot and storms away. Yeah, that's damn near an apology in her world.

I'm mid-chuckle when the entrance bell dings. My laugh fizzles in my throat as I watch Autumn and Aria approach the front counter. Both of them have backpacks on with flowy sundresses — Autumn's is a pale yellow and Aria's a vibrant pink. More like "grab a pair of sunglasses or risk blinding" pink. But the colors of their clothes aren't what truly shines. Autumn has always looked like she travels with her own bit of sun in her pocket. Like mother, like daughter.

With Autumn's frosty wisps of blonde hair and Aria's bouncing brown curls, they almost don't go together. But closer examination reveals matching button noses, and I swear their smiles are identical, although I haven't seen much of Aria's yet. My dark hair and eyes just might connect the dots of this family, and I feel a stab of longing at the thought. Brady's right, Aria is a perfect combination of Autumn and me. But hair and eyes are the easy part—that's just genetics. I've got a long way to go in winning my daughter's heart.

I do my best to tamp down the flood of irritation that follows. Yearning and indignation—these two emotions make strange bedfellows in my mind these days. I brush it all away and watch my daughter eye the goodie counter with wonder.

I've been antsy, waiting for them to show up, but seeing them has done nothing to calm my nerves. I texted Autumn last night after I left and asked her to stop by the shop for breakfast. I've missed so many firsts in Aria's life. Today's her first day of school, and I want to grab onto this moment as a balm for everything I've missed before it.

As she climbs up onto a stool, I ready the plate I've set aside special, just for her. I place the banana nut muffin in front of Aria, candle flickering in celebration. I nearly pat myself on the back for a job well done, finding a candle on such short notice to celebrate the day. That is, until I notice Aria suspiciously eyeing said muffin with a scowl.

"It's not my birfday," she states matter-of-factly with a shake of her head. Her curls fall over her shoulder, and she brushes them away in irritation. She's a little tipsy in her chair due to the puffy backpack strapped to her shoulders. I guess Autumn decided to pick her battles this morning, and stuffed animals didn't make the list.

"Well ... no. But it's your first day of school, and that's a really big day." She squints at me and continues to frown. I grasp at straws. "The candle is pink. You love pink, right?"

Autumn clears her throat to catch my attention and gives me a pained look. The hand she's got gripping her neck makes a claw-like gesture. "Meow ... remember?"

"I remember," I say through clenched teeth. She's trying to be supportive, but the pessimist in me hears conde-scension.

"What do you 'member now?" Aria eyes me expectantly, the candle on her muffin already blown out. Between the nerves and Autumn's catcalls, I've missed it.

But for the first time, Aria's got all of her attention focused on me. I can't screw this one up.

"I remember..." I search for something to say, but Aria loses interest quickly. Her gaze darts away from me, and I've been dismissed.

"Hey, can I see your pictures?"

"Sure, short stuff," Lexi says from behind me. She hip

bumps me out of the way and outstretches her arms for Aria's perusal.

"Whoa." Her eyes grow big and her lips round into a surprised "O" as she runs a finger over Lexi's arm art.

Her Wonderland tattoos are mostly black and white with the faintest tint of color throughout. She's been adding to it for years, and there's not a spare spot on either arm, wrist to shoulder.

Aria gasps and points to this quasi-hidden sharp-toothed grin and iridescent eyes. "I know him! That's the Cheshire Cat!"

Lexi laughs and taps Aria's nose. "It is. Do you like *Alice in Wonderland*?"

She nods, eyes wide in wonder. "You drawed this?"

"Well no, I didn't draw those, but I *could* draw them." Lexi leans over the counter and whispers in her ear. "Do you want me to draw a picture of Chessy for you?"

"Yes!" she squeals and puts her hands over her mouth to squelch her excited giggle. "And I have colors in my backpack. Momma, get my colors for the lady."

Aria scoots farther up in her seat to allow Autumn to grab a zipper pouch from her book bag while Lexi grabs paper from under the register.

"You know," I say to Aria, tapping the counter to get her attention. "I helped Lexi pick out a lot of those pictures on her arms."

She stares at me for half of an awkward second and then refocuses her attention on Lexi as she approaches. She oohs and ahs over Lexi's drawing as I disappear into the background. Every part of me wants to fast forward my way into Aria's life, and I feel so helpless at making it happen. My mind knows this is only the second time we've met, but my heart says, "See me! Hear me! Love me!"

Damn my starving, needy heart ...

Muffin demolished, and her new drawing carefully tucked into her book sack, Aria and Autumn ready themselves to leave for their first day of school. I come around the front of the counter and shove my hands into my jean pockets. The eager part of me wants to ask, but my hopeful side wishes Autumn would offer.

Do you wanna come with me to drop her off for her first day?
YES, YES, YES.

But I don't ask—I can't. As much as I want to, I can't shove open the door and insert myself into every part of their lives.

I'll be patient. I'll try to be content with peeking through the crack in the door and waiting to be invited in. I may spontaneously combust in the meantime, but I know it'll be that much sweeter in the end.

I crouch down to Aria's level and rack my brain for sage advice like what I offer Isaac. Well, maybe not exactly like that...

"Never trust boys who want to sit next to you in the lunchroom. Or the library. You know what, it's probably a good idea to beware of *all* boys, okay?"

Blank stare.

"Okay," she says, looking confused. With that, she turns on her glittered Converse-covered heel and heads for the door.

The sympathy in Autumn's smile doesn't help a bit as she hesitates for a moment then follows after Aria. My shoulders slump in defeat as I offer them both a silent wave. I place my hands on my knees to stand and come face to face with Lexi's irritated scowl.

"Stop acting so fucking weird."

I release the long-suffering sigh that's been building up inside of me. I'm not in the mood for her shit right now.

"Lexi, just this once, I need you to give me a break. That

little girl?" I point to the door Aria just skipped through. "She's my *daughter.*"

I wait for surprise to wash over her face, maybe some well-placed expletives, but she only rolls her eyes.

"Uh, I got that Einstein, but it doesn't mean you have to act like a weirdo. Trust me, I know what I'm talking about. She thought *I* was awesome. You should follow my lead."

"Trust *you?* You eat kittens and babies for breakfast. I can't think of anyone less qualified to coach me into my daughter's life."

"Do you remember Mr. Beglio's Yorkie, Puddles? Mr. B would read for hours at the outside table by the entrance, and that damn dog would growl at every single person who passed. People tried to pet him, give him treats—didn't matter. Dog was fricking Cujo in Jiminy Cricket's body. Except for me. Know why?"

"Why the hell does everyone keep comparing my daughter to animals?" I tip my head and squeeze the bridge of my nose, searching for the tiniest bit of patience.

"Because both children and animals can smell two things —fear and fucktard. And forgive me for saying it, but you've got both going on times ... like a hundred."

I groan in frustration but can't really argue.

"I was a fucktard, wasn't I?" I plop down onto a stool and bury my head in my hands. "I'm usually a hit with the ladies, but a four-year-old girl? I'm completely clueless."

While I wallow, Lexi slides a warm blueberry biscuit onto the counter and hands me a fork.

"So, Puddles." She pours a thin ribbon of honey onto the top of my biscuit, and I bristle at the conversation change. "Down boy. Anyway, while everyone else showered that little shit with attention, I basically ignored him. I'd say hello when he got there and walk away before he had a chance to get grumpy. While waiting on the surrounding tables, I'd drop a little something-something on the ground next to him. Bacon, cinnamon roll, ... pot brownie."

My eyes dart up to meet hers, and she laughs.

"Just kidding about the last one," she says in a less-than-believable tone, then pops her honey-laden finger into her mouth.

"So you're telling me I should win over Aria with pig, sugar, and drugs?"

"Ugh! Do I have to spell everything out for you? You win her over by not trying so hard. Tone down the pushy and let her come to you. At this point, you reek of desperation." Lexi fans her nose and scowls.

I roll my eyes.

"Thanks," I mutter as I stab the biscuit with my fork. The burst of sweetness explodes on my tongue as the buttery biscuit melts in my mouth. "If you're going to call me hopeless, at least you sugar-coated it. This biscuit is delicious, Lexi."

"I know, of course it is, but back to the matter at hand. This is what you need to do." Lexi holds up a finger. "Number one, don't try to impress her. It won't work."

I open my mouth to argue, but Lexi silences me with her finger. "Trust me. Just play it cool. Number two, you can give her small treats, but don't make a big deal out of it. Like, just for example, lighting a candle and sticking it in said treat."

Damn.

"All right, point taken. No candles."

"And nothing extravagant. That'll just piss off the mom, and then you're really screwed."

"Autumn, her name is Autumn," I growl, and Lexi lifts her eyebrows in surprise.

"Ooh, I'll have to investigate that response a little more. But later. Number three ... and listen up because it's the most important rule of all. Whatever you say you'll do, wherever you say you'll be, do it … be there. Don't let her down, for fuck's sake, or so help me, I'll drug you with pot brownies, douse you with this honey, and leave you for dead in the nearest forest."

A cold shiver runs down my spine at the tone of Lexi's voice … the chill in her eyes. I don't think she's joking, and if I didn't know any better, I'd swear she's speaking from experience.

Do I actually know better? Has she … nah …

I shrug off the eerie sensation and get back to the matter at hand. Getting the green light from the finicky Aria, my cat-like daughter.

I will be standoffish, but available. I will shower her with gifts, but tiny ones that aren't too showy. I will always, always follow through.

"It sounds like I'm trying to land a girl." I chuckle as I devour the last bite of my delicious biscuit.

"You *are* trying to land a girl, dumbass. You're trying to land *the* girl—the most important one."

CHAPTER 22

Autumn
Present Day
Haven, LA

Aria tugs my hand just before I open the door to the college's elementary lab school. I motion to the front door, and she shies away. My brave girl looks timid this morning.

It's been one change after another for Aria over the past few days, and she's taken it like a champ. She's putting on a good show at the very least, but I wonder what's going through her mind. New town. New home. New ... Sebastian.

And now a new school. Just one of those things is a lot to handle. All of them at once is like a steamroller in my little girl's life.

And not only is this a new school, but it's actually Aria's first year at big girl school. Between keeping my classes on Tuesdays/Thursdays most semesters and the help of my Aunt Dorothy, Aria was an infrequent visitor at Mommy & Me in Providence. Five days a week is a whole new ball game.

I have a savings account with a meager balance set aside just for Aria. I've been putting away what I'm able to while repeating the mantra "every little bit helps." Every teeny little bit. Only time will tell if the money will go toward college or therapy. Motherhood is hard. I'm ninety percent sure I'm doing it wrong fifty percent of the time.

I crouch down and meet her doe eyes, both trusting and a teensy bit frightened. "What's the matter, poppet?"

She places both hands flat on my cheeks and widens her eyes. "I don't know, Momma. I'll go to school today, but what if I don't like it? We can talk tonight, okay?"

My negotiator. I lay my hands on top of hers, and she pushes on my cheeks until my lips pucker.

"Aria, this is the best school in town. Momma's already checked. The best teachers ... best toys. And guess what? You won't just have one teacher, you'll have lots of them."

Neither my reasoning nor my strange fishy voice wins her over. I lean in and place a juicy kiss on her nose, and I'm rewarded with a well-earned giggle.

"You're going to have a fun day, I just know it. Okay?" I nod my head, hoping she'll return the gesture.

Instead, she scowls and wipes at her wet nose.

"Can you at least show me the bafroom?"

What am I going to do with this one?

"Yes, Aria, we can check out the bathroom," I say with a sigh, then mutter, "but I'm not putting up a fresh coat of paint or setting out potpourri if it doesn't meet your standards."

Before she can argue, I whip out my phone and tap my head with hers.

"First day of school pic for Uncle Bray?"

"Bunny ears! Bunny ears!"

"All right, all right." I laugh as I bring up the filter.

Aria pokes out her tongue while I make a mean bunny face, and it brushes away some of the nerves.

I pull up Brady's number and attach our silly photo with the message, *Rockin' the first day of school!*

My finger hovers over the send button, and I have the sudden urge to add Sebastian to the text.

I'm not an idiot. I saw the look in his eyes when we left the coffee shop this morning. I know he wanted to come with us, and part of me longed to ask him. That girl who still wonders *what if* and *how come* wants to forge ahead and figure out *what's next*. But the bigger part of me has spent the last four years protecting my daughter, and I'm still so unsure of what's right for Aria.

Of course, knowing her father and having a relationship with him is what's right, but there's something to be said for timing. I'm trying my best to balance Sebastian's understandable anger and Aria's fragile heart, and I feel as if I'm failing at both. As for my feelings, I've stowed that hot mess up on the highest shelf in my mind. Or at least I'm trying to.

For now.

Tired of overthinking every single thing, I add Seb to the text and hit send.

"Come on, poppet," I whisper, clasping her hand in mine and standing. "Let's go meet your new friends."

"How'd it go, little sister? Did you cry your eyes out? If you did, I expect photographic evidence."

"Don't be a douchebag. It's a big d-day." My voice cracks on the last word, and Brady bursts out laughing.

"I knew it! I knew you couldn't hold it together. I can't wait to tell Aunt Dorothy I won."

"Won what?"

"Nothing, never mind. Now for the real question." He clears his throat then pauses dramatically. "Was there a bathroom inspection?"

I groan, and Brady starts up another bit of raucous laughter.

"She'll grow out of it, right? Tell me she'll grow out of it. Wait, why am I asking you?"

"You doubt my knowledge?"

"I caught you trying to burp Aria when she was two years old, Brady. Yes, I doubt your knowledge."

"I was lovingly rubbing my niece's back. That's all you saw. I think your germ-addled brain, due to your daughter's frequent public bathroom inspections, I might add, was confused."

"Shut up."

"Hands on your head. Hands on your head," he chants in a girly voice.

"Give me a break! If I have to visit every bathroom between here and Timbuktu, I at least need to keep her tiny mitts in check."

"Ah, ya know I'm just giving you a hard time. If it were me, I'd have scooped her up and brought her for a banana split breakfast. No way I could have left her there," he admits in his "aw shucks" voice.

I turn on the car and set the AC to high, letting the cool air dry my damp eyes. I glance at my watch nervously. I've still got an hour before my first class but finding parking on campus can be tricky.

"Saw you sent Seb the picture, too." The words dangle between us as if he's waiting for me to fill in the blanks.

"Yeah." I lean my head on the window and sigh. "This morning at the coffee shop was kind of a disaster. I mean, it wasn't terrible or anything, but you know how Aria can be around new people."

"Uh, yeah. I swear that kid side-eyed me from the day she was born until at least six months old. Doesn't give an inch, that one."

"She really took to the girl who works there, though. Lexi, I think her name is," I say, and Brady scoffs.

"Of course she did," he mutters.

"What does *that* mean?"

Is there something going on between Sebastian and Lexi? The thought makes my insides roil. She's gorgeous, edgy, sexy-as-hell ... everything I'm not. I couldn't blame him if she were his type these days.

Oh yes, I could. I could blame him all damn day.

"Never mind. Just give Aria some time. She'll warm up. I mean, we're talking about Seb here. He's awesome. I'd love for him to be *my* dad."

"So, you're all good with the 'cut and run' variety?" The words fly out of my mouth at light speed, and I wish I could snatch them back and keep them to myself. "Shit, sorry. That was uncalled for and only half the story. I know that. I *do* know that."

"Say it to me, Autumn. Say it to me so you won't say it to him."

Just like Brady to push me to vent without taking a side. When your best friend and your sister are in opposition, Switzerland is the smartest approach. He may be trying to smooth things over, but his request is like waving a red flag at a raging bull. It's all the provocation I need. I stamp my hoof and take off for the races.

"It may make me an asshole, Brady, but I can't deny the fact that I'm still hurt. What happened in the past doesn't just wash away because we want it to." I wait, fully expecting him to counter my argument, but he remains silent as I gnaw on my cuticles. "But then I see Sebastian gazing at Aria like she's a princess, because she damn well is, and I feel like a thief. How can I be so right and so wrong, all at the same time?"

"Because real life doesn't come with a rule book and red pen, Autumn. There are five thousand different explanations on the way from right to wrong, and most things fall somewhere in between the two. It's entirely possible to be the victim and the thief, and you're allowed to have feelings about both. What you can't do is negate everyone else's perspective but your own. And why's that? Because you may be a thief, but you're not an asshole."

"Can't I just be right?" I grumble, feeling knocked down a peg or ten.

"No, but you can't just be wrong either, so chin up, little sister."

"Yeah, yeah," I grumble, glancing at my watch again. Fifty-five minutes. "I should have asked Sebastian to come with me to drop her off this morning. I knew he wanted me to and I just ... ugh, I couldn't do it. I need to be careful with Aria. She's fragile, Brady."

"Uh, I think you've got that mixed up. Aria's a laser beam away from being a Marvel superhero. Strong as they come. *You're* the fragile one."

I huff. And sputter. And release the most exasperated of sighs.

"Beatbox all you want, but it's true." I keep my mouth shut, and he lets out a victorious laugh. "You know, you've raised that little girl pretty much on your own. I mean, yeah, you had Aunt D and me, but I burp grown ass children ... and Aunt Dorothy? Much longer and she'd turn Aria into a degenerate gambler and a cheat."

"It's only cheating if you get caught," I interject.

"You've been living with Aunt D for way too long."

"Whatever."

Tuesday afternoons are for card games with the ladies,

and Aria has been a permanent fixture there for as long as I can remember. Aria's poker face is award-winning, and she can slide an extra card to her Aunt D with uncanny precision. Her game of choice is bourré, and she'll strip grown men of their pride with a twinkle in her eye and a card up her ruffled, pink sleeve.

"Anyway, point is we're not exactly Mr. and Mrs. Rogers. And don't get me started on the negative amount of help Mom and Dad offer."

"Please don't get started," I groan.

Before Brady's accident, he was too busy with football to notice everything my parents didn't notice—mainly me. At some point, I stopped caring and did what any teenage girl would do. I took advantage.

Throughout my pregnancy and after Aria was born, my parents were a check that came in the mail every single month, without fail. They thought their actual presence was only required on major holidays and birthdays—Aria's birthday, not mine—and phone calls were few and far between.

This time around, it's Brady standing smack dab in the middle of my family, frantically waving his arms to the sound of stubborn pride and parental disappointment. I couldn't find it in me to care. At least that's what I tell myself. It's what I've always told myself. I don't have the energy to wave frantically anymore.

"The point is you've been doing this thing alone for all these years, and now there's someone standing on the sidelines, begging you to tap him in. Betting if you really think about it, you'll have to admit that the only thing harder than doing it alone is letting someone help. And that someone being Sebastian? Yeah, you're terrified. But you're going to have to swallow it down and shake it out because Aria's got another person in her corner wanting to love her. And you've got to let him."

CHAPTER 23

Present Day
Sebastian
Haven, LA

The first day after my talk with Lexi, I placed a reserved sign in front of a barstool just for Aria. She and Lexi decorated it with markers from her backpack. One side Wonderland, for Lexi, and the other side mermaids and unicorns, for Aria.

The next day, I hung a pocket organizer from the back of her chair and filled the smaller compartments with scented markers. Her favorite was the watermelon, or waterlemon, according to her. Before leaving for school, she gave me a quick half smile and a scrunch of her rainbow dotted nose.

Every day, I've added to her stash. Sketch pad ... pink bow to decorate the pocket organizer ... glittered princess stickers. Those were the clincher. She found the biggest crown on the page and slapped it on my chest with a hasty "thanks" as she darted out the door to school.

It's after lunch, and I'm still wearing my glittery crown, along with a goofy grin I just can't seem to shake.

Not too shabby for the first full week of being a dad. Or kind of a dad. She may not know I'm her dad yet, but if she found out at this very second, there's only a fifty-fifty chance she'd balk. That's a marked improvement from just a few days ago.

After Lexi's pep talk about winning the girl, I called Autumn and asked if we could make breakfast at the coffee shop before school a regular thing. Surprisingly, she was all for it. Sounded downright enthusiastic.

I refuse to obsess about what that means.

I've spent each morning, eyes trained to the side window of the shop, waiting for those two pairs of feet to make their way down the stairs from their apartment.

The day after the hot pink tulle bow, Autumn texted me and asked me to meet Aria at the staircase. She was too excited to wait for her mom to finish getting ready.

She met me at the bottom, a wide pink headband attempting to tame those wild curls and excited eyes. I told her she'd need to hold my hand until we got inside, and when those tiny fingers slid into my hand, tickling the inside of my palm, my ribcage could barely contain my heart. I put on a brave face, but my inner-dad-yearning-to-break-free wept with joy.

Earlier in the week, Brady had called and asked if he could visit for the weekend, and I was all for it. Then he talked Autumn into letting Aria come over so she could study, and it took a great amount of effort to keep my fist pump and girly yelp to myself. So, when he asked how I felt about a slumber party at my house, I had to put the phone down for a minute. I don't know how he got Autumn to agree to it, but gift horse and all that.

My emotions hang precariously from a spinning yo-yo, and my daughter is holding the string.

"The urge to knee you in the balls to bring you back to

reality is so strong, I'm literally trembling from restraining myself."

My hand covers my fly on instinct because restraint has never been Lexi's strong suit, and I shoot her a scathing look.

"You're fired."

"Okay," she deadpans as she continues to manhandle the espresso machine.

"Mind if I leave early this afternoon?"

"Please. Leave. You're oozing happiness, and it's starting to fuck with the vibe of this place. I can't take it."

"What the hell are you talking about? This is a place of business. We serve happiness in a steaming cup. That's why the people keep coming back."

"We serve *fuel*," she growls, pointing to the store sign. "We play …" she points to the speakers in the ceiling. "Rap music. We give them…" She points to herself. "Attitude. We serve java with an *edge,* and you're, you're…" She waves her arms in my direction with a disgusted scowl on her face. "You're nothing but a puffy cloud of goo right now. I'm glad your daughter kind-of, sort-of is starting to like you, but keep that shit to yourself." She lowers her head closer and whispers, "Keep your personal life out of the workplace, man. Your employees shouldn't have to tell you this."

Before I can respond, a familiar voice joins the conversation.

"Who's ready for a sleepover? Lexi?" I hear the tease in Brady's voice and feel the menace in Lexi's glare. Brady lifts up a DVD case. "I even brought *Moana.* Grab your bikini, sexy Lexi, we're going to Hawaii."

"Don't ever call me that again."

"So sensitive, that one," Brady says, pointing the DVD at Lexi.

"Out. Now. You're a fluff ball up my nose, and he's sandpaper on my nipples. I don't know whether to sneeze, shout in pain, or both."

I round the counter, pointing an accusing finger at my barista. "Don't scare away my customers."

"Ugh!" She rolls her eyes and huffs. "You don't get it. They come back *because* they're scared."

"She's right, dude. I can't explain it," Brady mutters as we leave the shop, only loud enough for me to hear.

"Yummy," Aria says with a smack of her lips as she swallows and puts down her mug. Chocolate rings her tiny lips, and she tries to lick it clean with little success. I'm surprised any hot chocolate made it through the mound of marshmallows she piled on top.

Star marshmallows, of course, because I'm awesome. Only the coolest things for Aria.

Her monogrammed duffel bag sits by my front door with a pint-sized pillow looped into the top straps. I keep glancing at it and wondering how my solitary life became so full.

Isaac.

Brady.

Then Aria.

I'm not sure where, or if, Autumn fits into this list of blessings, but this wave of happiness I've been riding all week has made a minuscule crack in my dashed hopes and dreams where she's concerned. If I can morph from a loner into a guy who has sleepovers, then anything's possible, right?

My anger has been doused with hot chocolate and marshmallows. What felt like a raging fire only a week ago is starting to resemble dying embers.

Can it really be that simple?

"Been waiting all week to hear about this amazing school,

Aria." Brady nudges her elbow. "Tell me about your new friends."

She sucks in a deep breath, and her shoulders rise from the effort.

"Well, Manda is my bestest friend. She's got a guinea pig named Meatball and eats macinroni for lunch. My other friend, Kylie, has a Wonder Woman lunch box and she talks about her daddy taking her fishing *all the time*."

"Meatball," Isaac parrots with a smirk.

"And Henry sits next to me on the story mat. He smells like hot dogs and already lost a toof."

"Old Henry's keeping his *hands* to himself, right?" Brady shoots me an amused smirk, and his mouth twitches with the effort of *not* making a hot dog joke. "Do I need to go to that school and put the smack down on that little jerk?"

He scrunches his face and leans in, nose-to-nose with Aria. She giggles and taps his shoulder sweetly. She reaches across the table and grabs the cards I'd placed there earlier at Brady's request.

"You shuffle the deck, Uncle Brady. Then I'll deal." She slaps the cards in front of him, and he chuckles.

"All right, but I can't play this round. I need to finish up a few things with this new app I'm building," he explains, pointing to the laptop open in front of him. "It's crunch time for Uncle Bray, but I'll be done soon. You'll have to play with Sebastian and Isaac."

Aria steals a glance at Isaac sitting next to her at the table and whispers shyly, "You know how to play bourré?"

Isaac shakes his head. While she quietly explains the rules of the game, I collect all the things I've learned about her like golden eggs.

Aria is the girliest of girls, the complete opposite of her tomboy mom. She's got glittered barrettes in her hair. Autumn usually had errant twigs. I see Autumn's strength

141

beneath the surface, though. It's just wrapped in ribbons rather than smudged with dirt.

Her favorite muffin is cinnamon chip, but she won't sneeze at a strawberry glaze one either. And she'll lick every bit of glaze left on her hands, right down to the wrist. It would be atrocious to watch if she wasn't so darn cute.

She brushes her unruly curls out of her face constantly, but waves Autumn away any time she attempts to wrangle them.

Her voice is firm and commanding. It becomes the sweetest whisper when she's overwhelmed, though. And when she's got a crush ...

Which is the newest golden egg, because she's definitely crushing on Isaac.

Since she's four, I'll think I'll wait until much later to break her heart with a talk about cousins. In the meantime, Isaac eats up the attention as Aria flutters and coos.

She kneels on her chair and grabs the deck Brady just shuffled for her.

"You know how to play?" she asks, cocking her head to the side.

I nod and tap the table in front of me, signaling for her to deal the cards. Her lips quirk up into the smallest of smiles.

The cards slide in front of each person with practiced ease. Once they're dealt, she places the deck in the middle of the table and flips over the top card. Five of clubs.

"Clubs are trumps," she states, all business as she swipes the card and places it in her hand.

Honestly, it's a little eerie. I'm half expecting her to ask me to ante up.

"No betting tonight, Aria," Brady warns, and my eyes widen.

Shit...

The ace and king of clubs sit pretty in my hand, but I

discard the ace with my throw away cards and ask for three new ones. Beating the crap out of Aria won't gain me any points toward winning her heart.

She inches her mug across the table until it hits my hands. "Can I have some more hot chocolate please?"

"Of course." I jump up and make her drink just the way she likes it. Heavy on the marshmallows.

There will come a day, very soon I'm sure, where I'll have to put my foot down or say no to Aria. And I'll do it, because that's part of being a parent. Lucky for me, today is not that day. Today, I plow her with marshmallows.

The table is silent as I sit down and give Aria her drink. I shrug it off and grab my hand off the table and fan out my cards.

The ace of clubs is back in my hand.

My head pops up, and I glance at Brady. He won't meet my gaze, but I see his shoulders shaking. Isaac shrugs his shoulders, but his eyes dart to the smallest player at the table. Aria is a statue.

"Don't need help winning," she says while examining her fanned out cards.

Aria was right. She didn't need one bit of help winning. She wiped the floor with Isaac and me and left us begging for mercy.

My daughter is a card shark. I'm oddly proud.

"Uncle Seb, can I go to my friend Tristan's house for a little while? They're playing Call of Duty, and he only lives three blocks away on Elm." Isaac stands and checks his watch. "I'll be home before eleven, if that's okay."

Aria pokes Brady in the arm, but he waves her off with a gesture.

"Sure. Do you want me to drive you?"

"Nah, it's not far."

Aria keeps poking, and Brady finally turns to look at her. She leans into him and whisper-yells the way only kids can do, "Can I go wiff him?"

Her front teeth tap her bottom lip when she makes the "f" sound, and I wish I had a camera so I could see that exact expression over and over. Etch it in my brain. Tattoo it on my heart.

Remind myself that I'm here, with my daughter, and I'm part of this moment. Part of this family.

Brady gives her a sad smile and pecks her on the cheek. "Nah, sugar. It's too late for little girls to be running the roads. Plus, it's nothing but a bunch of dirty boys playing video games. What fun is that?"

She peers over at Isaac and drops her eyes to the ground. His shoulders sag at the sight.

"Hey Aria, how about I meet you at the coffee shop for breakfast before school sometimes? What if I sat with you?"

She gives him a nearly imperceptible shrug as she mutters, "All right."

"Cool." Isaac taps her nose and smiles, and that's all it takes for her to perk up.

"Time to bathe, Aria," Brady says after closing his laptop. "Can you please grab your bag by the door, then give Isaac and Sebastian back a little of their dignity?"

"Okay." She giggles as she skips across the room.

"That was a helluva ass-whooping she gave y'all," Brady mumbles out of the side of his mouth.

Neither one of us comment. What is there to say? She annihilated us.

She climbs up into Brady's lap, and he pops a wheelie to get an extra laugh, then takes off for the bathroom.

"She's a pretty cool kid," Isaac says as he clears the kitchen table.

"Since she thinks you are responsible for the rising and setting of the sun, not surprised you think so." I pop him in the stomach with a hand towel, and he dodges the hit.

"I *am* pretty great."

"You're all right." I follow him into the kitchen. "So, first weekend after school's started and you've got plans. I take that to mean it was a good week, yeah?"

"Yeah."

"And Tristan? Good kid? Good parents?" I hold up my hand to stop him from talking. "Swear to God, if you 'yeah' me, I'm walking with you to this kid's house and introducing myself to the family."

Isaac's eyes bug out, and he shakes his head. "Aw, hell no. You can't do that."

I gesture for him to continue as I walk to my shoes by the front door as an obvious threat.

"He's in my honors classes, so he's got to be pretty smart. On the basketball team. I'm not sure about his parents, but I know his dad went to Temple when he was a kid." I move away from the front door, and Isaac sighs in relief.

I point at him as I pass. "Eleven o'clock. If there's any trouble, anything feels off, you call me, and I'll be there, no questions asked. Got it?"

"Got it."

CHAPTER 24

Sebastian
Present
Haven, LA

The faintest whisper tempts me from sleep, but I burrow deeper into the blankets. The sun is far from up. I've got hours of glorious sleep to go before morning.

Until the whispers get louder ... and my bottom lip pulls away from my face.

I jerk awake in a flurry of covers, and my groggy eyes meet identical sleepy ones.

"Aria." I cough, trying to clear the gravel from my throat. I run a hand over my mouth and sit up. Then I cover my naked chest ... because what are the rules here? I'm wearing running shorts, so I think I'm good. Maybe?

Shit, I'm too dazed to think about this shit.

I drop the blanket and focus on Aria, whose eyes look a little more than sleepy. They're glassy and on the verge of spilling over with tears.

"What's wrong? Are you sick?"

"I want my momma," she whimpers, and a fat tear splashes onto her cheek.

"Oh no, don't cry. Don't cry. Please don't cry."

I wipe a thumb across her wet cheek and scoop her up into my lap. She lays her head on my bare chest while I rub her back.

As I cradle my daughter in my arms and rock back and forth, I know one thing with complete certainty. I would slay dragons ... tackle lions ... throttle teenage boys ... kill anything or anyone who ever dared to hurt this little girl.

"I can bring you home, baby, it's not a problem. I'll call your mom right now," I say, squeezing her tight.

"Okay, I'll go get my bag." She untangles from my arms and hops down. She wipes her eyes as she sprints back to the bedroom she was sharing with Brady.

I call Autumn as I get dressed and grab my keys, but the phone goes straight to voicemail. I try again, but no dice. When I look up, Aria's standing in the doorway in her pajamas, bag packed and in hand. Horns poke out of her feet.

"Nice unicorn slippers."

"Fanks."

"Your mom isn't answering, so I bet she's probably asleep." I pause and wait to see what her response will be. None at all. "Well, I guess we could drive over there and see if she answers."

"Okay," she says quickly and skips down the hallway.

The skip is a bit bouncy for a kid who was just crying her eyes out, but what do I know?

I tap on the door to the guest bedroom and call Brady's name. He grunts.

"Aria says she misses her mom and wants to go home."

Brady reaches over and illuminates his phone on the bedside table. "One-thirty. Yeah, right on time. She's like clockwork, that one. She knows better than to wake me up with that shit now. She's played that card one too many times with Uncle Bray."

"Wait, you knew she would do this?"

He scoffs and rolls toward the wall. "She does it every damn time. She's all big britches until the house goes quiet."

"Why the hell didn't you tell me this beforehand, douchebag?" I whisper, peeking behind me to make sure little ears are out of range.

"It was a test. You passed."

"Are you serious?"

"No, I honestly forgot. Sorry."

I leave Brady with a parting growl of frustration and open the front door for Aria to pass through. Instead, she raises her arms to me.

"I don't want to get my unicorns dirty," she explains in an exasperated tone.

"Oh, right." I lift her up onto my hip, and she wraps her arms around my neck. I'm all too happy to snuggle her tight, if only for a few minutes. Come Monday, I'll probably be lucky to get a wave hello, so I need to enjoy this while I can.

Dang cat …

I settle her into the car seat, and she helps me with the latches, chanting, "Don't pinch me. Don't pinch me," while I secure them between her legs.

Once we get moving, Aria calls to me from the back seat. And by "calls to me," I don't mean she calls me by my name. Or any name at all. At this point, I'm "Hey" to Aria. My daughter calls me "Hey."

"Yeah?"

She's quiet for long enough that I peek in the rearview mirror to see what's she's doing. Her head's turned, staring out the passenger window, watching the street fly by.

"Do you want to take me fishing?"

I pause at the strange question, remembering back to

earlier in the night when she talked about her friend at school and how her *dad* takes *her* fishing. I wonder what exactly Aria is asking me … and if *she* even knows.

"Do you want to go fishing?"

I check the mirror again and watch her, face scrunched in deep thought. "I don't fink I would like fishing. Fish are slimy and squirmy. And stinky. I don't fink I'd like it."

"Then we won't go."

"Okay."

"But if you ever want to go, I would love to take you."

I park in front of the coffee shop and turn in my seat to meet her gaze.

"Do you have a boat?"

"No, I don't," I say, keeping my eyes fixed on hers. "But I'd find one. For you. When you're ready to go fishing."

She's silent for a moment. Then two. Then her lips quirk in to a half smile, half laugh.

"Okay."

I scoop Aria and her overnight bag into my arms and climb the stairs. A faint glow shines from the window of the apartment, and a thought that hadn't occurred to me jumps to the forefront of my brain.

What if Autumn's got company? Shit …

I'm mediocre at training my face on a good day. At this point, I'm tired as hell and punch-drunk from riding the yo-yo of emotions that comes with spending time with my daughter. My heart is so full at this moment, and if a man opens this door right now, it may just explode and splatter blood all over his fat face.

"Are you gonna knock?" Aria asks as she leans forward in my arms and bangs on the door.

"Shit," I mutter, summoning all my strength to keep a neutral face.

"Huh?"

"Nothing," I say quickly as a shadowy figure moves closer to the door.

Autumn peeks through the curtains, eyes bleary and unfocused. The latch clicks, and she opens the door. Aria launches herself into her mother's arms.

"Mommy!" She squeezes Autumn's neck and buries her face into her cheek. "I missed you and wanted to come home."

The words come out muffled since her mouth is smashed into Autumn's face and they both laugh.

"That's all right, poppet. I was getting lonely anyway."

"I tried to call and let you know we were coming, but it went straight to voicemail."

Autumn's sleepy expression turns panicked, and she darts inside the apartment. I peek through the doorway, and she grabs her phone off the table.

"Dead. I can't believe this. I'm so sorry. That's completely irresponsible of me. It keeps dying an hour after I charge it—I don't know what's—"

"Hey, no worries," I say, reaching out and touching her arm. "She was with Brady and me. Pillars of responsibility. No harm done."

She presses her lips together and nods. Aria wriggles from her arm and takes off across the living room.

"Can you say thank you for the sleepover?" Autumn calls out to her retreating back.

"Fank you!"

"Goodnight Aria," I say, loud enough for her to hear.

Autumn leans back, watching her retreat, then laughs.

"Little shit. She's in my bed. She'll have a whole speech prepared about how much she missed me and needs to be close to me now."

I can imagine Aria putting on the charm, and the thought makes me grin.

"Yeah, I kind of feel like I got played tonight."

"Oh, for sure. Like a fiddle." She smiles and leans her head on the frame. "Used to do it to Brady all the time when he lived in Providence."

The thought of Aria yanking Brady's chain gives me a warm and fuzzy feeling, I can't lie. He deserves it for keeping me in the dark tonight.

A comfortable silence falls between us, and we both smile tentatively. Part of me wants to fill the void with every single thing I couldn't say for the past five years. But the largest part wants to sit in the pocket of just being here, standing next to the girl who knows every groove and crack of my heart. The grooves she helped mold with her love. The cracks she dug deep with her silence.

No doubt she's got cracks courtesy of me as well. I hope the grooves left a more lasting impression.

Only time will tell. Only time can heal.

Autumn's brow furrows in confusion, and she tilts her head in question. "What? Why are you looking at me like that?"

"It's been too long since I've had the luxury of just looking at you. I'm going to need a minute." The words tumble from my lips unchecked and laced with longing.

A flurry of emotions flits across her face. Surprise … adoration … irritation … betrayal.

Always betrayal.

She shakes her head, and her eyes flutter shut. "You … you're like a loaded rifle with no safety, Sebastian Kelly."

"I'm going to prove you wrong, Autumn. Just you wait. I'm so much more than you give me credit for."

"I won't make you any promises," she whispers, stepping away from the door, her eyes shiny with unshed tears.

I blink back my own emotions and smile with a confidence I only feel in half measures.

"The possibility of something more ... I've lived on less, so much less than that over the last few years. I think I'll take my chances."

The door clicks shut, and I can't walk away. The shadowed silhouette on the other side of the door tells me neither can she. My knees feel weak as I place a hand on the door and lean my head on the frame. I close my eyes and just breathe.

The air feels heavy with the truth we've spoken and strung tight with the things left unsaid. The door bows with the emotion pulsing from both sides.

I hate you ... I love you ... I need you ... I don't want to.

Then, with all the effort I can muster, I turn around and go home.

CHAPTER 25

Sebastian
Present
Haven, LA

"Not sure what the kitchen sink has to do with the price of tea in China, but I'd trade Marge in for a dozen of these cookies." Joe shoves another bite into his mouth while his wife gives him the side eye.

"Wouldn't even need payment. You can take this old goat off my hands for free," Marge mutters, throwing an accusing thumb in Joe's direction, then goes right back to her crocheting.

He stops chewing for a fraction of a second, but his stomach wins out over the butt hurt. He turns his body away from hers but doesn't make much progress with the sliver of loveseat Marge's size affords him. He harrumphs and takes another bite.

At a glance, the two are opposites in every way. Joe, wearing a crisply starched Western shirt with pearl buttons and a pack of cigarettes perched in his front pocket. Lean as a green bean and just as pointy. Marge, billowing and rounded, with her pleated house dress extenuating her already more-than-ample bosom while her feet overflow her Sas shoes like overbaked loaves of bread. Puffy as cotton candy and squat as a sumo wrestler.

One look at Lexi's ballerina corset and spiky black hair, along with my trendy lumberjack attire and two-month-old scruff, and it's safe to say we are four of the most oddly matched people to come together and make a family. We're like four mismatched socks at the bottom of a clothes dryer. But looks can be deceiving, and hearts come in all shapes and sizes. And some of the largest, squishiest ones are guarded with dynamite and barbed wire. Many times, those are the best ones.

"Well isn't this cozy." Lexi's gaze takes in every detail around her with a disapproving gaze and an I-smell-shit scowl.

The tiny apartment smells faintly of moth balls and stale smoke, and there's hardly enough room to house all of us in the cramped living room. One look at the peeling wallpaper and shag carpet matted with God knows what, and it's obvious Evangeline Apartments has seen better days.

Don't get me wrong, not a pillow is out of place, and courtesy of Marge, I can see my reflection in the cracked Formica counter in the kitchen. She's always kept a spotless home. Leaving a stray sock or food wrapper laying around meant you ran the risk of having your ear twisted right off.

But there's not enough spit to shine this turd.

"Seb, did you know the house I rent has two bedrooms?" Lexi's eyes are fixed on me, but she throws her voice across the tiny living room, directly at Joe and Marge.

"Hush it, little girl," Marge warns, never looking up from her yarn and needle.

"Split floor plan. Bedrooms are on opposite sides of the house from each other."

My silence earns me an elbow to the gut, and I yelp in pain.

"You don't say," I mutter through gritted teeth.

"You wouldn't happen to have a cookie jar in this house, would ya, Lexi Lou?" Joe raises a brow in question while visions of sugar plums and an unlimited supply of cookies glitter in his eyes.

"Joe!" Marge drops her crochet like it's on fire and stares at her husband, horrified.

"Maybe she's got a magic kitchen sink, Margie. Spits out these golden goodies with a tap of her wand. That'd be worth moving for, wouldn't you say?" He reaches for another cookie and takes a monstrous bite.

Smack. "We will not." Smack. "Be a burden." Smack. "I take care of you." Smack. "You take care of me." Smack. Smack.

Joe rubs his battered shoulder and scowls.

"I don't care if cookies rain down from the ceiling after supper every night."

Joe's expression brightens at the thought.

Smack. Smack.

"Woman, I'm about to take care of you all right, but I'm not sure it's in the way you mean. Now stop slapping me!"

"Hold on, hold on," I say calmly, trying to be the voice of reason. "I think what Lexi's trying to say is we're worried. When you sold your house, we knew you'd be downsizing to something smaller, but ... well, you've got to admit, this place has seen its better days."

"And so have we." Marge crosses her arms in a huff, offended on behalf of their apartment. "Just because something isn't as shiny as it used to be doesn't mean it's worthless. Even run-down things have their place on this earth."

"Speak for yourself. I ain't run down. *Some* things get better with age." Joe barks out a raucous laugh that quickly morphs into a rattling cough.

"Christ," Marge mutters.

"You've done so much for Seb and me," Lexi says, shooting a glance in my direction. I nod. "You took us in when we had nowhere to go. What would it say about us if we let you live in this dump? Let us be there for you like you were there for us."

I watch in wonder as Lexi pleads with them, and I can't help but smile. Every day, I watch her chew people up and swallow them in one gulp. A true cannibal at heart. But Joe and Marge get down to her gooey center unlike anyone else can. It's actually beautiful to watch. If it weren't for these two, I'd wonder if Lexi was absent the day God handed out feelings.

"You two do enough. We don't need you to take care of us in the way you think. Margie and me," Joe says as he reaches for Marge. She slides her hand in his and smiles. "We take care of each other. Been doing it for fifty years."

"When you're not trying to kill each other," Lexi mutters and rolls her eyes.

"Hush that right now. We may not always see eye to eye, but there's no one else in the world I'd want to yell at every day other than Joe. And that includes you." Marge sniffs and pats her and Joe's clasped hands. "Love doesn't always look like you think it should. Doesn't make it any less real."

Lexi looks apologetic as she picks at invisible lint on her jeans, but she says nothing.

"Besides, we've got friends here. Margie plays dominos with the ladies every Tuesday, and I run the elevators in the afternoon." Joe nods and puffs his bird chest proudly.

"Run the elevators?" I wonder aloud, because I'm pretty

sure I got on the elevator and pressed the button to their apartment just fine on my own. No assistance needed.

"The point is," Margie says, raising her voice and interrupting my train of thought, "we're doing just fine, thank you very much, and we expect weekly visits from both of you, just like always. Don't care if you like this place or not. Do you hear me?"

"Yes, ma'am," we both mumble as Marge mutters under her breath. "Don't know who made these two yo-yos president of the Good Housekeeping committee. Pretty sure neither one of 'em even owns a vacuum cleaner."

Before I can argue the point, because I damn well do own a vacuum cleaner no matter how infrequently I use it, my phone buzzes in my pocket.

I'm surprised to see Autumn's name lighting up the screen.

Autumn: Are you busy?

Me: No, what's up?

"Boy, you come visit me and my wife and sit on that damned old phone, looking googly eyed? No manners, that one." I look up to find Joe scowling in my direction.

Lexi barks out a laugh. "Speaking of love ... that goofball face sums it up nicely. For Sebastian, love is looking about three-foot-tall with brown eyes and bows in her hair. Pretty sure the mom is part of the equation, too, if you know what I mean."

"Stop telling the boy's business—"

Before Marge finishes taking up for me, my screen lights up again, but with a call this time.

"Hey, is everything okay?"

"I'm so sorry, but I didn't have anyone else to call," Autumn says, sounding way too frantic for my liking.

I step out into the hallway and close the door behind me.

"No, you did the right thing. What's wrong."

"The school just called me, and Aria is sick. She threw up at recess, and then again in the classroom. I still have two classes, and one of them is a lab with a fifty-point assignment."

"I'll leave right now. I can be there in ten," I say, judging the fastest route to Aria's school at this time of day.

"Oh God, thank you so much. I didn't know what I was going to do. I'm used to having Aunt D and Brady—"

"Now you have me. I'll take care of everything until you can get home." I pull my keys out of my pocket and walk back into the apartment. "Is there some kind of approved list I need to be on to pick her up?"

"Um, yeah. I added you on the first day of school," she admits.

And I grin.

After promises to fill Marge in later and a few well-placed jabs from Lexi, I hop in the car and take off across town.

"Hey," Aria mumbles as she slides off the chair and walks toward me. "I frew up."

"I heard." I run a hand over her hair in comfort while looking for the principal or secretary ... or basically anyone who can give us the go-ahead to leave.

"Two times."

"That's awful."

She nods.

"Want to go home?"

She nods again, and her head flops to the side, resting on my thigh.

"Hi, can I help you?"

I startle at the proximity of the voice because I never heard anyone approach, but a five-foot-nothing woman with a mess of gray hair knotted on top of her head is smiling across the counter from me.

"Yes, I'm here to check out Aria…" I stumble over the last name, not knowing if it's Norris or Kelly. Hoping that it's Kelly. Knowing my hopes will most probably be dashed.

"Of course. You must be Aria's father. Ms. Norris told us to be expecting you."

I stiffen at her words, and the hand that had been soothing Aria's head comes to a standstill. Over the last few weeks, I've imagined hundreds of ways of telling Aria who I am. This particular scenario never crossed my mind.

I look down and find Aria staring at me, face scrunched in confusion. Her lips twitch imperceptibly, and her arm snakes around my leg and squeezes. She sucks in a deep breath, and her shoulders quake with the effort.

Then she bends at the waist and pukes all over my shoes.

CHAPTER 26

Autumn
Present Day
Haven, LA

I turn off the ignition, and my forehead falls to the steering wheel. This day has been fast-approaching, but I figured we had a little more time. Seb's text blew that thought right out of my head.

Seb: Not positive, but I think the dad's out of the bag.

After four years with Aria, I wish I could say I know exactly how she'll react. But the truth is she's a shocking little thing. I never know what she will think, say, or do at any given moment. She's a mixed bag, really. That's one of the best parts of her ... most of the time. At this moment, it's got me freaked the hell out.

There are worse things. As I gather my purse and the six-pack of Gatorade I grabbed on my way over here, I remind myself there are worse things than my daughter finding out she has a father and he's aching to love her. Wishing she would love him.

Actually, there is nothing better than exactly that.

I shake off the nervous energy that's plagued me since I made the move to Haven and let the wonderful warmth settle in my chest. Since my talk with Brady, I've been making a concerted effort to let the past go and let people in. At least where Aria is concerned.

When it comes to Sebastian and me? That's a completely different story. What we are to each other ... what we've done to each other ... "let the past go" is too flippant and simple to deal with the scars we've inflicted.

We were two separate trees nurtured together in the same backyard. The roots have crossed and intertwined, looped about and driven deep into the earth. Even fused together in some places, like toes touching under the covers. It's not so easy to extricate your life from someone else's. It's impossible to deny the pain when one of those trees is ripped from the ground.

And it's unimaginable to think two lives can be transplanted and reinvigorated after that amount of carnage.

But one look at the perfect little girl we created together, with love, and hope undoubtedly creeps its way into the roots and crevices.

"Get it together, Autumn. You're not a freaking teenager anymore," I whisper as I hurry up the sidewalk.

I've never seen the inside of Seb's house, but last week when Aria stayed over, an incognito drive-by on a takeout run gave me a sneak peek from the road. Don't judge. When weighing the importance of propriety with sheer curiosity, there's really no contest.

And for the record, his house is ... I don't know what it is. Surprising? Adorable? I mean, Sebastian Kelly, the boy who used to throw lizards and go skinny-dipping now has a flower bed. With actual blooming flowers in it. And wind chimes hanging from the front porch. It's crazy.

And all kinds of cute.

Elton John filters through the door as I knock, followed by the telltale squeal of a little girl. A little girl who doesn't sound very sick.

The door opens to reveal a floppy haired Isaac with Aria wrapped around him like a spider monkey. At second glance, Aria's wearing—

"What are you wearing, poppet? And how do you feel?" I brush her curls back and press my lips to her forehead. "No fever …"

"I feel better, Momma. Isaac is teaching me to dance," she says, tucking her head in the crook of his neck and batting her eyelashes.

He shrugs. "More like swaying."

"Come on in," Seb calls out from beyond the living room. "She's wearing the smallest T-shirt we've got, and boxers cinched together with a clothespin. We had to improvise."

I step inside and shut the door, then reach my arms out to Aria. She doesn't take the bait.

"Well," I say, surprised as hell.

Isaac shrugs again.

"We can still go to Aunt D's, Momma, even though I'm sick?" She says "aunt" like "ain't," and it never fails to bring a smile to my face.

"We'll have to see how you're feeling later this week. We don't want to give her a virus."

She lifts her head to look at Isaac. "I'm going to my Aunt D's to spend the night. My Nana and Poppo will be there, too."

"No Nana and Poppo this time, poppet. They had to change plans," I explain, shooting a glance in Seb's direction.

Aria frowns, and Seb looks like he wants me to explain, but thankfully keeps quiet on the subject. I'm glad because that conversation is destined to end badly.

"I just put her clothes in the dryer. Things got, shall we say, messy." Seb's eyes grow wide at the admission, and I can imagine how messy things got. Aria's got the aim of a blind sniper when's she sick. She couldn't hit the broad side of a barn.

"I frew up a lot. My clothes were yucky." She points across the living room to Seb in the kitchen. "His shoes were yucky."

"Oh no," I whisper, and cover my mouth.

"We had to frow those shoes away. They stunk bad," she explains, nodding her head and frowning. "His socks, too."

"Oh my gosh. I'm so sorry. I'll replace them, I promise." He's shaking his head before I even finish talking. I meet him in the kitchen, ready to argue the point.

"You're not replacing anything." He looks over my shoulder, presumably checking for little ears. "I feel like I was christened into the family. I chucked those shoes in the dumpster with a smile on my face. How old were you when Aria first peed or pooped or spit up on you?"

I laugh. "We hadn't left the hospital yet."

"Exactly. So, no shoes. Just welcome me to the family."

"Welcome to the family, Seb," I whisper, trying with all my might to keep that warm feeling in my chest from settling smack dab in the middle of my heart. I shake it away, put a bookmark in it to obsess over later, and change the subject. "Did she uh ... did she say anything about ... you know?"

Realization dawns in his eyes, and he shakes his head. "Nah, not a word. The secretary at school mentioned d-a-d, but Aria was ten seconds from spewing her guts up. She may have been in a vomit-induced haze."

"Well, that's ..." I search my brain for the right word while I sneak a peak at my cooing daughter. "Disgusting. Yep, that's disgusting."

"Disgusting, yes, but timely all the same. May have bought us more time, right?"

"Right." I shrug and give him a tentative smile.

I should be relieved, but instead, my insides feel like a deflated balloon. It's as if we're standing at the starting line, poised and ready to start the race. Up until today, I've been the one holding the starting revolver. Now, I'm not sure I want the job anymore.

"We're getting good at this, right?" he asks with a grin. "You and me? I was afraid this would be awkward, but it's not. I mean, you don't think it's awkward, do you?"

"No, not at all," I say with a half nod, half shake of my head. "Nope."

But it is. Awkward, I mean.

Part of me knows Sebastian like he's my favorite novel I've read until the pages are smudged and worn. But then again, years have changed the both of us, and those new parts are crisp pages I've never seen before, and I have no idea what comes next. That can be both frightening and exciting at the same time. It can also make for uncomfortable and difficult situations.

But Sebastian says awkward like it's a bad word, and I don't believe it is.

Awkward isn't alone, trying to find the words to tell my parents I'm pregnant.

Awkward isn't afraid, praying I'm not doing this parenting gig all wrong.

Come to think of it, I look forward to awkward these days.

Because awkward is starting to look like the makings of a family.

Seb's eyes brighten, and he wipes his hands on his jeans. "Oh, I almost forgot, I have something for you."

He places a bag in front of me and pulls out a cell phone.

Shiny, new, and way more expensive than what I can swing right now.

I shake my head and take a step back, but he doesn't give me the chance to protest. "It's something you need, and I want to give it to you. It's not a big deal, so let's not make it one."

"I can't accept it."

He slides the box open and pops the phone out of the casing. "You can keep your plan with this new phone or I can just add you to my plan. I've got unlimited everything, so no worries there."

"Wait … what? No, I told you I can't—"

"Autumn, I've got two questions for you, and then we're done with this. First, what percentage battery do you have on your phone right now?" He crosses his arms and waits. When I don't react, he waves me on.

I pull my phone out of my purse, roll my eyes, and mutter under my breath.

"What was that? I couldn't hear you?" He taunts, cupping his hand to his ear.

"Nine."

"Percent?"

"Yes."

"Right, okay. So, you need a new phone." He raises his hand and shows me two fingers, before whispering, "Second thing, how many years of child support do I owe you?"

"Stop."

"No."

"Sebastian—"

"Autumn, I wish I could go back in time and be there for you, for her, but I can't. But I need to be clear about this, so we don't misunderstand each other going forward. I'm going to take care of Aria, which means I'm going to take care of you. And you're going to have to let me." Seb releases a gigantic breath and waits for me to respond.

"Just let me do my job, okay? That's how we make this right. That's how you can help me move forward."

I press my lips together and nod.

"I can do that. Thank you."

"No thanks necessary," he says as the music changes behind us.

"Isn't She Lovely" by Stevie Wonder.

Aria lets out a soft giggle, and Isaac replaces the old record into its sleeve.

"A record player? I'm impressed."

I walk over to the entertainment center and peek at the stack of albums sitting next to the player.

Rod Stewart, Etta James, Patsy Cline.

"Yeah, there's a great record store down the street from the shop. The guy who owns it is a piece of work. Strange, but really cool. He reads people's vibes or some shit and picks music for them. It's uncanny how right he gets it. It's like he knows the soundtrack to everyone's life." Seb pulls a pot off the stove and pours noodles into a strainer. "I made spaghetti for dinner if you're hungry. I mean, spaghetti for us. Just toast for Aria until we figure out if the worst has passed. Her clothes won't be dry for a bit longer, anyway."

"Okay," I say distractedly, still flipping through the albums. Sam Cooke, Rolling Stones. I gesture to the records in my hand. "So, is this the soundtrack of your life? Is that why you have them?"

"I actually pulled those out for Aria. I'm hoping one day, decades from now, she'll hear one of these songs and remember that one time when she danced with her cousin and puked on her dad's shoes. I hope she hears 'Tiny Dancer' on the radio and knows how special she is." He shrugs as he grabs plates down from the cabinets.

Awe. There's no other word to describe how I feel right now. At this moment, I'm in complete awe of him.

The relationship between a parent and a child is so complex and textured. It's layer after layer of words, emotions, memories, and secrets. Words whispered, frustrations shouted, and even those things that are given no voice at all. Some are sweet, like wisps of cotton candy while others are stubborn and unwavering. All of it adds up to a magnificent kind of love, the whole being infinitesimally more valuable than the sum of its parts.

And Sebastian Kelly is wrapping his daughter in freshly spun sugar.

I smirk at the thought of these two clashing like battering rams. That particular layer will be a battle for the ages, I'm sure.

This kind of love and dedication can't be taught from a parenting book, and yes, I spotted a stack of them on the coffee table when I arrived. It comes from within. It takes shape over time.

It's the difference between a father and a daddy.

"Look at this pitcher," Aria interrupts as she shoves my new phone at Sebastian. "It's the fish we caught. 'Member that one time?"

Sebastian crouches down to her level and looks at the blank screen and smiles. My girl has such a wild imagination.

"I remember. It was a really big fish."

Aria chuckles and brushes her curls out of her face. "You said I couldn't do it, but I did. I did it. 'Member?"

"Yes," he whispers, head bent over the phone and his daughter.

"Next time, can we go swimming instead?"

"Of course. I'll take you swimming whenever you want."

She drops the phone to her side and meets his gaze. She narrows her eyes and purses her lips. "Do you have a pool?"

"No, I don't." His words are soft and even but dripping with intent. "But I'll find one. For you."

She smiles and hands the phone over to him before skipping across the room. I watch the man she's left in her wake and wonder, if Seb had never left town, if he knew his daughter from the start, how would things be different now? I watch him, now sporting a beard much thicker than the few measly whiskers from his teenage years and his muscles corded and lean—he's fully grown into the man he was meant to become. When I look at present-day Sebastian, it isn't very hard to imagine how things would be at all.

Probably a lot like *this* ...

The thought startles me, sneaks into my mind, and grabs center stage with absolutely no warning. The thought leaves me unsettled, but it doesn't make it any less true.

Aria jumps up next to Isaac on the sofa, completely oblivious to her father, kneeling frozen on the floor right where she left him.

All the while, Seb is completely oblivious of me, present-day Autumn seeing him in a completely different way.

And I'm not positive, but I think Aria just ripped the starting revolver from my hand and pulled the trigger.

The race is on.

CHAPTER 27

Autumn
Present Day
Providence, LA

"Hello?" I call out after a knock on the screen door with no answer. Aria sneaks around me and darts into the house like a shot. "Aria, wait a minute!"

"She's on the swing. I hear it. Aunt D!"

The frantic stomping of little girl feet mixes with the rhythmic creaking of chain links, and I know she's right. The patch of concrete underneath that porch swing gets more traffic than anywhere else in the town of Providence.

I can sum up Aunt Dorothy with a few words. Swing. Coffee. Cards. All the things she loves.

And her great-niece, of course. Aria sits proudly on the top of that list, crown firmly in place.

I hear the squeal before I make it to the sliding door, and the rhythm of the chains goes wonky.

Aria.

"Hold on, little girl, you'll throw Chessy and me right off

this swing. And believe me, if this big butt hits that little ground, there will be an earthquake."

Chessy, her twenty-pound tabby cat. Another thing to add to her list of loves. A healthy diet of freeze-dried shrimp and table food means there's a whole lot of Chessy to love.

"Sorry, we're a little late. We made a stop by the office to check on West and the girls." I'll always have a special place in my heart for West. He taught me so much when I interned at his practice. "His wife's pregnant."

"Huh, about time. They'll make pretty babies."

I nod because it's true. They'll be absolutely gorgeous.

Aunt D howls as Aria puts her neck in a death grip of a hold and peppers kisses all over the side of her face. The cat lets out a low growl from the pit of that cavernous belly. Aria is undeterred.

"Slow down, poppet, or she'll drown to death in your spit." I lean against the porch door and laugh. Seeing these three reunited brings on the type of happy I feel from the top of my head down to the very tips of my toes.

"It's all right, let her kiss on her old Aunt D. I haven't put on my face yet."

Aria turns her attention to Chessy, who looks less than impressed.

"Did you miss me, Chessy? Did you miss me? Huh, boy?" She scratches behind his ears and pats his wide load and puffs of fur fly with each tap.

"I don't know when that girl's gonna realize Chessy is *not* a dog. He ain't ever gonna lick the side of *your* face, girl. We'll leave the licking to you." I roll my eyes as Chessy lets out a warning hiss, undone with all the attention he's receiving. "I've already got a cup but go inside and make some cafe au lait for both of you."

"Because that," I say, pointing at the bundle of excitement sitting next to her, "needs coffee?"

"Oh, shush that. A little bit of coffee milk never hurt a child. My momma made it for me and your dad. Your mom made it for you and Brady." She shoos me with a waved hand and amused scowl. "Now go on."

"Not to mention it's a hundred degrees out," I mutter as I walk away to do her bidding.

Aria chants, "Coffee. Milk. Coffee. Milk" in the background while jumping up and down on her knees.

"I've got the fan on. You'll be fine," Aunt D calls out, followed by another hiss from Chessy.

~

"School?"

I nod my head slowly and press my lips together. "Good. Really good, actually."

"Aria's school."

My lips curve into an automatic smile. "Great. She's the belle of the ball."

"Of course she is," Aunt D huffs as if any other answer would have been pure blasphemy. "And the living situation?"

"Hmm..." I search for the right words to sum up the messiness of our lives since we've moved to Haven. We swing and sip together, watching Aria climb between the branches of an oak tree. Chessy lounges on the ground beneath.

"Better than expected, I have to admit. It's an adjustment for Aria, letting someone new into her life. You know how she is, Aunt D. She can be so aloof and unaccepting of new people. But she's slowly coming around. Maybe it's time to explain to her who Seb really is."

She slaps her knee and lets out a peal of laughter like I've just told her the funniest joke she's ever heard. She places her hand over her heaving chest and tries to catch her breath.

"Whew, that's a good one, girlie. I haven't had a laugh like that in years."

"What in the world are you laughing at?"

"You. I'm laughing at you." She wipes the tears from under her eyes and chuckles. "Coming around. My Aria is 'coming around.' That little girl has *come* and *left*. She's just waiting on you."

"Left? What?" I turn sideways on the swing and wait for some kind of explanation of what the hell she's going on about.

"When you were making coffee, Aria spilled it *all*, girl. Told me she has a daddy. Told me I needed to meet him soon." Peals of laughter erupt from Aunt D as my eyes widen in shock. "Asked me if she should tell you the secret because she's afraid … sh-she's afraid you'll be upset if you knew."

Cue the howling laughter from Aunt D. Cue the tidal wave of embarrassment from me. How could I have been so oblivious?

"Oh God."

"You got that right. And he better be calling the Lord, too. Because you know what I've always said." She points at me and wags her finger. "The minute there's someone in this world calling you Momma … or Daddy … your fat's in the fire. You let him know."

Me: FYI-the dad is definitely out of the bag.

Seb: ???

Me: Turns out she's known for a while. Was afraid to tell me she had a dad. Let that sink in for a minute.

Seb: …

Seb: So I guess the birds and the bees talk comes some-time AFTER four years old. LOL

Me: I'm glad you see the humor in this. I, on the other hand, feel like an idiot. That little girl has been HANDLING me.

Seb: Now, now, give her credit. You're a helluva lot to handle. She's got skills.

Me: Christ...

Seb: So you know.

Seb: I know.

Seb: She knows.

Seb: But she doesn't know that we know she knows.

Seb: Confused yet?

Me: Shut up.

Seb: I think it's time we take the dad out of the bag and let him prance around the room for everyone to see. Don't you think?

Me: You've always been good at prancing.

Seb: Shut up.

"Momma!" Her whine-yell filters down the hallway, just as it's done a hundred times before. "Chessy won't lay in bed wif me. He keeps trying to run away!"

The hiss and accompanying yowl tell me Aria's gotten hold of a leg or a tail. The little girl growl that follows tells me he's evaded her once again.

"Eyes closed, Aria! Right now."

She groans, then quiets down. I take my own advice and snuggle into the blankets, thoughts of daddies and family and boys I swore to forget peppering my thoughts and dreams.

Two o'clock. In the morning. What the hell am I doing, wide awake? My thoughts are so alive and churning, I can't even physically shut my eyes. My brain won't allow it.

Shit ...

I swipe my shiny new phone off the bedside table and type before I can talk myself out of it.

Me: So what was your song?

I lock the screen and throw it back onto the bedside table. No way Seb is up at this time of night.

Ding!

Seb: Huh?

Seb: And why are you still awake?

Me: What song reminds you of when you were a kid? Like "Tiny Dancer" for Aria?

Me: And because I'm a fool, obviously. Aria shows no mercy. Six AM.

Seb: "Sailing" by Christopher Cross. My mom used to play it when she cleaned. Drove my dad nuts.

I remember it, could almost swear I've heard Mrs. Kelly play it before. I close my eyes and play the song in my head. The words make me smile.

Ding!

Seb: You?

Me: You'll laugh but … "You're the One That I Want"

Me: Grease

Seb: LOL! That's so perfect.

Me: I'm going to regret this … but … I had a whole routine.

Seb: I'm dying! How did I not know this?

Me: You don't know EVERYTHING about me.

Seb: I got chills

Me: Shut up.

Seb: They're multiplying.

Me: I'm two verses away from kicking a hole in your sailboat.

Seb: All right, all right.

Seb: And I do.

Me: Huh?

Seb: Know everything about you. Cheesy musicals notwithstanding.

I drop the phone onto the mattress and raise my hands in some sort of silent surrender.

I pick it up.

I drop it.

Pick it up. Drop it. Again. Again.

Two simple sentences, but there's not one simple thing about them. They open doors that might be better left locked tight. They leave the light on, in wait. They leave me to ponder the question *what if.* Entertaining those two simple sentences with a response isn't only giving into temptation, it's inviting it over for coffee.

Were we ready for that? Was I?

Love is a lot like snow. A wonderful idea in theory, but reality brings about something altogether different. Black ice instead of snow angels. Frozen mounds covered in exhaust in the place of white wonder. Snow doesn't always deliver on its promise of beauty. Just like love. It's a lesson I learned the hard way a long time ago.

But if anyone or anything deserves a chance to begin again, it's Seb and me. Maybe that's the key to it all. Not fixing the past, but letting it go. Beginning again. *What if …*

Me: Maybe we

Delete, delete, delete.

Me: I think we should

Delete, delete, delete, delete.

My thumbs hover over the screen, scared and nervous and thoroughly giddy at the possibility waiting for me at the other end of that screen. *What if* has me acting like an awestruck teenager all over again. This is harder than I thought.

Me: What if I told you I wanted to learn everything about you … again?

I hit send and release a nervous breath. I drop the phone and curl into a tiny ball, trying to squelch the adrenaline pumping through my veins as I wait for a response. I clench my eyes shut, fearing that ding almost as much as I anticipate it.

I roll over to sunlight painting the bedspread. I click my phone and see the time blinking back at me.

Five-fifty AM.

What I don't see is a response from Sebastian.

Snow and love—two things more magical in theory than practice. Which is why I live in Louisiana.

And why I never should have gotten my hopes up in the first place.

CHAPTER 28

Sebastian
Present Day
Haven, LA

I roll over in bed, trying to escape the wet spot my filthy body has made, but going as slowly as possible as not to wake the spewing volcano in my gut.

Am I dead? If not, can I go ahead and do that now?

"Gatorade?" Isaac calls out from the door.

It's as close as he'll get to me in this condition. Smart kid.

"I'll just throw it up," I mutter into the pillow, and my lips leave a trail of spittle behind.

"Better than all that heaving you're doing."

"Stop. Talking." Every word out of his mouth feels like a tiny dagger right in my eye, the throbbing in my head drumming out a victory song for Satan himself.

He keeps jabbering, but thankfully death is merciful and pulls me under before the daggers really get going.

"He's been like this since I woke up this morning. Found him on the floor of the bathroom, arms wrapped around the toilet like it was a teddy bear."

I let out a loud groan, partly to stop the tiny daggers, and partly in anger at the fact that I am still indeed alive.

"A bucket?"

My brain perks up at the sound, less knife-like and more ... feminine? My brain may have come to attention, but the rest of me continues to melt into a pile of disgusting sludge. Lifting my head and opening my eyes is equivalent to wrestling a pack of starving grizzlies at this point.

"He stopped making it to the bathroom hours ago."

"I'm glad Lexi told me he was sick when I stopped by the coffee shop. He looks really awful."

"Ha! You can say that again."

"Isaac, shh. My head," I grumble as I bury my face deeper into the pillow.

Until ... the volcano awakens with a vengeance.

"Oh no." I roll toward the edge of the mattress with all the effort I can muster and reach blindly for my bucket of destruction.

"He's gonna do it, he's gonna do it," a tiny voice chants with either horror or excitement, I can't say for sure.

Then Mount Sebastious erupts with maximum damage.

CHAPTER 29

Autumn
Present Day
Haven, LA

"You fine, you fine, you okay, you fine," Aria whispers as she runs her flat palm down Seb's calf in time with her words.

Too bad he's oblivious to her affection. He's been longing for Aria to jump into his outstretched arms like every Hallmark movie in existence, and now he's missing the whole thing. Every so often, we get a quirk of an eyebrow or a long, suffering groan, but I'm pretty sure those don't count as signs of life.

"Should we call somebody?" Isaac asks, still standing at the threshold of the door with eyes wide and clueless. No amount of coaxing is getting *that* boy in *this* room. I'm pretty sure if Seb had asked for anything before we got here, Isaac would have pelted him in the head with it while standing beyond the doorway.

"Nah, it's actually worse than it looks," I say as I carry the bucket of death to the bathroom to dump. "You're looking at his reward for taking care of Aria last week when she was sick. This virus has made the rounds at her school. Looks like another one bites the dust."

"Nuh-uh. No way this is the same thing she had last week," Isaac protests while shaking his head. "She spit up a couple of times then pranced around for the rest of the afternoon. This?" He points at the half dead lump in the bed. "This is the *Exorcist* with a side of *Walking Dead*."

"Something you should know about kids, Isaac. They are a host of germs and dirt. The first time Aria got ringworm, the doctor just shrugged and told me, 'Children are filthy animals,'" I call out from the bathroom. "Seb hasn't been around a lot of kids lately, or schools. He's like a bubble boy who got thrown into a cesspool. Basically, Aria's immune system kicks Seb's immune system's ass. That's why she bounced back so quickly. That and she's a four-year-old spring chicken."

Aria sits on the corner of the bed, beaming as Isaac watches her with fear in his eyes. An elephant cowed by a teeny, tiny scorpion.

"A-a-am I a bubble boy, too?" He lays a hand on his chest in a "Who me?" type gesture.

I chuckle and shake my head. "No, you're probably good. You're still in school, so you're a filthy animal in your own right."

He looks insulted by my accusation and poised to argue the point.

"What? Would you rather be filthy or sick?"

"Good point." He grins and shoves his hands deep into his jean pockets. "How can I help?"

"From a distance, you mean?"

He smirks sheepishly. I toss him my keys.

"Take Aria for a snack at the coffee shop, then you two

cesspools hang out at our apartment for a while. I'll take care of the *Exorcist* over here."

"Yay!" Aria hops off the bed with a clap and bounds toward Isaac.

He gives her a wide berth and a light tap on the head. She giggles, oblivious to his terror as she grabs his hand and pulls toward the front door.

~

It's nearly dark before Seb shows any real signs of life, and most of those are moans and grunts as I clean him up and change his wretched sheets. The actual retching seems to have tapered off, which I'm eternally grateful for. I have a strong stomach most of the time, but a girl can only take so much before she breaks.

As he sleeps off what I hope is the last of this virus, I take a look around his house. I mean, I don't open any drawers or anything. I'm not a total creeper. I only scope out what's in plain view, like I'm a cop without a warrant. No harm in that, especially if he never finds out.

So, here's what I gather from my quick perusal: Seb's a whole lot neater than he ever was before, he's got great taste in art, and an album collection that would rival any musician's. The only photograph in the entire house is of Aria—the one he nabbed the night he learned of her. It sits on his bedside table, along with a lamp, his wallet, and his cell phone. That's the extent of the personalization of Seb's house. A bedside table.

I take a second glance at his cell phone, then I accidentally trip and press the ON button. Oops. The screen illuminates, and my last text lights up the screen.

Autumn: What if I told you I wanted to learn everything about you … again?

He never saw it. He never saw the text, so he wasn't ignoring me … or blowing me off … or being a complete douche. A sense of relief washes over me, followed closely by a wave of panic. He hasn't seen it and, holy hell, what if I'm here when he finally does?

Shit, shit, shit …

"No need to panic, I promise not to puke on you," Seb mumbles, and I jump at the sound of his voice. "Wait, maybe I already did. Have I? Puked on you?"

He pushes up to sitting and runs a hand over his still-pale face. He looks down at his bare chest in confusion then turns to me.

"I, uh, took it off when I gave you a kind-of bed bath. I didn't put a new one on because too much movement, and you'd…" I gesture to my mouth theatrically, and he flinches in shame. "Figured it was best not to tempt fate."

"So, I *did* puke on you. Shit, sorry."

"No, no, you've got a much better aim than your daughter."

I shove my hands in my pockets, trying to stow away some of the nervous energy vibrating down to the tips of my fingers. I ball them into fists and take a deep breath.

"Bed bath, huh?" Seb grimaces and shoots me a sympathetic smile.

"It was all on the up-and-up, I assure you." I laugh at his obvious disappointment. "Although I did notice you have a lot more bulging than before."

He lets out a choking sound, and I gasp.

"Muscles!" I shout at the top of my lungs and cover my face. "I meant muscles. Shit!"

"Sure, right. Sure, you did." He throws his head back in laughter then clutches his stomach. "You gotta tone down the jokes, woman. My stomach is sore from the revolt."

"Gatorade? Something to eat?" I offer, thinking of anything to keep my idle, twitching hands occupied.

"Shower?" My eyes widen, and he lifts his hands in protest. "No, not shower *with* me. I meant do you mind if I take a shower? Bed bath aside, I feel like a greasy dirtball."

"Sure, of course." I turn to leave the bedroom, but he calls me back.

"You'll ... you'll stay, right?" he whispers, and the vulnerability in his voice unnerves me. "We still need to discuss that dad. You know, being out of the bag."

"Right. Yes, I'll just," I point toward the door, "wait in there."

I mosey out of the bedroom but turn my head just in time to see him swipe his phone off the table before heading to the bathroom.

Shit, shit, shit.

~

"Shower accomplished without passing out or hurling, so maybe the worst is behind me?"

Sebastian plops down onto the sofa next to me with more bounce than he's had all day. I'll take that as a good sign.

He runs a hand over his face, his palm scratching the stubble of his beard. The sound draws my eyes to his mouth and my imagination to those full lips.

What would it be like to kiss a man with a beard? No, that's not the question on my mind. What would it be like to kiss a bearded Sebastian? Yes, that's the one.

Damn that man. Damn his gentle brown eyes and damp sexy hair. And definitely damn his sweet and flirty texts, because they were the beginning of the end for me. Out walked levelheaded, single mother Autumn, and in skipped swooning Autumn, batting her eyelashes and twirling her hair.

Seb scratches at the collar of his shirt, and a patch of skin comes into view ... with finely dusted chest hair ... and I blush like he'd just walked out here in assless chaps and a hula hoop.

Get it together, girl.

"Can I get you something to eat? Drink?" I ask, my voice sounding screechy, even to my own ears.

He chuckles and places a hand on my knee. Squeezes. "Let's not tempt fate just yet."

I nod, burning a hole in said hand with my gaze. Do I want him to leave it? Take it away? Gah!

He pulls it back, propping his elbow on the back of the sofa and leaning his head on his fist.

"So, do you think we need to have a discussion?"

"Huh?"

"Do we need to sit Aria down and talk through the 'dad' thing?" He makes air quotations then points a finger at himself.

"Honestly? Nonchalant is the key to Aria. Cat, remember?" Seb rolls his eyes at my reference, then nods grudgingly. "Give me a crack at it, then we'll go from there, okay?"

He nods, even more grudgingly if that's possible. With slumped shoulders and a deflated smile, he picks the invisible lint from the couch cushion. "I just thought there would be this moment where everything would be revealed. Like on Maury Povich ... but way classier." He laughs and shakes his head. "Sorry, this is coming out all wrong. I just want that moment, you know? Where I finally feel like her dad. And then it'll all be real. But it doesn't happen like that, does it?"

I can't help it. I grab his stray hand between both of mine and squeeze.

"No, it doesn't. I know you feel like you need validation,

and I get it. But I think we're doing the right thing, letting Aria guide us through this."

"I don't need it. I'm just ready for it. I'm ready for it all."

"It is, you know? Real? It always has been. I'm just sorry you're having to play catch up now." I smile at the memories Seb has been making in just the last few weeks. He's been hard at work, for sure. "If it's any consolation, you catch up like a boss."

"Tell me about it," he whispers, head bowed but eyes lifted, meeting mine. "Tell me about when you gave birth to her."

CHAPTER 30

Autumn
Present Day
Haven, LA

"Oh," I breathe, a tiny rush flowing through me at the memories of that day. "Okay, um…"

He inches closer, his knee coming into contact with mine. "You're not the only one who wants to know everything again."

My head jerks as he tosses my words back into my lap, and my breath stutters in my chest. He smirks, then his lips morph into a crooked smile. He doesn't say a word, just waits patiently for me to continue. So, I do.

"True to form, Aria was late to the party. After I was a week past my due date, my doctor scheduled me to come into the hospital for an induction. You know—" I gesture to my stomach. "Where they give you medication to start labor."

He nods, eyes trained on my stomach as his Adam's apple bobs with a stiff swallow.

"Two days before I was supposed to go to the hospital, it

happened. I was standing in line at the Texaco with my Slushee—I craved Slushees something fierce when I was pregnant—and my water broke. It wasn't a trickle or even a gush. It was a freaking tsunami. I just stood there, wishing the ground would swallow me whole so everyone would stop gasping and staring. Aunt D strolls up behind me with her fountain drink, takes a sip, and says, 'Well shit, you don't ever do anything by half, do ya? Gotta pay for my belly washer and get my Power Ball ticket before we head to the hospital. Pot's eight hundred million, girl.' Then she hollers, 'Anybody got a picnic blanket in their car we can borrow?'"

Seb's eyes widen, and I'm not sure if he wants to laugh or scowl. I'm not sure he knows either. "She's a piece of work, huh? Your Aunt D."

"Oh yeah," I laugh. "The best kind, though, I swear. She's a little hard on the surface, but the inside is squishy and awesome. She's been like a mother to me these last few years."

Seb snorts at that, and I pick up where I left off, hoping to bypass any talk of my parents.

"So, we head to the hospital to get checked out, but I'm not hurting or having contractions. The nurse tells me that even though my water broke, they may have to give me medicine to start the contractions."

The further I get into the story, the closer Seb and I find ourselves. Our drawn-up legs are lined up shin to shin. We lean into each other, mere inches separating us. My hands are clasped in his, pulled tight into his lap.

"Then she checked to see if I had dilated, and I was two centimeters."

"Is that good?" he asks, his voice low and hopeful.

I chuckle, then frown. "It would've been if there wasn't a teeny foot sticking out where there should have been a head."

Seb's hands tense in mine, and his jaw goes stiff. I shake

my head, smiling at his concern. I'd be lying if I didn't say it felt good.

"C-section. I promise it sounds worse than it was. The nurses and doctors were great and kept me calm the whole time."

"What, um ... did, uh, was ..." Seb clears his throat and whispers, "Was she okay? Were you—uh—were you okay?"

"Oh yeah." I nod emphatically, lowering my gaze to meet his downcast eyes. "She came out screaming like the champ she is. And I was good, too. A little scared once they took her to the nursery, that was all. It's unnerving, spending nine months with someone, feeling every move and kick, telling her things I've never said aloud to anyone else, and then she's just ... gone. We were separated, and I didn't know what was going on."

"Where were your parents? Brady?"

"They came later that night, but this was all of a sudden, remember? They planned to be there for my scheduled induction, but Aria blew that to pieces. It was just Aunt D and me," I say, and he shoots up off the couch and releases my hands.

"Shit, I have to—" He paces the length of the living room, and his flat palms hit the front door with jarring force. I wait for his hands to curve around the waiting doorknob.

I wait for him to run.

His forehead meets wood as he drags in a ragged breath. "You were alone. You were alone. You were fucking all alone. *And so was she.*"

I reach him. Place my hands on his heaving sides. Lay my forehead on his trembling spine. And I speak the truth.

"So were you, Seb. So were you."

He shakes his head and sniffs. His palms drag down the door, then curl into fists at his sides. "It's not the same thing, and you know it."

"I never meant to hurt you by telling you these things. I'm trying to fill in the blanks so you won't feel so—"

"Empty?" He scoffs at the word and turns to me, everything in his expression saying, "Fat chance of that."

"No. I wanted to make you feel a part of all this. I wanted it to be *real*," I say emphatically, using his own words against him. "Her legs were so long and spindly. And her hair? Gosh, I'll have to show you pictures. Jet black, I shit you not. It looked like I'd grabbed the wrong baby from the nursery. And no amount of combing would tame it. It was like one big cowlick—I finally had to slide a baby bow through that mess and call it good."

He rolls his eyes up as if taking a look at the mop on top of his own head and gives me the slightest smirk.

"Yeah, somehow you both manage to pull it off." I laugh. "Her lips were bright red, like she was already wearing lipstick, ready for the party. And they'd purse like she was sucking her pacifier, even when there was nothing in her mouth."

I pull him back to the couch. He follows, sitting hunched over with elbows to knees and head hanging low.

"And when I'd run my thumb across her forehead, her eyes would flutter closed, for just a moment."

My mind flits to the stacks of albums stowed at the top of my closet, and I wonder if they would do more harm than good. The last thing I want to do is hurt him. I think there's been enough hurt between us to last a lifetime.

As if he can hear my thoughts, Seb grabs my hand and meets my eyes. "Will it always be this way? Will every conversation about the past always be drenched in this guilt?"

He says "guilt" like it's poisonous, and for the two of us, it truly is. Seb and I have learned the hard way just how greedy and cavernous guilt can be, especially when the only thing filling the eternal void is regret. Another word dripping with venom.

"It won't be if we don't let it. I'm not saying it'll be easy. God knows it's been a bitch up until now, but I think you and I are due for a few breaks in this life, don't you?"

He pushes up off his knees to stand and nods. Even manages a small smile. "I think you're right. And we're the lucky ones really. We've been through so much, haven't we? But at the end of all that pain, we get this precious gift. I'd endure it all over again for the chance to know Aria. I've got to start thinking of it in those terms. Forget about the years I've lost and focus on living this life, in the here and now. I mean, how blessed are we?"

"*So* blessed," I whisper, sucking in my lips to hold back the rush of emotion threatening to break free.

"When you found out you were ... did you ever think about ... that maybe—"

"No." I shake my head. "The timing wasn't great, but I wanted Aria. Loved her. There are a lot of things I regret, but she isn't one of them. I wanted our baby from the very beginning, no matter the circumstances."

He leans back a bit, looking confused. "What do you regret?"

"Not trusting my gut, for one. Why couldn't I see the one thing I've known my entire life? You would never just leave." I shake my head, the tears surging forward in earnest. "You're the only thing I've ever believed in, and when it really counted, I couldn't trust myself to know the truth. I'll always be ashamed of that. I'll never forgive my father for driving you away, and I'll never forgive myself for believing it."

He pulls me close then, tucking my head into his neck, and I let go. The frustration, the sorrow, the memories he's missed—I feel it all like a punch, and I know he does, too. But he soothes me with soft whispers and holds me with strong arms. And I cling to him, wishing we could have comforted each other in the times when all felt lost. It feels like mourning a death, and in a way, I suppose it is. I wish I knew how to let go of this pain and move forward with our lives, whatever that might look like.

Sobs become hiccups, whimpers fade to sighs, and Seb holds me through it all, being the rock I've always needed him to be. I draw in a deep breath and sit up straight, unraveling from his embrace. I wipe my ragged eyes and give him a watery smile. He runs his thumb across my damp cheek.

"We've built entire lives on top a mountain of unresolved feelings," he says as he takes my hands in his. The corner of his mouth tips into a half smile, then falls. "I don't know how to dig through to what lies beneath and see what's left. I don't know how to rebuild … or if it's even possible."

Hope and despair war within me at the thought, but I can't deny the wish that pushes its way through.

There's nothing I want more than to try.

But before I give voice to my wish, the front door swings open and tiny feet scamper into the house.

Aria, face smeared with what must be chocolate, her wild curls looking teased and matted. She screeches to a halt in front of us and squints her eyes at Seb.

"Are you done?" she asks with wide eyes.

And we all laugh.

CHAPTER 31

Autumn
Present Day
Haven, LA

"And Lexi—"

"Miss Lexi."

"Gave me a cookie, and it was dis big," she says, stretching her arms as wide as they can go. "And chocolate sauce for dipping."

I scrub the shampoo deep into her scalp while she winds up her submarine monkey for a swim. She hasn't stopped talking since she and Isaac returned to Sebastian's house. Seb and I barely squeezed in a quick goodbye, so there definitely was no chance to continue our conversation.

I don't know how to rebuild...

Just the thought, which runs on repeat through my brain, turns my insides to mush. The sweet and gooey kind—the very best kind of mush.

"Did you dip the cookie in the chocolate sauce or your hair? This mop is a hot mess tonight."

She giggles, completely unconcerned.

"And Lexi—"

"Miss Lexi."

"Made me hot chocolate wif whipped cream dis high." She raises both hands over her head, letting out a screech as she reaches for the ceiling. "And sprinkles. Rainbow ones."

"Yes, I see," I say, picking bits of colored mush from her hair. "Did you tell Miss Lexi anything?"

She stops splashing, and the only sound between us is the buzzing monkey submarine. She gives me a confused look.

"Huh?"

"Did you tell her any … secrets?"

I raise my eyebrows in question, and Aria drops her gaze from mine. One shoulder lifts then drops without a word.

"It's okay if you did," I say quietly, but Aria shakes her head, still not meeting my eyes. "Or maybe you could tell me."

Not a word. Complete silence.

"Or maybe … maybe I already know."

Her head jerks up, and her eyes widen in surprise.

"You do?" she asks, her voice filled with shock.

I nod my head and fill the pitcher with fresh water from the faucet.

"Head back."

She tilts her head back as I wash out the shampoo, then turns back to me.

"Are you mad, Momma?"

Aunt D had already told me this was Aria's worry but hearing the words straight from her undoes me. I swallow back the tears for my little girl who loves so hard and smile.

"No, poppet, of course I'm not mad. Someone in our family was lost, and we found him. That's wonderful, isn't it?"

Her smile grows to match mine, and she claps excitedly.

"Yes, yes, yes."

"And do you know what else that means?" She freezes and waits impatiently for my reply. "It means Isaac is family, too. He's your cousin."

She gasps again, her mouth dropping in awe. "Cousin?"

I nod, trying to hold in my laughter. "Yes, poppet."

"And do you know what cousins do?" She picks up her submarine and winds the engine. "Cousins eat breakfast togever, and cousins play all the time. Cousins go everywhere. Togever."

"Not sure where you got the definition of a cousin from, but I think Isaac will be surprised by all this togetherness, don't you think?"

The enthusiasm bubbling up inside her is palpable, and I'm afraid her head may just pop right off. Or her curls may frazzle to the point of no return.

"You 'member when cousins would eat supper togever, too? And daddies would spend the night? You 'member dat?"

"Mmhmm." I keep my lips pressed tightly shut, mentally refusing to respond to that particular land mine. Nope, not today, not this time. I raise the towel, signaling to her that bath time is over, and she stands.

Her head bobs up and down as she chants, "I'm excited, I'm excited, I'm excited." She gasps and slaps a hand over her mouth, her elation rivaling that of Christmas morning. "I never had a daddy before. Or a cousin."

She steps out of the tub, and I wrap her like a burrito, hugging her into my arms. I kiss her forehead. The top of her nose. And both cheeks.

I meet her joyous eyes, trying to hide the emotion brimming in mine. Then I whisper, "You've always had a daddy, poppet. It just took us a while to find him."

The next morning, Aria bounds down the steps to the coffee shop for our usual breakfast and grins when she sees Isaac sitting next to her special chair. She climbs up and plops down, scanning the coffee shop at the same time. She hops onto her knees and cranes her head behind the counter.

"Be careful, poppet," I say, touching her back to steady her.

"Where is he?" she asks Lexi, hands perched on her hips.

After sliding a glass of milk and muffin in front of Aria, Lexi's hands go to her hips as well.

"Simmer down, half-pint. We don't need Seb and his rotten guts infecting the place, so I've kicked him out for the day."

"'Cause she thinks she's the boss lady," Isaac mutters under his breath.

Then his half eaten muffin disappears right from under his nose. Isaac scowls. Lexi glowers.

Then she turns her attention back to Aria.

"But he came by to get some paperwork to work on at home." Lexi leans down and meets Aria eye to eye, then whispers, "And, of course, to wait for you."

Aria's eyes brighten as she peers around curiously, but then gets distracted by her muffin and milk. And Isaac, of course. She informs him about his new cousinly duties, which he appears to find as surprising as I did. But Aria is firm … and a tiny bit bossy. And Isaac takes it in stride, backing away slowly, nodding his head and slipping his book bag on his shoulders.

"See you tomorrow!" Aria calls out as she digs into her breakfast. Isaac takes off like a shot.

When Sebastian emerges from the back, I make myself scarce by taking an extra-long bathroom break. When I return, Aria hops down from her chair as Seb helps her put her book bag on. He leans down, and she whispers in his ear.

He watches me the entire time, his eyes changing from bright to the deepest of chocolate. His faces goes slack, and Aria runs away before he can respond. I raise my eyebrows in question, and he crosses the room to meet me.

"She uh ..." he says in a froggy voice, then clears his throat. "She said that you're not mad, so it's okay if I'm her daddy now."

I reach for his arm and squeeze. He runs a hand over his scruff and lets out a relieved laugh. It's funny how one sentence from a little girl can untangle a slew of complication. So much is still unresolved, but the most important thing, our daughter, is happy and loved. What more can we ask for?

I don't dwell on that particular question, because the answers are equal parts scary and exhilarating.

"Well, I—"

"Momma, hurry up," Aria calls from the door. "Manda's bringing her guinea pig for show-and-tell today, and I want to be early."

We both sigh, shrug, then laugh. Because interruptions have been the name of the game lately. Whether it be school, or Aria, or a raging virus, there's always something keeping Seb and me from talking things through.

I toss a thumb toward the door and scowl. "I guess I better—"

"Mom!"

"Aria!" I fuss, and she's got the nerve to giggle.

I grumble when I see Seb's admiring grin—at Aria, not me.

With a grudging wave and a parting mumble about two peas in a pod, Aria and I head off to start our day. I don't notice Sebastian's text until I sit down in my bio lecture.

Seb: To be continued. Yesterday, this morning ... five years ago.

CHAPTER 32

Sebastian
Present Day
Haven, LA

"You got only," Aria says, pointing at my piles of cards, then whispering, "One, two. Two tricks. I got ... one, two, free. Free tricks. I win!"

She smiles smugly and corrals all the cards into a pile. After five games in a row of losing my shirt, I admit defeat. Aria is the princess of bourré, and I bow down to her majesty.

Win or lose, I never want this day to end. An afternoon, just my daughter and me.

"I win," she singsongs, counting off each treat with her fingers. "Ice cream, hot fudge, whipped cream, sprinkles, and a cherry."

"Yes, Princess Aria, you win all the things," I chuckle, straightening the cards and putting them back in the box. "Why don't you go wash your hands while I fix your sundae."

"Wif soap?"

"Yes, with soap."

She releases a labored sigh and wriggles off her chair. "Okay."

Turns out, getting the green light from Aria on the daddy front isn't quite the same as getting a membership to the gym —it's definitely not an all-access pass. Much like before, she doles out her acceptance in tiny slivers, but somehow, I find them much more satisfying than before.

That chunk of muffin she saved just for me at breakfast? It was an eight-tier birthday cake in my eyes.

Begging Autumn to do her homework at the coffee shop with me after school? It felt like a million "I love yous."

And I have to admit, making these tiny steps forward is much more satisfying than an all-access pass. I don't mind working for it. It's the ultimate labor of love.

Aria may be opening the door to her heart a centimeter at a time, but her mother? She's not budging. At least I don't think she is, but she's avoided every situation that may give us even a second of alone time. Ever since our breakthrough … breakdown … whatever you want to call it, she's eternally indisposed. Studying … class … dyeing her hair. I thought the hair excuse was just a joke. Shit, maybe it is …

She's not openly rude to me, but she's been way too unavailable this week for it to be a mere coincidence. My mouth waters as I grasp for what I've always wanted, only to have it slip through my fingers again and again.

I'm determined to open her eyes to the possibility of us. Hell bent and unwavering. I've come way too far to walk away now. I've been starving for the past five years, and I refuse to go hungry again.

Never again.

I spend half my time walking on clouds of cotton candy and little girl glitter, resisting the urge to stop people in the street and show them pictures of Aria, and the other half scratching my head and wondering where I went wrong with Autumn. I can't put my finger on it, and I'm not sure how to fix it, but something's got to give.

"Hey, hey, hey, where's my favorite niece?"

Brady's voice booms through the house as he wheels through the front door. I grin as part one of my plan tosses his duffel bag in the corner.

"Uncle Bray!" Aria shrieks as she bounds down the hallway, her hands dripping the entire way. "I didn't know you were coming to see me."

"Forgot to dry your hands, little one?" He laughs as he dusts water off his suit jacket.

Aria's eyes widen, and she covers her mouth with her hands. "I forgot," she mumbles through her damp fingers.

He waves off her worries and attacks her belly with gusto. Curls fly everywhere, and giggles ricochet off the living room walls.

"And yes, I came to see my favorite girl." He looks across the room at me and winks. "Among other things."

"Well? How did it go?"

"Great. Better than great. The dean started the conversation by telling me it was more of an invitation than an interview. And it got better from there."

"I should have known. Who wouldn't want you?"

"Who indeed?"

"Cocky much?"

"Why shouldn't I be? I'm awesome." He shrugs, then resumes the tickle fest to a rain of laughter. "Tell him your Uncle Bray is awesome."

"No, no, no," she chants, trying to get away. "I'm gonna pee."

He drops her onto the carpet and scowls. "Way to break up a party, Aria."

Then she darts off to the bathroom.

Brady wasn't lying when he said the apps he's created really took off. He's made quite a name for himself as a free-lancer in the industry. Recently, Southern Louisiana University contacted him about heading up a student think tank to bring together different departments of the university in the creation, implementation, and marketing of apps. The teams would be made up entirely of Southern U students with the guidance of the think tank team leaders.

"You gonna take it?"

He pokes out his lower lip and nods. "Sure, why not?"

"Don't get *too* excited, douchebag."

"What? It sounds like fun, and I can do my own shit from anywhere, so win-win. They've got on-campus housing for me that'll accommodate the wheels, so I wouldn't even need to drive to work. But we'll see."

"Sounds like a winner."

"Yeah," he whispers and then sighs. "Truth is, I just want to be where y'all are, so they could have told me I'd be shoveling shit at the uni stables and I would've said yes."

His words hit me square in the chest, and I'm left momentarily speechless. In a matter of weeks, a family exists where for so long there had been nothing but tumbleweeds and hard feelings.

A family … *my* family.

"You all set for tonight?" he asks, waggling his eyebrows like an idiot. "Gotta say, for a guy trying to land the girl, I'm dressed a helluva lot better than you. You plan on winning my sister in flannel?"

"I'm going to shower now, ass. You've got Aria, right?"

"Shut up."

I'm halfway to my bedroom when Brady calls my name.

"Hey, didn't you say Lexi's last name was Lansard?"

"Yeah, why?"

He shrugs and scratches his face, looking confused. "I

don't know. It's just that—well never mind. But … I mean, is that the name on her W-2?"

I flinch, aggravated, and more than a little put out by his questions. I also hate to admit the truth to him. "Well, I kind of, sort of pay Lexi in cash, so she never filled out a W-2?"

It comes out as more of a question than a statement, and Brady's eyes widen at my confession. He huffs and shakes his head.

"Are you shitting me?"

"Look, it's not a big deal. When I bought the shop from Joe and Marge, Lexi was the only stipulation. She kind of came with the business."

"Like the espresso machine?"

"Yes … but not nearly as amenable," I joke, but Brady doesn't laugh. "Aw, come on, it's not that big of a deal."

"She could be one of Charles Manson's followers." A look of sheer fright takes over his expression, and I roll my eyes.

"She's about forty years too young."

"She could be the daughter of El Chapo … or Pablo Escobar."

"Or she's more than likely a kid who needed a fresh start. And now she's an adult, living that life. Leave it alone, Brady. I know you mean well but leave it alone."

"Fine," he grinds out, shaking his head in aggravation.

"El Chapo … where the hell do you come up with this stuff?" I chuckle as I head to my bedroom.

"The ID channel, dude," he hollers down the hall. "Maybe you should watch it."

CHAPTER 33

Autumn
Present
Haven, LA

"One more run through before we pack up?" Mary asks, pushing her glasses up the bridge of her nose and chewing on her pen cap.

"No, nope, no way, I'm done," Marcus chants, waving his hands in defeat. "My brain cannot accept one more ounce of information. I literally need to plug my ears to keep words, letters, and anatomical phrases from falling out onto the floor." He leans over and scribbles on his notebook. He lifts it up, proudly displaying his "closed" sign. "Marcus's brain is closed for business. With the appropriate amount of beer and wings, I may open the doors tomorrow."

I toss a crumpled piece of paper at his head, but he ducks just in time. "You're such a doofus."

"Me need beer. Me need hot wings. You come," he says, gesturing to me while doing his best Tarzan impersonation.

I shake my head as I pack my stuff. "Sorry, no can do. I've

got a little princess to pick up. It's been hours. Aria probably has Seb's nails painted and a clown-worthy amount of lipstick on his face by now. He'll need rescuing."

"I bet he will." Mary waggles her eyebrows and nudges Marcus.

"It's not like that," I say, trying to figure out how to explain the unexplainable. "It's ... complicated."

"I bet it is." More eyebrow waggles and lascivious smirks.

"Shut up." Mary chuckles. I frown.

My phone lights up as if on cue, displaying my parents' home number. A perfect example of how complicated all of this really is. I decline the call and toss my phone back into my purse. One of the many things I've been avoiding like a boss.

And when I pick up Aria in just a few minutes, I'll come face-to-face with the other object of my avoidance. I doubt I'll get away with it for much longer, but I'm not ready to have my heart broken just yet. I saw the look in his eyes when I told him about Aria's birth. I could feel his anguish like a living, breathing thing. It's not behind us—it's alive and well in every fist he pounded and breath he dragged into his ragged lungs. He'll never truly forgive me, and I don't blame him in the least.

The part that kills me is I know he wants to let this go and move on together. Hell, I bet he thinks he has. But it will always be there, waiting to rear its ugly head during a fight or pop up when we least expect it. Some ghosts can't be exorcised. Some ghosts linger for a lifetime.

"Come on. All work and no play make Autumn a dull girl," Marcus chants, bringing me back to the present.

I toss my book bag over my shoulder and stand.

"That's what a bachelor like you doesn't understand, Marcus. Being with my daughter? That *is* the fun part."

Marcus's face scrunches in confusion, like he honestly

can't think of anything that would be more fun than alcohol and chicken legs.

Mary's face goes soft. She and I were in undergrad together in Providence, so she's met Aria a time or two.

"Aw, give that cutie a kiss and a cheek squeeze for me. Her butt cheeks, I mean. She's got the cutest little hiney I've ever seen."

∼

I leave the library in a rush, digging my keys out as I head out to the parking lot. I debate texting Seb to tell him I'm on my way, but it would only give him the opportunity to ambush me when I arrive. Avoidance is key, I remind myself.

"In a hurry?"

I stop short at the sound of his voice, gravelly with a hint of mirth. I whip around, and my mouth drops open at the sight of him, propped against the building, arms crossed and smirk firmly in place. He's dressed to perfection. Dark jeans hugging his trim thighs, midnight blue button-down tucked into his cinched waist. Shirt sleeves rolled up showing corded forearms dusted with dark hair and a bundle of leather straps circling his wrist. His dark, tousled hair is damp, probably from the shower, and begging for my fingers to dive in and tug. Hard. I'm ten feet away, but I imagine he smells like he looks. He's a deadly combination for a reluctant romantic like me—pure temptation with a pinch of the boy I used to know.

I wish I were the girl I used to be. The girl who would break out into a run at the mere sight of him, electricity crackling over her skin and horses galloping in her heart. I wish I could wrap my legs around his waist and bury my face in the warmth of his neck. Feel his strong arms envelop me, crushing my torso to his. That girl was impulsive and foolish. But she was also *loved*.

I wish that girl, sitting in the dark corners of my mind, whispering that anything is possible, that love should win out in the end, would rise up and punch logical Autumn in her smug little face. Logical Autumn sucks the fun out of everything.

When he sees the question in my eyes, he pushes off the column and walks to me. "She's with Brady. He came into town for business and wanted to spend the evening with her."

At my doubtful expression, he smirks. "I may have suggested it, yes, but it's not like I twisted the guy's arm. Have you met our daughter? She's pretty irresistible."

Our daughter...

"Yes, she is," I whisper. I bite my lower lip to rein in the smile pulling at my lips.

"Her mother is irresistible, too. When she's not running in the opposite direction, that is." He stops, looks up at the sky and shakes his head. "I take that back. You running in the opposite direction gives me a great view of your ass."

"Shut up." I bark out a laugh and shove his shoulder. "You clean up nice, Kelly."

Understatement of the year.

"Thanks. I have plans." He grins, then shakes his head at what I assume is my fallen expression. "With you, doofus. Plans with you."

Crossing my arms and shrugging, I lower my head in an attempt to hide my reddening face. "I don't remember agreeing to any plans."

He tips my chin and meets my eyes, his soft and warm and everything I want to dive into. As his smile spreads, I feel the fall—my resistance, my resolve ... my heart.

"Come on now, Autumn, when did we ever need to make plans? You and me? We just *are*."

It's a simple thing, saying words so true, they're written in the stars. Seb stands in front of me, wide eyes, open arms, exposed heart, and the tears well inside me. What I long for and what I know play tug-of-war with my heart, leaving it with that all familiar ache I've lived with since moving to Haven.

My uncertainty is met with Seb's obvious determination, as he's showing no signs of backing down. He grabs my hand and tugs. And that's all it takes.

"Where are we going?"

He squeezes my hand and bounds forward, to the parking lot. "You'll see, soon enough."

He opens his car door, and I slide inside, my nerves river dancing in my stomach. Before I get ahold of myself, he sits in the driver's seat and closes the door.

"I feel underdressed," I say, tugging at my worn, denim sundress, wishing I was wearing something else. I look across at him and feel muted.

"You look amazing."

I smile, loving the closeness and the opportunity to inspect him. "Did you trim your beard?"

He turns the ignition and chuckles. "Like I said, I have plans."

Cue the encore of frenzied river dancing.

"Seb? Should I be worried?" I ask as his car ambles down a deserted dirt road, reeds of overgrown grass scraping the undercarriage as we go. "Kind of looking like the latest horror movie set up, from where I'm sitting."

The farther we go outside the city limits of Haven, the

higher my curiosity piques. I have no idea what Sebastian has planned.

His eyes dance as he drives, one hand on the wheel, the other resting on the shift. So nonchalant and cool. His stick shift hand reaches over to my knee for a gentle squeeze. My breath hitches and my whole body locks. His hand is warm and calloused against my bare knee.

Why did I wear a sundress today? Thank God I wore a sundress today. Gah!

"Don't worry, I'll protect you."

"That's what all the serial killers say."

The tremble in my voice is mortifying. Seriously, who gets hot from a simple squeeze of the knee? Obviously that girl is me, but also, nothing with Seb is ever "simple."

I watch his hand with complete focus as it drags across my skin and back to the shift, a trail of sizzle left in its wake.

"Just trust me."

The road clears in front of us, and a barn comes into view. A-frame, red with white trimming, but eerily abandoned.

"Umm ... mighty dressed up for an abandoned barn, don't you think?"

He shuts off the car and opens the door. "I didn't dress for the barn. I dressed for you." His boyish smile and hungry eyes melt my insides. "Come on, let me show you."

After Seb grabs an ice chest and blanket from the trunk, we make our way inside.

"You know, I've been looking for the perfect spot to take Aria swimming, because I promised her, and one of the shop's patrons heard me asking around. She gladly offered, and I came by earlier this week to check it out. It's perfect. Aria will love it, and I thought we could make a little party out of it. What do you think?"

"All right," I say, surprised by his suggestion. And

honestly, I shouldn't be. He's made every effort to forge a relationship with Aria from the beginning. She'll be over the moon, and Seb will be the one to have made it happen.

He slides the barn door open, and it widens with a deafening metallic scrape. I peek inside, and it's wide open and completely empty. No stalls or hay; no equipment to speak of. The floors are even swept clean. Sunlight filters in through the foggy windows, making the dust particles suspended in the air sparkle like bits of glitter.

"Mr. and Mrs. Martin live just over the field there, along with their swimming pool," he says, gesturing to the far end of the barn. "After we checked out the pool, she brought me here."

I walk to where he's pointing and look through the window. Far in the distance, I see the pointed roof of a house pushing past the oak trees.

"They don't use the barn anymore, but she insists Mr. Martin keep it spic and span. They ride out here a few times a week to watch the sunset. Done it for decades." Seb looks at the sky peeking through the opened barn door and smiles. "It looks like we're just in time. Have to admit, I was getting worried. I didn't think you'd ever leave the library. We nearly missed the show."

I turn from the window and take him in. Alone in the center of the barn, blanket in one hand, ice chest in the other, he waits for me. The truth of it is he always has. Waited for me, I mean. And although I can't see it with my eyes, I'm all too aware of the heart on his sleeve. I feel his vulnerability reaching for me, pulling me closer, and who am I to resist?

"I'd love to watch the sunset with you." The words spill from me without preamble.

Right here, right now, with nothing between us but dusty sparkles and fading sunlight, only the truth will do. Our love is one of grimy feet and snowcone-stained tongues. I've never been here before, but no place has ever felt more like a physical representation of who we are. Empty but cared for. Unused, but not forgotten. Dusty, but somehow, after all this time, still magical. Not now, but maybe someday ...

No, nothing but the truth will do tonight.

Sebastian gestures to the ladder leading up to the hayloft and raises his eyebrows in question. "Shall we?" I nod. He gestures again. "Ladies first."

I laugh. "Nice try, hot stuff. You'll have to work harder than that to get a peek at my ass."

He shrugs, unfazed by my rejection. "I may not be a teenage boy anymore, but I'm still a man. Can't blame me for trying."

Once we get into the hayloft, me trailing behind Seb with the blanket, he lays out an impressive spread of snacks. Cheeses, fruit, fancy crackers, and cloth napkins.

"Swanky," I say as I sit down on the blanket and pop a grape into my mouth.

Then he breaks out the six pack of cheap beer, and I bust out laughing.

He smirks. "You can take the boy out of Prosper ..."

I smile at his joke, but it's short lived as I think of a far more painful interpretation of his words. He's right, Prosper will always be a part of him—of us—and it rips my heart to pieces. Tears build behind my eyes thinking of all the hurt we've caused each other.

Seb takes in my expression, and his face falls.

"Talk about an awkward segue."

He twists the top off my beer and hands it to me.

"Yeah." I take a long drink, the fizz burning a trail down my throat. "But that's the thing of it, isn't it? You're exactly right. All that's happened—the mistakes, the regrets, that toxic town. It's all still here, sitting between us."

"Wait—"

"I look at you, Sebastian, and it hurts." My voice breaks, and I push my palm deep into my chest, trying to massage away the ache that comes from seeing what I can't have. What I'll never have again. "It physically hurts to know I can't be with you."

CHAPTER 34

Sebastian
Present Day
Haven, LA

Can't be with me? What the hell is she talking about? With one word, one simple gesture or provocation from her, I'd have her pinned beneath me in this hayloft. I know she feels it, too. I see it in her eyes. I feel it like barely bridled energy, thrumming between us.

There's nowhere in this world I want to be more than right here with her. Why can't she see that?

"Hold on, hold on." I take hold of her shoulders and meet her eyes. Eyes brimming with unshed tears. "What in the hell are you talking about, Autumn?"

She lets out a long sigh and slumps her shoulders. Tears streak her cheeks, and she shakes her head in defeat. "We both know it's true. No matter what, I'll always be the one who kept your daughter from you. The thief who stole five years of memories. Nothing will ever change that."

"And what? I'll always be the guy who ran away and left

you without a word? Is that how you see me?"

Confusion flits across her face, followed closely by frustration. She shakes her head furiously and huffs. "No, no, that's not what I'm saying. I've forgiven you for that, Sebastian. I'm not trying to throw it in your face. I know my father threatened you. I know that now."

I run the palms of my hands up and down her arms, trying to calm her, trying to stop the centripetal force of this tailspin she's so intent on putting herself into.

"So, you're capable of forgiveness ... but I'm not?"

"It's not the same thing."

"It's exactly the same thing."

"I know you think that, but it's not true," she whispers, shaking her head and averting her eyes. "This is one of those things that will always be lurking, waiting for the most inopportune moment to punch us in the gut. A baby picture of Aria, an offhand comment, or snuggles she gives me willingly but shies away from giving you—who knows what will spark it? But you'll lash out, understandably, reminding me of what I've taken from you. And I can't even blame you, because I deserve that anger. Some wrongs can never be made right. Some wrongs are bigger than forgiveness."

I know she believes what she's saying, every single word, and it guts me. After the last five years of isolation, I finally have a chance at a family. A chance with *her*. And she thinks I'd give all of that up, for what? For some one-upmanship game in who's hurt who more?

Never. Never again will I let my life be run by something so insignificant and petty. But how do I make her see that?

"Nothing is bigger than forgiveness, Autumn. I hope, deep down, you know that."

Silence.

It's a tangled mess of hope and heartbreak. Who will win out in the end is anyone's guess. But I've always been a dreamer, and when it comes to Autumn and me, I've always dreamed big.

I let go of her arms and smile despite her sorrow. I shift away and watch another of her tears fall.

"Why don't we table this," I say, standing up and moving toward the hayloft door. "Why don't we eat, drink, and watch the sunset together without a thought of what's to come. Let me just be with you, Autumn."

She nods, sucking in her lips in an attempt to curb her tears. I unlatch the hayloft door and open both shutters wide.

Golden warmth bathes the loft, stealing the breath from my chest with splashes of fiery orange and smears of deep purple. Fields of vibrant green sugarcane stretch as far as the eye can see—the colors alive in a way no photograph or artist could ever capture.

I crawl behind Autumn for the show, pulling her between my legs, her back resting against my front. I interlace our fingers and hug her close, feeling the catches in her breath and watching her pulse jump under her skin.

"This is breathtaking," she whispers in awe.

"It definitely is," I reply, without attempting to hide my real meaning as I run the tip of my nose down the curve of her neck. I ache for my tongue to follow the same path, but I hold back, afraid to scare her away. Goose bumps erupt on her skin, and she shivers, then she settles closer into my chest.

Silence falls between us as we watch the remnants of the day fade into smoky dusk, and I silently wish for more time. I never want this feeling of her, content in my arms, to fade away.

She sucks in a deep breath, then closes her eyes as she breathes out slowly. She tips her head back onto my chest, and I press my lips to her temple.

I tip her chin, forcing her eyes to meet mine, and as

always, I'm a goner. Those baby blues own every part of me. Always have and always will. I shift her in front of me, turn our bodies so we're face-to-face. Nowhere to hide.

"Just hear me out, okay? You say there's too much in our past to have any kind of future, but I refuse to believe that. You're focused on the wrong things." Her expression is hopeful but cautious, as if she'd give anything for me to have the answer that would fix all of this. "Maybe we don't need to sift through the ashes of the past. I look at you, Autumn—I look at my daughter, and the answer is so clear. We leave the past behind and build a new fire. All this time, I thought I was waiting for you to show up, so I could explain, tell you I'm sorry. Maybe I was just waiting so we could … begin again. We need to let go of the past and focus on the future. I can do that. I *am* doing that. The question is … can *you?*"

I see the war raging behind her eyes. The tug-of-war between her truth and mine. One leads to a lifetime of longing, while the other gives us a chance at true happiness. Is there really any question?

"But—"

I touch my fingers to her mouth, her lips parting at the contact. Her breath dances on my fingertips, warm and silky. I trace the curve of her jaw, then tuck a wisp of her hair behind her ear. My hand lands on the curve of her neck, palm resting on her fluttering pulse.

She sighs.

I wish.

I wish she would open her heart to the possibility. I hope she can see there is more to us than the mistakes of our past. More to us than shattered pieces of the most exquisite glass I've ever known. We can be whole again if she would just allow it.

"There's a lot to be learned from the crooked line between right and wrong. There's even more to gain by just letting go." I lean in closer, a breath away from pressing my mouth to hers. Her gaze lowers, settles on my lips, and her lashes flutter like delicate butterfly wings.

Open.

Closed.

Open.

"Let go with me, Autumn. Just let go," I plead, my lips brushing hers with every syllable whispered.

Her misty eyes dart back to mine, and that's when I see it.

Hope.

Release.

And finally, acceptance.

A strangled cry escapes her as she bridges the gap, pressing her trembling lips to mine. Her fingers dive into my hair, and I run my thumbs over the apples of her cheeks in reverence. I want to revisit every inch of her I've missed so deeply. I want to commit every new dip and curve to my memory. I want to kiss her so long and deep, the last five years evaporate into mist, and all we can see is each other.

Our lips brush, our tongues dance, and the feeling unfurls through every cell in my body like a mantra.

I remember you …

I remember you …

I remember …

"Yes," she whispers as her lips leave mine for the smallest second. "Please. Yes."

"So damn good." I groan, hungry for more of her.

I pull her closer, fitting her in my lap, legs draped over mine.

"Even better." She runs her fingers over my cheeks and giggles softly. "Your beard."

My mouth smiles against hers before taking a gentle bite of her lower lip. I lean back slightly and scowl. "What? You don't like it?"

She grabs my ears with both hands and shakes her head. "I think," she says, pulling my lips back to hers. "I think I love it."

"Yeah?"

She sighs, and I feel her body go boneless, completely melting into my chest. "Oh yeah."

I wrap my arms around her and nuzzle her neck, her ear, her apple-scented hair. She squirms as I hit her ticklish spot, then settles with a contented sigh.

Her eyes are hooded, her expression sated, positively drunk with kisses. I'd forgotten how lovely Autumn is when she's cherished. Loved.

Only then do I raise my eyes to the setting sun and realize the moon is taking center stage. The warm of earlier is replaced with breezy moonlight, and the barn darkens by degrees with each passing minute.

I groan inwardly, give Autumn a tight squeeze, then release her.

"I'd rather be ripped limb from limb by a pack of starving lions than let go of you right now, but I don't see any way around it. Pretty sure we'd break our necks going down that ladder in complete darkness."

She nods grudgingly and pecks my lips before pushing up to her knees. She tosses our uneaten food into the ice chest while I gather up the trash.

"Pride."

"Huh?"

"It's a pride of lions. Not a pack." She shrugs, her lips pursed into a mischievous smirk.

I pop her ass with a napkin, and she yelps. "Know-it-all."

Another shrug, her eyes dancing with delight. I stand, gathering our supplies and gesture for her to go ahead.

"Ladies first. Wouldn't want to get an uninvited glimpse of that hot little ass of yours."

She passes me, brushing lightly against me as she goes. "And what a show it would be." She smiles shyly before heading down the ladder. I can only see her face as she makes her descent, and she stops to deal her final blow. "Black thong."

And just like that, what was already at half-mast is at full attention. She continues down the ladder with ease as I resist the urge to yank her back up and finish what we started.

Patience, man. You've got to be patient with her.

But she needs to stop poking the bear. Oh, the innuendo in that statement is killing me.

"Coming," I call from up above, smirking to myself. "Watch out for the bats, okay?"

She lets out a terrified shriek, then slaps her hand over her mouth as if the sound will wake the coven of blood-sucking creatures. I calmly climb down the ladder while she spirals into an epic frenzy.

"Bats? There are freaking bats in here?" she whisper-yells. "Hurry the hell up, Sebastian Kelly, before I maim you ... or the bats maim me. Just ... hurry up!"

When I hit the ground floor, she races to me and slides under my arm for protection. I lower my lips to hers and kiss her once, twice, then chuckle and shake my head.

"Maybe you don't know it all then," I whisper.

When realization dawns, her eyes widen, and she smacks my chest hard. I let out an oomph then peck her lips again.

"You're nothing but a bully," she says as she stomps away with a huff, arms crossed over her chest.

"Come on, Autumn, flash me a little peek of that black thong," I call out as she storms to the car. "You know you wanna."

Instead of flashing me her gorgeous cheeks, I get a saucy one-finger salute. God, I love riling her up.

CHAPTER 35

Autumn
Present Day
Haven, LA

"So…" I unlock the door to my apartment and turn to face Sebastian.

He watches me like I'm some precious thing. Touches me like I may disappear at any second. Little does he know, there's nowhere in the world I'd rather be than here with him.

I want this to be real. I *need* it to be real. There comes a point where the future is so bright, so radiant, the past that once seemed so important becomes completely inconsequential. I think, I hope, with everything in me, that Sebastian and I have reached that point.

"So," he counters, grabbing my hands and intertwining my fingers with his. He lays a soft peck on my nose and bathes me with the most adoring gaze. Prickly warmth crawls up my neck, blushing all the way to my cheeks.

"Aria, uh," I whisper-choke, then clear my throat. "Is it all right if I hitch a ride with you to the library tomorrow to get my car?"

He nods. "Of course. I'll bring you first thing."

"Aria's probably fast asleep. I mean, it's after ten and all. I guess she'll just sleep at your house tonight."

Hint, hint ... please, for the love of all that is holy, take the hint.

"And if she pulls her middle-of-the-night stunt?" He arches an eyebrow, and I laugh. Aria, my little master manipulator.

"After the tenth ... or hundredth time, Brady finally got her number. He's got tricks to distract her until morning, don't worry."

He leans back, looking incredulous.

"What? Where were these skills a few weeks ago when I was dragging my ass out of bed at one AM, huh?"

"Hmm ... I think your best friend had ulterior motives that night. My bet is he was trying to nudge things in the right direction, or more accurately, shove us together."

Sebastian tips his head back and laughs, then leans down and nuzzles my neck.

"I knew there was a reason I loved that guy."

The tip of his nose blazes a trail up the side of my neck, his tongue following closely behind. My body spasms, and my nipples push against his hard chest as I arch into him. He groans, long and deep, before nipping my ear with his teeth.

"Look, I need to go. I really don't want to rush you into anything, I don't. But five more seconds standing in this door, and I'm pushing you up against it."

My brain is fuzzy, and I struggle to hone in on his words instead of his lips brushing the ridge of my ear. My brain says, "You, me, door? Yes, please." But my lips only let out a contented sigh.

He presses a kiss to my temple, and his fingers dig into

my hips with a territorial squeeze, then he steps back, releasing another tortured groan.

Wait, is he leaving? Why is he leaving?

"You, me, Aria. Breakfast at the shop in the morning?"

I nod dumbly, my racing brain going entirely too fast for my mouth to catch up. Weren't we about to ... did I read that all wrong? My fuzzy, lust-filled mind stammers with objections but all that comes out is "Um ... uh ... okay?"

He's backing away, leaving me standing on the doorstep, speechless and dumbfounded. He turns his back and bounds down the steps, looking back twice with a questioning glance, but not saying a word.

I step inside and shut the door, wondering where I went wrong and why in the hell my mouth refused to work. I turn the dead bolt, listening to it click with finality.

My mind reels, trying to think of what signal I gave that made him leave and coming up empty. I did everything I could to give him the green light ... well, short of actually saying the words, that is.

Why in the hell did I not just say the words?

Before I think better of it, before stupid-ass propriety shows up to the party and ruins everything, I unlock the dead bolt and throw open the door with steely determination.

"Wait!" I call out before my eyes focus on the man standing directly in front of me.

"Thank God," he groans as he crashes his lips to mine.

Fumbling hands, searching lips, and labored breaths fill the room as we slam the door and he shoves me up against the wall. His tongue dives into my mouth as he hitches my knee on his hip and grinds into me.

"Yes," I hiss, my body rolling into his, trying to chase the delicious ache that's already building inside of me.

He sucks my bottom lip into his mouth and pulls, sending a jolt of electrified heat straight to my core. His hands run along my waist, my back, my ass, eating up the expanse of my skin with heavy palms and frenzied fingers.

My love for him is a current pulsing through my veins, flowing between my legs ... the all-encompassing emotion of it, the feelings erupting inside of me are almost too much to bear. I grasp blindly at his shirt, looking for buttons, zippers, any damn thing that will unwrap the present in front of me.

"Is it too soon?" he rasps between open-mouthed kisses, pressing his forehead to mine. "Tell me it isn't too soon, Autumn."

Is he serious right now?

"Not soon enough, Seb. Not. Soon. Enough," I chant, each tug of his belt, shirt, jeans punctuated with impatience.

He rips his lips away from mine and steps back, his clothes a disheveled wreck hanging off his body. He grabs the hem of my sundress and slowly drags the fabric up and over my body. Fabric silently hits the floor, and Seb's eyes turn molten.

"Damn," he whispers, his eyes never meeting mine, never tearing away from his heated perusal of my body. He charges forward, his lips crashing into mine as his shirt meets my dress on the floor beside us.

Skin on skin, his chest meets mine, and I groan into his mouth. He swallows it down, takes everything I give him, and wraps my legs around his waist. We stumble to the bedroom, a tangled mess of longing and need, attacking each other's mouths the entire way.

I unlatch my legs and slide down the front of him, Seb unlatching my bra on the way down. Cold air hits my nipples, followed by wet heat and sweet, sweet suction.

"Yes," I rasp, throwing my head back in ecstasy, pushing my hips into his denim-covered, rock-hard cock. Too much material stands between me and what I want. What I desperately need. I fist his hair between my clenched fingers, and he nips me with his teeth.

Belt buckles clang.

Bed springs creak.

Old memories intertwine with new, and the enormity of this moment ... this man ... wraps around my heart and squeezes.

I've been waiting for you, Autumn. I've been waiting for so long.

His tongue trails down my stomach as thumbs loop around my panties and tug. I shut my eyes, anticipating his hips settling between mine. Craving the pressure of him, heavy and full, pushing against my entrance.

The elastic drags down my thighs, slow and teasing, biting into the skin on the way down, down, down. Until he stops cold, my panties tangled and knotted at my knees.

I open one eye and find Seb kneeling between my legs, boxer briefs half shoved down one hip, arms helpless at his sides as he stares down at me.

At my uncovered skin.

At my scar.

Shit...

I raise a hand to cover my belly, and he bats it away. His fists clench and unclench as too many emotions flit across his face. I hold my breath, waiting for what comes next. He blows out a breath, finally meeting my gaze with sorrowful eyes.

A car alarm sounds from down below, stopping time, stretching the moment like a rubber band, keeping us in this place of bittersweet memory and regret.

I saw you, and I loved you.

I left you, and I'm sorry.

I lied, and I can't take it back.

A decisive beep-beep restarts the clock, and an electrified silence fills the room. I reach for him. He pulls away and bows over my stomach.

"I'll never leave, Autumn. Never again."

He runs a reverent thumb over the scar that stretches across my abdomen. A frisson runs across the cinched skin as he presses his lips along it. It always feels a bit numb there, tingly, like the scar has fallen asleep. But not today. Every touch soothes hurt feelings, sands down the edges of resentment that have sharpened over the years.

His touch is healing. His kiss a promise for the future.

My heart will accept nothing less.

He lifts his eyes to mine, lips hovering over my skin as his breath dances across it.

"Big moments. Little moments. I'll be here for all of them." His thumbs press into my belly, and I give him my eyes. "Do you know that?"

"Yes."

"Do you trust me?"

"Yes, I trust you." I reach down and run a hand through his mussed hair and tug his ear. "I trust you, and I *love* you."

He shuts his eyes, and his body goes limp in relief. He nuzzles his face into my stomach, and I giggle. He jerks up, looking offended by my laughter.

"What? It tickles," I say, another peal of laughter rolling through me as he tickles behind my knees. "Come here, you big jerk!"

He grabs behind my knees, rips off my panties, then pulls himself up until we're nose to nose, his eyes dancing. His hips settle in between mine, and I shiver.

My anticipation feels like cotton candy—airy and melt-in-your-mouth delicious.

He runs his nose along the ridge of mine and grins. "I love you, Autumn Norris. Always have, always will. How I feel about you has been the one constant in my life."

"Always," I whisper.

My hips roll underneath him, craving the friction, needing a physical release to follow the flood of emotions humming through my veins. I run a palm down his back, then smack his half-covered ass. He scowls, doing his best to look insulted.

"I need these off and you inside me," I whisper, teasing his lips with my tongue.

I tug at the fabric with my toes, pulling the waistband then letting go with a pop. He hops up from the bed and grabs his discarded jeans from the floor.

The cold air hits my skin, and I resist the urge to cover myself. It's been a long time since I've seen Sebastian this way. Since he's seen me. There's a fair amount of nerves that come with that knowledge.

The scar on my belly isn't the only thing that's changed in five years. Same for Sebastian. The years have been kind to him—long, lean muscles, sexy, bearded scruff, and a textured depth to his eyes that suggests there's more to him than meets the eye.

Everything about him, old and new, is intoxicating.

I hope he feels the same about me.

He jumps back onto the bed, a condom dancing between his fingers, and I laugh.

"Carrying condoms around in your pocket? Aren't we confident." I smirk, and he shrugs.

"Sometimes I have more hope than sense." He throws off his boxers and tosses them onto the pile on the floor. "Worked out this time, didn't it?"

My eyes widen at the sight of him, but he doesn't notice

me gawking. His body is beautiful, hard and jutting, ready for me. My body spasms at the thought.

He trails his hands up my legs, widening them on his ascent. His thumbs graze my center, light pressure, barely dusting across my skin. He continues the gentle torture over and again. I push into his thumbs, try to increase the pressure, but he backs away every time.

"Please Seb, you're killing me," I groan.

"Please what? Where do you need me?" I hear the tease in his tone as his thumbs brush half a centimeter away from where I'm aching. He drops a kiss to my knee. "Here?"

"Jerk."

Kisses my stomach.

"There?"

I whip my head to the side and cover my face with my hands. "You're evil."

"You're gorgeous," he volleys back. "I can't stop looking at you. I can't stop touching you."

His fingers push inside me, and my body grips him with ferocious need. He lowers his head between my legs and sucks, and I detonate, my body exploding into white, hot heat. My inside pulsating with a rhythm so intoxicating, it feels like drowning. My breath is lost, my muscles tight like a bow, my legs clenching Sebastian's head like a vice.

I come to in waves. Smell first, sex and sweat. Then sound, panting breaths and the telltale ripping of a wrapper. Then sight, as Sebastian comes into view, eyes filled with lust and hunger.

"You and me," he whispers.

"Me and you."

"Yeah."

"Always."

He nudges against my entrance and brushes his stubbled

cheek against mine. "I'd have waited forever for you, Autumn."

"I think we've waited long enough."

His lips brush mine as whispered I love yous tumble between us. He enters me in one swift thrust, and my body catches fire, knowing its match, feeling how right we are for each other, deep down to my soul.

CHAPTER 36

Sebastian
Present Day
Haven, LA

"Who brings one condom to the party?" Autumn slaps my stomach before laying her head on my chest and laughing.

"I said I was hopeful. Bringing a pocketful is overly ambitious if you ask me. Not to mention, tempting fate. Show up for a date with a string of condoms, guaranteed you're whacking off alone at the end of the night."

"You're not whacking off alone." She lifts her head and raises her eyebrow in challenge.

"I didn't show up with a pocketful of condoms, either."

She sighs contentedly as I run my index finger up and down the length of her spine. My phone chirps from the pocket of my jeans, and I reach down to grab it off the floor. I see Brady's text illuminating the screen, and I bark out a laugh, then show it to Autumn.

Brady: Cry baby thwarted. You owe her hot chocolate—

lots of marshmallows. See you at the shop in the AM. You're welcome, fucker.

"Told you he had tricks."

I grunt, my mind already moving to tomorrow. Breakfast with Aria, Autumn, and the expertly skilled Brady ... planning Aria's pool party ... buying a monstrous crate of condoms.

Autumn's fingers slide over my chest, ruffling the hair. I place a hard kiss on the top of her head.

"Got a thing for chest hair?"

"Sort of," she says, then giggles. "I mean, yeah, I think it's sexy. The feel of it when you rub against my chest ... and you look like a real man."

I burst out laughing, and she shoves me hard.

"I know that sounds ridiculous, but it's true. I have all these memories of young Seb, and I'm trying to marry them with this version of you. So much has changed."

I lift my head and quirk an eyebrow. "Really? Tell me more."

"Shut up. You know you're sexy as hell. Your chest, muscles, beard ... your—" She stops short and sniffs.

"No really," I cough out, my body quaking with laughter. "You *must* tell me more."

"No really, *shut up.*" She hides her faces, then peeks through her hands. "I mean, who knew it would keep on *growing*. You were eighteen the last time I saw it. It should have been fully grown by then."

"Okay, stop. You've got to stop talking, or I might suffocate from laughing at you." I give her a tight squeeze, and she hides her eyes again. "There are things about you that are different, too, you know?"

Her body tenses, and her hand absentmindedly moves to her belly. I grab it and return it to my chest.

"That's the change I love the most. It gave us Aria." She

sighs and presses her lips to my skin. "There are other things, too."

"Do I want to know?" she asks, cringing.

"Your breasts are fuller, a little more than a handful now. Not complaining, for sure. And your nipples are bigger, too. Perfect for sucking."

She drops her head, her hair sheltering her face, but I brush it away. "Of course, you'd go straight to boobs. Such a man."

"I love it. But I also love the things about you that haven't changed."

"Yeah? Like what?"

"Your smile is still the brightest thing in any room. And no matter how much powder you put on, the freckles on the bridge of your nose still peek through. I love that when something happens—good, bad, funny, whatever—you're the first person I want to tell. It's always been that way, even when we were apart. It was like a little stab, even on the best days. Like it wasn't great or even real unless I shared it with you."

"That's why it's so hard for me to let things go," she whispers, meeting my gaze for a split second, then focusing on my chest. "Every laugh, smile, step ... it was all so bittersweet because I wanted to share her with you. Every milestone was a reminder of what I'd taken from you. Every memory something you'd never get back."

"So you'll tell me. And I'll tell you. And we'll all live happily ever after." She laughs despite the tears swimming in her eyes. "Why are you laughing? Isn't that the way the story goes?"

"Sure, if this were a fairy tale," she says with a laugh.

"Listen, I know we'll have tough times. I know we won't always agree. But I know that I love you. And you love me. And that little girl we've made together ... God, Autumn, I never knew my heart could be so full. So, we'll make new memories. And nothing about them will be bittersweet because we'll be together. Right?"

She nods, pressing her lips together, swallowing back the tears she needn't shed anymore. We're done with regret as far as I'm concerned. We're finally moving on with our lives.

"So, speaking of new memories, let's talk about Aria's pool party. Not this Saturday, but next? I thought we could invite her class and make it a back-to-school type of thing. Is that cool?"

"Sure, that should be fine. I think. Shit." She cringes. "School and Aria have me pretty swamped, so I don't have a lot of time to plan something big."

"You don't need to do anything. That's just it, Autumn. You're not alone anymore. I've got this."

It's going to take time; I know it is. She's so used to doing everything on her own, but she's got me now. It's hard to rely on another person, to trust them to pick up where you've left off and carry part of the load. But I'm willing to be patient and ready to earn her trust. I know she knows it in her heart, but it just may take a while for her head to catch up.

She nods, but her face is ridiculously doubtful.

"What? You don't think I can plan a party?" She quirks an eyebrow in question. "All right, I may have roped Lexi into helping me. She's filling in some of the girlie blanks."

"Lexi?" Autumn's eyes widen. "She's probably going to sneak switchblades into the goodie bags."

"I swear, underneath all that bloody and black, she's got a gooey center. She'll do good. She was a little girl once, too."

"Are we talking about the same person?"

"Just trust me."

She sighs but settles back onto my chest and snuggles into my side.

"I thought I'd invite Marge and Joe to come out, too. I

really want them to meet you and Aria." I pause, draw in a deep breath for what's next, and go for it. "I thought I'd invite your parents, too."

"No."

"If we just—"

"No."

"Autumn."

Silence.

"When was the last time you spoke to them?"

Long sigh. "The day I told them I was renting an apartment from you."

"Is that really how they want it to be? They'll turn their backs on you—on their granddaughter—if I'm in the picture?"

"They threatened you and your family and ran you out of town. Honestly, what wouldn't they do?" She closes her eyes and shakes her head, like she's tossing the idea out of the room. "I don't want to know. They've caused enough hurt, don't you think?"

"Okay," I say, brushing my hand across her cheek and running my fingers through her tousled hair. "Okay."

I let it go for now. I see her frustration amping up with every question I raise, and I'm getting nowhere fast. I'm not willing to ruin this night, so I put a pin in this topic, saving it for another time. But as far as I'm concerned, the conversation isn't over.

CHAPTER 37

Autumn
Present Day
Haven, LA

Aria crashes into my legs, a full body hug the second we hit the door of the shop. Seb's right behind me, and I fall back into his chest. He wraps an arm around my shoulders and presses his lips to my temple, chuckling the entire time.

"Good morning, poppet. I see Uncle Bray hasn't gotten any better at fixing your hair." I run my fingers through her wild curls but get stuck in a tangle of knots almost immediately.

She looks up at me and grins. "I fixed my own hair."

"Ah, now that explains it."

Seb lets me go and crouches down to Aria's level. "I think it looks beautiful."

She brushes it out of her eyes. "Fanks."

She taps his shoulder like she needs to grab his attention. Like he isn't completely mesmerized and starstruck by the little girl in front of him.

"I didn't ask for my momma at all last night," she whispers, raising his eyebrows like he should be impressed.

"Not even once?" The tone of his voice is one-part humor, one-part disbelief.

Aria flinches and scrunches her nose like she's trying her hardest to remember.

"Well, maybe one time, but it's okay. I still get hot chocolate," she says matter-of-factly like she makes the rules.

Sebastian nods. Aria grins.

She leans in, close to his ear, and whisper-yells, "You got star marshmallows here, too?"

He nods again, and her grin grows even wider. She whips around and runs across the shop, a flurry of matted curls and glitter shoes. "Isaac, do you want star marshmallows?"

Only then do I notice Sebastian's nephew at a table in the far corner of the shop. Aria hops up on the chair beside him, stars in her eyes, Seb and me all but forgotten.

"Wow, she really missed the hell out of me," I mutter, shaking my head.

Seb squeezes my shoulder and chuckles. "Yeah, Isaac walks on water as far as Aria is concerned. No way you could top that."

He gestures over to the counter where Brady and Lexi face each other in some sort of stare down. Lexi's leaned over the counter, way in Brady's space, eyes on fire.

Shit, that girl's scary. I flinch a tiny bit, even though her glare isn't directed on me. Even though I'm way across the room. Yeah, she's that intense.

Seb walks over to Brady, and I follow closely behind, only hearing the last bit of their exchange.

"I said it's none of your fucking business, so back the hell off," Lexi says through gritted teeth.

"And what if I say it is?" Brady's tone is more menacing than I've ever heard it.

"Hey," Seb interrupts, laying a hand on Brady's shoulder. "What's going on here?"

Lexi stands and crosses her arms, ice replacing the blaze from moments before.

"First-degree murder if you don't get him the hell away from me." Not a flinch, not even a hint that she's joking. I honestly don't think she is.

My gaze lands on Brady's shoulder just in time to see Sebastian squeeze much tighter than what could be considered friendly. Brady's eyes dart to Seb's, and he lets out a frustrated grunt.

"You harassing my employees? I've already told you about this one, Brady. Her bite is just as ferocious as her bark." He lowers his head, only slightly, and whispers, "Leave it alone, all right?"

"Fine," he says, expression looking like it's anything but fine. He swipes his coffee off the counter and starts toward Aria and Isaac's table.

Lexi turns her back to us and stalks away.

"What was that all about?"

Sebastian's expression lightens as he shrugs. "Who knows. Those two are like oil and water. Go ahead and have a seat with everyone, and I'll fix our drinks."

I nod, quickly peck his mouth, and head toward the table. I turn back to see him disappear into the storeroom in the back.

～

"And you're gonna live wif us?" Aria screeches, standing on the seat of her chair.

"Poppet, sit down before you fall."

Instead of heeding my warning, she launches herself into

Brady's chest. He catches her with an oomph and returns her high-five.

"I'll be really close, I promise. But I can't live with you, munchkin." Aria's shoulders slump, and her lips poke out in a dramatic pout. "Sorry, Aria, but those stairs aren't Brady-friendly."

"Trust me, I lived with your uncle for nearly two decades. It's not all it's cracked up to be." I nod slowly and make a disgusted face.

Aria giggles.

Brady does not.

"I'm delightful," he growls.

"He eats all the food."

Aria squints her eyes at him. "Not cool, Uncle Bray."

"Stinky socks."

"Ewww." She giggles when he tickles her side.

"Poots."

She bursts out laughing, nearly falling out of the wheel-chair, but Brady catches her by the arm before she makes the plunge. She settles back into his lap, cups her hand by his ear, and whisper-yells, "I poot, too."

Brady and I burst out laughing. Isaac is the one that blushes instead of Aria. She looks downright proud of herself.

"But you say excuse me," I say, just as Sebastian walks up with a handful of cups.

"You gotta use your manners, Uncle Bray. Then you could live wif us." She takes her hot chocolate from Seb with an excited grin. "Fanks."

"Stairs, munchkin, stairs. But I promise to find a place close to you so we can visit all the time. There's a place I'm looking at this afternoon. Already modified and everything. I'm almost afraid to get my hopes up. It seems too good to be true."

"Wow, things are moving fast," Seb says as he takes the seat next to mine and drapes an arm over my shoulder. I look to Aria for a reaction, but she doesn't seem to have one. She just keeps sipping away at her drink.

"The university wants the program up and running for spring semester, so we need to hit the ground running. As soon as I accepted the position, I put in a call to a realtor." Brady shrugs and smiles nonchalantly. "And hey, if the place doesn't work out, there's wheelchair accessible housing on campus. I could always live there for a while if I needed to."

"I can't believe this is happening. And that you kept it from me." I shrug and roll my eyes. "I mean, yes, I would have been so disappointed if it hadn't have worked out, so you were right to wait. But still."

"I'm happy for you, man," Seb says, then squeezes my shoulder. "Hell, I'm happy for me, too. It's like the old gang is back together."

"Plus a few additions." I smile at Isaac, then turn my gaze to our daughter.

Seb lifts his cup to Isaac, and grins. "Very welcome additions."

Isaac hits his cup to Seb's with a sheepish grin, then takes a sip. This prompts a round of cup bumps from Aria, her having to hit everyone twice.

With an overflowing heart, I take in each person sitting at our table. I never thought we'd get here. I never dared dream of it, for fear the wanting would overtake me. Sometimes coming full circle feels more triumphant than the place you originally started. Second chances are like first chances with a rearview mirror—you respect where you've been and know the future will be better for it.

"What do your folks think of the move?"

I bristle at Seb's question, his words deflating my good mood in an instant.

"Who cares what they think," I mutter under my breath.

"Eh, I've been living in Providence for years now. They've gotten used to me doing my own thing."

I scoff, knowing my parents will never get used to Brady doing his own thing. Before the accident, after the accident … it doesn't even matter. He's the dream my dad will never let go of. His dream, not Brady's.

"So how about this," Brady says in an overly cheerful voice in an obvious attempt to change the mood of the room. "Why don't my two favorite girls come with me to see the house this afternoon?"

I give a tight smile and nod while Aria cheers excitedly.

And I don't miss the serious looks exchanged between Seb and Brady.

CHAPTER 38

Present Day
Sebastian
Prosper, LA

I roll into town as the morning dew is burning off the grass, leaving nothing but oppressive heat and the stifling judgment this shit town is known for.

But I can't find it in me to care anymore. It's a pesky gnat buzzing around, but I can swat it away and move on, no problem. Old demons no longer hold me hostage. I feel freer than I ever have before, even within the confines of Prosper city limits. I feel like Jerry McGuire singing Tom Petty with the windows rolled down, one-handing the steering wheel, sporting a shit-eating grin.

Now I just need to get Autumn to the same place. She thinks she's there. She thinks she's let go of all that's happened and is ready for the future, but this anger and resentment for her parents will eat her from the inside out. I saw it plain as day at the coffee shop, and I want more for her. More for us.

Their blatant dismissal of her, of our daughter, is abhorrent to me, and I can't just let it stand. If they choose to continue on this way, I guess that's their dumbass prerogative, but they will hear what I have to say.

She may not thank me. Hell, she'll probably be downright pissed, but I need to do what I can to help her move on from this.

My timing is purposeful, mid-morning when I know Mr. Norris will be at the office, and hopefully, Mrs. Norris will be home alone.

My phone dings in my pocket just as I pull over in front of their house and kill the ignition.

Autumn: You're picking Aria up from school today, right?

Me: Yes. Ice cream and pool toy shopping, remember?

Autumn: <thumbs up> Meet up at your house after?

Me: Our house?

I chuckle, knowing she's huffing as she reads my text. I'm relentless about what I want—she and Aria living with me—but we've lost enough time together already. When it comes to our future, I don't believe there's such a thing as "too fast." I'm more of an "it's about time" kind of man.

Autumn: Shut up.

Autumn: And I love you.

Me: Insanely.

Autumn: Stupidly.

Me: Always.

~

"Sebastian." Mrs. Norris's eyes are as wide as saucers as she hesitates for a split second, then widens the door. "W-what a surprise. Please, come in."

I can't describe it. It's a mixture of a dozen different

239

things, but the Norris's house smells exactly the same as it did when I was a teenager. One breath in triggers a flood of memories —all the good ones.

Wrestling Brady on the living room carpet while Autumn refereed.

Holding Autumn's hand under the table at Sunday lunch.

Stealing cookies with Brady while Mrs. Norris's back was turned.

Stealing more than cookies with Autumn when her parents weren't looking.

"Can I get you some coffee? Tea maybe?"

She gestures to the kitchen, and I see the faint tremble in her hand. When I shake my head, she leads me into the living room and sits on the edge of the couch, wringing her hands. She's hesitant, but also eager in some way. She's like a sneeze on the verge, but unsure whether to let it loose or stifle the urge.

"I'm sorry to show up unannounced this way, but under the circumstances, I thought it would be best."

She nods her head and presses her lips together. She smooths the skirt of her sundress then tucks her hair behind her ear. It's still the same golden blonde that Autumn's used to be. Her eyes skirt over my face, then she laughs nervously. "You'll have to forgive me for staring. You've grown into such a handsome man. I knew you would be, but to see you sitting here…" She blows out a breath and fans her watery eyes. "You'll have to excuse me. I'm an emotional old woman these days."

"I don't mean to upset you, but there are a few things I need to say. I would appreciate it if you'd hear me out." Her lips tip into a watery smile, and she nods. "And then I'll leave."

My last words bring back the pressed lips and wringing hands. The slightest touch of a feather could push her over the edge, and I don't understand her reaction. I expected terse nods and cold shoulders. Where is the blatant dismissal I was prepared for?

"I didn't come here to rehash the past, I really didn't. We both know what happened. The accident … me leaving town … the pregnancy. I can't change any of it. None of us can change it, but we can forgive. And that's what we've done. We're moving forward, Mrs. Norris, and leaving the past in the past, where it belongs."

"So, you and Autumn," she interrupts. "You're together now?"

"We are."

She chokes out a sob and covers her mouth with both hands.

"I love her."

"Of course, you do," she whispers, crying and laughing at the same time. "You always have."

Complete and utter confusion. What the hell is going on here?

"And my sweet grandbaby? Aria?" She gives me an open-ended look. "Has she stolen your heart yet?"

"Completely," I whisper.

She grabs a tissue from the side table and blots her eyes, drawing in slow breaths as she tries to calm herself.

"I miss her so much. I miss both of them."

I feel as if I've entered an alternate universe, where black is white and up is down. One thing is for sure, I'm missing something here.

"Then why did you turn your back on them? Autumn told me you haven't spoken to her since she moved to Haven. Like her even renting an apartment from me was more than you'll tolerate. If you miss them so much, then what the hell are you doing?"

The horrified look on Mrs. Norris's face tells me all I

need to know. I went too far. But honestly, I don't care. It needed to be said. If it shakes some sense into her, makes her see all she's giving up, then it's worth it.

Tears track her cheeks as she shakes her head and grabs my hand out of my lap. It's still trembling, and she squeezes tight as another sob breaks free.

"Oh Sebastian, no. You've got this all wrong."

CHAPTER 39

Present Day
Sebastian
Haven, LA

Autumn's car is already in the driveway when Aria and I pull up, and she takes off like a shot the second I unbuckle her car seat, shopping bag waving wildly in her clenched fist.

I gather the rest of our purchases out of the trunk, with both hands because we bought that much shit, but I couldn't pry that one bag out of Aria's hand.

I hit the front door just in time to hear her yell, "I got a new baving suit! A bikini!"

Autumn and Isaac are sitting in the living room, one with a goofy smirk and the other with a scowl. I'll let you guess who's scowling.

Footsteps clomp down the hallway as Aria calls out, "I'm going try it on."

I drop my bags by the front door, the crinkling of plastic the only sound once the bathroom door slams shut.

"A bikini," Autumn whispers, looking incredulous. "She's only five years old."

"Calm down," I say, before thinking better of it, then cringing at the glare those words earn me.

"I'm just gonna—" Isaac mutters, pointing to the back and slinking away.

Lucky shit.

"Okay, I did not mean to say, 'calm down.' I'm smarter than that," I say, doing my best to back pedal.

"I don't like this, Seb." She shakes her head. Stands. Rubs her hands on her jeans while watching the bathroom door. "I figured she'd be about—oh, I don't know—thirty before I let her wear a bikini."

"I think that's supposed to be my line," I chuckle.

She raises her arms in question. "I thought so, too."

Before I can respond, Aria races into the living room, arms wide and grinning.

"Isn't it pretty?" She spins in a circle and runs a reverent hand over her bathing suit. "Pink is my favorite color."

She's so fucking adorable. Heart-stoppingly so. She flicks the tulle ruffles on her butt, and then shakes it like a little wet duck. She stands up tall and sucks in an excited breath, the halter top showing about an inch of her rounded belly.

"It's the best swimsuit I've ever seen, poppet," Autumn whispers. "You look like a pool party princess."

"I am." She giggles, before racing back down the hall. "I wanna show Isaac."

Autumn's shoulders slump as she watches me through lowered lashes. I sit down next to her on the couch and draw her legs over my lap. She drops her head to my shoulder and sighs.

"I overreacted," she whispers.

"Yes," I say, unable to hide the laughter in my tone.

"I'm sorry."

"I know."

"I'm a jackass."

She looks up at me with puppy dog eyes and an apologetic smile. I can't resist. I press my lips to hers.

"But you're the cutest jackass I know," I say before deepening the kiss, letting her tongue brush against mine.

It'll never get old. It'll never be enough. If we live to be a hundred, I'll still love her like the starstruck teenagers we once were. Because just like them, I still believe anything is possible, as long as we're together.

"Do you trust me?"

"Yes." No hesitation.

"Do you love me?"

"You know I do."

"Then you know I want what's best for Aria. We won't always agree when it comes to her, but I'll talk to you. I'll see your side." I brush my thumb across her cheek and settle my hand at the base of her neck. "And you'll have to see my side. You're not alone anymore. I'm with you all the way. But it also means you have to take me into account. We're a team."

"You and me."

"Me and you."

"Yeah," she whispers, watching me with trusting eyes and an open heart.

I hope she feels this loving when I tell her where I've been today. We'll need more than a couple of minutes for that conversation, so I hold off for now.

"Check out the cool shit we bought today," I say, getting up to grab the mountain of bags by the front door. I grab random things out of the bag and toss them on the couch. "Squirt guns ... dive rings ... inflatable donuts."

"Inflatable donuts?" She laughs as she picks up the package to inspect it.

"Yup. Because a princess pool party isn't complete without donuts. With sprinkles."

"You are such a pushover," she says with a grin, leaning in to peck my lips.

"Oh, and check this out. It's a puddle jumper. It's like old-school floaties, but better. She squealed when she saw this thing." I hold up the contraption, and her eyes brighten. It looks like a hot mess to me.

"I forgot hers at Aunt D's. She loves the thing. Makes her feel like a big girl, swimming all on her own. Oh, speaking of, we should totally ask Aunt D to come to the pool party."

"Already done," I say while I shove everything back in the bags.

"Wow, I'm impressed. You've got this all under control."

"I do." My lips meet hers as I fall onto the couch and pull her back into my lap. "Why don't you stay here tonight? You and Aria."

Indecision wars behind her eyes as her hands nudge my chest. Her heart is all in, but her head can't let go. My girlfriend says yes, but Aria's momma still isn't sure.

But Aria's dad is relentless and hopelessly in love. Not to mention, calling Autumn his girlfriend is a gross understatement and a term that in no way represents who she is to him.

And why am I talking in the third person?

"I don't want to give Aria the wrong idea. What exactly is the right idea?" Her lips are back on mine before I can answer, then she pulls away again. "I mean, the message would be that we're together. And this is happening. This is happening, right?"

Before she leans in to kiss me again, I slide my fingers into her hair and stop her.

"This is happening. Since the very first time I held your hand. Our first kiss. First fight. First…" I trail off and blush creeps across her cheeks. She lowers her head and giggles.

"Even the years we were apart, I kept hoping. Even when it hurt too much to think about, I never could push the thought completely away. It was always happening. It was always forever."

Tears well up in her eyes, and she bites her lower lip. Footsteps patter down the hallway, but Autumn and I stay put.

"Isaac wants to know what's for supper," Aria asks as she perches her chin on the back of the couch. Autumn shifts forward to hide her face while I pinch Aria's nose. She giggles and swats me away.

"What if we ordered a pizza and watched a movie?" Her eyes brighten. She hops in excitement, shaking her head the entire time.

Then I take a chance.

"What if … you and Mom just stayed here tonight?"

Autumn and I hold our breaths, waiting for the verdict of a pool party princess. She taps her mouth and cocks her head to the side, thinking … thinking … thinking. Then her eyes light and a smile slides into place.

"Let's do that, Momma! Will you go get our mermaid tails?" When Autumn nods, Aria takes off to the back of the house for round two. "Isaac, I'm sleeping at your house and eating pizza!"

I watch Autumn, and she watches me, both of us waiting for the bubble to pop. But it doesn't.

"Just like that," Autumn whispers, throwing up her hands and giggling.

"Damn straight. Even she knows it. You and me? We just are." I growl as I fold her into my arms and attack her neck, making her cackle with laughter.

She tugs my ears, pulling my face to hers, eyes full of love as she stares into mine.

"This is happening," she says, with complete conviction.

"Damn right it is."
I kiss her lips. Her nose. Both of her cheeks.
"Mermaid tails?"
"Don't even ask."

CHAPTER 40

Present Day
Sebastian
Haven, LA

"Come on, Seb. Quit playing hard to get," she whines, pulling her shirt up her chest until I thwart her attempt, shoving the shirt back over her belly. "What do you have against boobs? Free peep show, right here."

"I've got nothing against boobs. In fact, I want your boobs against me. All the time. Swear," I say, lifting her off my lap and placing her on the bed beside me. "But we need to talk."

"You're new to this parenting thing, so let me clue you in. When the child is asleep, that's when the magic happens."

I chuckle, loving the enthusiasm. Aria and Autumn are equivalent to birthday cake for no particular reason. A piñata on a Tuesday. Playing hooky in the middle of the week.

Peep shows at bedtime.

Shopping, pizza, and *The Little Mermaid* wore Aria out early tonight. She missed the ending credits, and I carried her to the spare bedroom, cheeks flushed with sleep and crocheted mermaid tail in place. Autumn ditched her tail, opting to straddle me instead.

I'm fully on board with the plan, and I'm hoping she agrees after we talk.

"I took a road trip today … to Prosper." All humor drains from her face, and she watches me cautiously. She scoots away to create some space, as if preparing for what she knows I'll say next. "To your parents' house."

If looks could kill…

"It wasn't your place. I didn't ask you to get involved. I didn't *want* you to." Legs swing over the side of the bed, but I catch her arm before she makes it very far. "Why couldn't you leave well enough alone?"

"Because it wasn't good enough. It was nowhere near good enough." Can't she see that? Even through her anger, she's got to know. "Why didn't you tell me you were the one to cut them off and not the other way around?"

"What difference does it make?"

"It makes all the difference, Autumn, and you know it. That's why you let me believe they wanted nothing to do with you and Aria."

She bristles at my accusation, and I know I've hit a nerve. I'm going about this all wrong. My intention is to heal old wounds, not pick at the scars.

Softening my voice, I try again. "If I've learned anything in this life, it's that things aren't always how they appear. So, I wanted to see for myself." Moments pass with tense silence, so I continue. "I only spoke with your mom."

"He was at work, I'm sure. Glad you didn't have to endure him," she scoffs, head turned back to me, but eyes averted.

Well, that's something, at least. If she were really pissed, she'd wish for her dad's shotgun between my eyes when the front door swung open, right? I'll take that as a win, however small it may be.

"He might have been at work." I wait long enough for her to look up and meet my eyes. I want to be sure she hears every word. "Or he could have been on Elm Street, in the apartment he's been renting since your mom kicked him out."

And now I've got her undivided attention. Her mouth falls open, her lips attempting to form words but falling short each time. She narrows her eyes to slits like she's trying to suss out if I'm screwing with her.

"W-what did you say?"

"She kicked him out."

She shakes her head and presses her lips together, rejecting the very idea of it.

"She would never—"

"On his ass."

"Is this some alternate universe?"

I tug her toward me, and she comes willingly this time, meeting me in the middle of the mattress.

"I told you, things aren't always as they seem. Do you know when she found out about your dad threatening me after the accident? Just a couple of months ago, when you confronted both of them and told them to stay away from you and Aria." Jaw dropped, Autumn shakes her head in total disbelief. "She didn't know anything about it, Autumn. She thought I just took off, same as you."

She runs a finger along the seam of my comforter. Chews on the side of her cheek while dropping her head to the pillow. I watch as the world she thought she knew shifts beneath her shaky feet. Her eyes close as she replays years' worth of interactions and arguments, realizing not all adversaries were real and some allies hide in plain sight.

"She was never the same after the accident," she whispers, emotion clogging in her throat. "She always let Dad run the show, yeah, but she pulled the reins when she felt he was getting out of hand. When needed, she had this fire that would rise up and be the voice of reason. After the accident, there was no fire left. Not even a flicker."

"Tragedy affects people in different ways. Some people shatter, while others rise up. I don't know what makes one or the other happen, but it's safe to say learning the truth relit that fire within your mom. She wants to stand up. She's trying to reconnect the family she sees slipping through her fingers." I slide my hand into hers and squeeze. She opens her eyes and sniffs. "She's been calling you for months. She's working up the courage to drive to Haven and sit on your doorstep, but she's petrified you'll turn her away."

"I wouldn't do that. I mean, now I wouldn't. Now that I know." Her eyes widen, and she releases a long sigh. "I just can't believe it, you know? Do you think it's really over? I bet he'll weasel his way back in."

"Well, she didn't file for divorce or anything, but she seems resolute. If he can't embrace his family as they are and let go of his anger, he can stay the hell away. Her words, not mine."

"He'll try to bulldoze her like he always does."

"Eh, I wouldn't count her out. He's in therapy, if you can believe it. She insisted on it."

"Honestly, I can't."

"Everyone deserves a second chance in life, don't you think?" I brush a thumb over her cheek, and she leans into me, still looking doubtful but showing the tiniest crack in her resolve. "There's good in him, too, Autumn. Even I can admit that. His anger swallowed it whole and buried it deep. But who knows? Maybe he can find his way back. It says a lot about your mother that's she's willing to let him try. And she's putting you, Aria, and Brady ahead of this shit. That says a lot about her, too."

"Yeah," she whispers, her mouth tipping up into a sad

smile. She draws in deep, her chest and shoulders rising from the effort, then blows out long and slow, and I feel the frustration and resistance seep from her body.

I gesture to her phone perched on the bedside table and give her an encouraging smile. "Maybe you could meet her in the middle? It's not that late—I'm sure she's still awake." She eyes it warily and chews her lip. "You can't pick the pieces you want to let go of and save some of the hurt for later. I want us to be a family, and we deserve a fresh start. So does she."

She lunges forward, pressing her lips to mine. Our foreheads touch, and she clenches her eyes shut. "I love you."

"I love you, too," I whisper as she rises and sits up on the edge of the bed. Running her phone through her hands, she lets out a long sigh before lighting up the screen and tapping.

It couldn't have rung more than once before she answers.

"Mom?" Her voice is shaky, her shoulders hunched. She lets out a long sob, then an almost happy laugh.

I take an extra-long time checking on Aria.

EPILOGUE

Autumn
Present Day

"How much time do we have?" Sebastian rasps, as his hands slide under my tank top, tweaking my nipples as his morning wood bruises my ass.

His teeth graze the curve of my neck, and our eyes lock in the bathroom mirror. Sleepy hair, hungry eyes, and stubble scraping my skin in the most delicious way—oh yeah, I'm wet and ready.

"Ten ... maybe twenty minutes."

Life with a five-year-old—you sneak in sex when you can, where you can, and you make every minute count. We're horny as newlyweds, but our flip-flop of life events makes things challenging to say the least.

We have fun with it. Lots of fun.

It's the day of Aria's pool party, and she and I haven't slept at the apartment once since our initial slumber party at Seb's. The only things left in the apartment are my furniture and our winter clothes. All the obsessing and overthinking about how Aria would take this transition, and her reaction to it, can be summed up in a flippant shrug.

Mommies and daddies live togever, Momma. No big deal.

I resisted the urge to tell her not all parents live together and *took the win.* If every morning could start off like this one, I'd explain family dynamics some other time.

As Seb rips down my tank top to prop up my breasts, the last thing I'm worried about is clothes, winter or otherwise. When his hand dives into my panties, fingers sliding inside, my eyes roll back in my head.

Boxers fall to the floor. Panties slide down my thighs. Palms hit the bathroom mirror. His hands meet mine, and our fingers intertwine as I arch into him.

"Need to fuck you. It's gonna be fast."

"You haven't started yet?" I taunt, just as he drives into me. My head drops back to his shoulder, and I moan, because *yes, right there, that's where I need you.* "I don't care if it's quick. I need it."

"I didn't say quick. I said fast." He bites my ear, then licks the burn. "Not the same thing."

Starving hands run down my arms, one stopping at my breasts and the other traveling between my legs as he pounds into me, each thrust longer and harder than the last. Root to tip, almost losing him as he pulls back, only to push in again and again. My legs turn to jelly, and I grab his neck, tug his hair, silently wishing this high would last forever.

"Hands to the mirror, Autumn." He wretches my fingers from his hair and slaps my hand back in place. "Hold on tight, baby."

It's not a build so much an active volcano, heated ecstasy rolling through me, a latent orgasm ready to spring to life without warning. My control holds like a hair trigger, one touch having the power to cause an eruption.

"Soon," he chokes out, head buried in my neck. "Soon … fuuuuuuck."

That dirty word … his sandpaper chin scraping my skin … his final thrust, deep and powerful, pushing me up onto my toes with the force of it, and I'm gone. I'm a ball of fiery sensation and pleasure and the only thing keeping me from melting to the floor is Seb's arm locked around my waist.

Cold tile stings my skin as he whips me around and plants me on the counter, our tongues sliding together as we slowly come back to reality.

Bang, bang, bang!

"Momma?" Bang, bang, bang! "Do you know what today is?"

I break the kiss and drop my head to Seb's shoulder. Hysterical giggles bubble up inside me, and I bite his shoulder to keep them inside.

"Pool party day, poppet. Are you ready?"

"Yes!" she cheers, then knocks again.

"Got your swimsuit on?"

Pause. Footsteps hauling butt out of the room and down the hallway. I let out a sigh of relief.

"I love that little girl, but she's the princess of all cock-blockers," Seb mutters as he runs his hands up and down my thighs.

"To be fair, she didn't block the cock this time," I laugh, holding up a finger. "Maybe just stuck a pin in the afterglow."

"This time being the key words there," he chuckles before brushing his thumbs across my cheeks and meeting my eyes. "Ready for today?"

"Yeah," I say with a smile, eager but nervous to see my mom. We've been talking a lot in the past week, but this will be the first time we've seen each other in months. "I should ask you the same thing. This is your first attempt at party planning. All set?"

He leans over to turn on the shower and gives me an overconfident wink. "We'll just have to see, won't we?"

~

Sebastian

Lexi may be the queen of mean, but she stowed the switch-blades and let loose the pink glitter, all for Aria. My prickly friend has outdone herself this time.

A sundae station armed with every confection a kid could imagine, a sandbox in the yard fully equipped with castle supplies, a giant cut-out of a shark around the diving board so the kids can jump out of its mouth ... it's so amazing. I confess to Autumn that Lexi's the mastermind out of sheer guilt. She's too mesmerized to care.

"Didn't know she had it in her," Brady mutters as he rips off a bite of licorice. "Who knew someone with a black heart could make something this festive."

He dodges my greasy spatula as I try to whop him upside the head. Flipping burgers is the perfect job for me. People stop by to visit, and I keep my hands busy. Looking over the crowd of friends and family gathered, my heart is full, but my nerves are churning full force. It's a lot to take in, especially Autumn, Aria, and her mother sitting at one of the tables, Aria perched in her grandmother's lap, and Mrs. Norris positively beaming. All of them are grinning ear to ear.

My girls—pockets full of sunshine.

"Give Lexi a break. And I don't just mean today." He scowls, but he knows what I'm talking about. I don't know where Brady got the bright idea to use his hacker skills to look into my friends, but he needs to cut it out. Lexi's good people—a crunchy outer shell with a gooey center.

257

I assume her center is gooey. I haven't actually seen that part of her yet.

"That's a good thing you did right there." He gestures to his mom and sister and shakes his head. "Still not sure why she didn't tell me all of this. I would have talked to Autumn. I would have fixed it."

"I know you would have, man."

"It's like she can't tell me anything bad. Keep up the smile for Brady, he's got enough to worry about," he says with mock sweetness. "I'm a happy motherfucker regardless. No need to put on airs for me."

"Who's putting on airs? People oughta be who they are, and that's that. Isn't that right, Marge?"

Joe elbows Marge in the ribs, and she slaps his arm in retaliation. "Keep your mitts to yourself, old man." She leans in and kisses my cheek, then pinches them so hard I flinch. "Love you hard, boy, but I see a little girl with brown curls and a tutu I gotta meet."

While I introduce Joe to my oldest friend, Marge teeters across the yard with a wobble and a cane. The cane is a new addition, and I don't like it one bit. Lexi runs to Marge's side, cradling her other elbow to help her to the table.

Parents and children from Aria's class trickle in, each classmate getting a bigger squeal from Aria than the last. I can't wait for her to point out Manda and the hot-dog-smelling Henry. I see my chance as she bounds toward me, pink puddle jumper bobbing in her hand.

Splashes fill the air behind us as kids take running jumps into the water. Aria slams into my legs, eyes wild with excitement. She raises her puddle jumper high in the air.

"Can you put it on me? I wanna swim wif my friends!" she yells like we're across the yard from each other, and I burst out laughing.

"All right, all right." I chuckle, crouching down in front of her. I hold out each hole, and she shoves her arms inside. I wrap my arms around her and fasten the latch with a click.

She grins, and so do I.

"Fanks, Dad," she whispers and runs away.

Like she didn't just blow a hole right through the center of my chest.

The raucous laughter and splashing fade as I blink back tears and fight the urge to fall backward on my ass. Brady clamps a hand on my shoulder and squeezes.

"You okay, man?"

I nod furiously and drop down, knees to elbows.

"First time she's called me that," I admit.

"It's a beautiful thing, the love of a child. Happy as hell you get to experience it, son," Joe says as he lights his cigarette and draws in a deep drag. "That little girl could charm the tits off a sow, so you're doubly blessed."

"I sure am."

"Deserve it," he mutters.

I shake my head. "Don't know about that, but I'll take it."

"I know it." He shoots me a dirty scowl. "Boy, don't argue with an old man. It's shit manners, and I won't stand for it."

Brady chuckles, and I fight back a grin.

"Yes, sir."

My eyes land on Autumn as she pulls up a chair for Aunt Dorothy. I watch as Mrs. Norris's smile goes from tentative to beaming as the other woman takes the chair and sidles right up to her, grabbing both of her hands.

"Give me that spatula before you serve us all charcoal briquettes for lunch." Joe wrangles the spatula from me as his cigarette dangles precariously from his lips. "Couldn't barbecue his way out of a paper bag, that one," he mutters.

When her eyes meet mine, silent words spoken often dance between us.

All this time. We're finally here.

You and me.

Me and you.

This is all I want from this life. Autumn and Aria at my side and our family surrounding us. Some made by blood, others forged with love. All more important than regret or guilt.

I smile at my future, and she smiles back.

I love you.

Always have.

I know.

THE END

ABOUT THE AUTHOR

J.A. DEROUEN RESIDES IN South Louisiana where she lives with her husband, son (aptly nicknamed "The Professor"), and her furry friend, Scout. She has earned bachelor's degrees in psychology and nursing. When she's not writing or inhaling romance novels by the stack, she works as a women's health nurse. She's been an avid reader and daydreamer since childhood, and she's never stopped turning the page to get to the next happily ever after.

Where to Find J.A. DeRouen:
SIGN UP FOR HER NEWSLETTER and stay up to date on all the latest book news, plus special, bonus content. Want to join her Facebook reader group? CLICK HERE to join the fun!

f facebook.com/JADerouen

instagram.com/jaderouen

a amazon.com/author/jaderouen

g goodreads.com/jaderouen

BB bookbub.com/authors/j-a-derouen

ALSO BY J.A. DEROUEN

The Over Series
Hope Over Fear (Book 1)
Wings Over Poppies (Book 2)
Storms Over Secrets (Book 3)

The Over Duet
Low Over High (Book 1)
Ever Over After (Book 2)

ACKNOWLEDGMENTS

First and foremost, thank you to my wonderful family for being the most awesome people I know. You're my most favorite thing. Even when my head is stuck inside my laptop, you're still my most favorite.

To my wonderful editor, Madison Seidler; proofreader, Mitzi Carroll; and cover designer, Mignon Mykal. I can't thank you enough for your time and patience.

To my early readers, thank you for your time, and most of all, thank you for your critique. I love all of your red pens the most! When you bleed all over my WIP, you make me better. I appreciate you more than I can express.

To my fellow authors, you know who you are, thank you for your undying friendship and support. But most of all, thank you for being the swift kick in the butt I need a lot of the times.

To all the amazing bloggers who took the time to review and post, thank you from the bottom of my heart for giving me a chance. Your kind words and efforts have meant the world to me.

To all of the wonderful readers out there, I hope you love Sebastian and Autumn as much as I loved writing about them. Thank you. Thank you. Thank you.